CW00541748

BURNING ANGEL

LAWRENCE OSBORNE

BURNING ANGEL

AND OTHER STORIES

HOGARTH
London

1 3 5 7 9 10 8 6 4 2

Hogarth, an imprint of Vintage, is part of the Penguin Random House group of
companies whose addresses can be found at global.penguinrandomhouse.com

First published by Hogarth in 2023

'Camino Real' was first published in the US in *Tin House*, Fall 2013;
'Volcano' was first published in the US in *Tin House*, Spring 2011, and also appeared in
Best American Short Stories 2012 (ed. Tom Peretta, Mariner Books, New York, 2012);
'Pig Bones' was first published as 'Kakua' in the US by *Fiction* magazine no. 58, 2012;
'The White Gods' was first published in the *New Statesman*, December 2020.

penguin.co.uk/vintage

A CIP catalogue record for this book is available from the British Library

HB ISBN 9781781090824
TPB ISBN 9781781090831

Typeset in 12.75/16.32 pt Fournier MT Pro by Jouve (UK), Milton Keynes
Printed and bound in Great Britain by Clays Ltd, Elcograf S.p.A.

The authorised representative in the EEA is Penguin Random House Ireland,
Morrison Chambers, 32 Nassau Street, Dublin D02 YH68

FOR NICHOLAS SIMON

Boats against the current

CONTENTS

GHOST

NEAR THE TOP OF THE MOUNTAIN, NOT FAR FROM the Victoria Peak Garden, Rowan Buford kept his company town house in the Overthorpe gated enclave. The $40,000-a-month rent had been paid by his employers, Gilby & Fitch, for seven years. His balcony overlooked the whole city, with glimpses of the South China Sea beyond, and his four bedrooms had accumulated over time artworks culled from nearly a decade of Christie's auctions, especially works of the Hong Kong 'New Ink' movement. The American community called him 'Party Hyena' behind his back and yet all the clubs welcomed his membership, and his reckless reputation did not diminish his allure.

Buford, now thirty-seven, had successfully petitioned the building's management to remove the tasteless decorative elephants from the development's front doors, but he had failed to limit participation in the Overthorpe's dismally claustrophobic communal pool. No matter. He belonged to two gyms in the city and shared a yacht moored in Aberdeen with a colleague of his own age. In the city's foreign hedge-fund world 'the young sharks', as they were known, constituted a small band – not of brothers, certainly, but at least of loosely mutual acquaintances. Buford had his tennis comrades, his drinking band, his cigar circle, his wine club and his girlfriend Lily, a finance worker from Shenzhen ten years his junior. He had found 'The Life', and each part of that Life had a compartment that suited a hundred different and variable moods. It was the dividend offered by quickly made wealth. What other city could pay those dividends so efficiently or let the earner enjoy them so completely? Buford had calculated at the beginning of his long stint at the firm that his town house on the Peak would place him in the middle of the highest real-estate prices in the world.

The Peak was more expensive than any real estate in human history. Knightsbridge or Central Park West and East were far down the mournful league table of dollars-per-square-foot. And the Overthorpe stood at the summit of the Peak, commanding in both the physical sense and in terms of its actual dollar value.

In the early morning he and Lily shared their croissants and cafetière with a little sniff of coke to start their day, lounging in the white deckchairs designed to offset a black wooden floor. They could watch ships moving silently across the harbour, the sun rising over Tsim Sha Tsui. For an hour at dawn the city was quiet enough for them to talk without haste. An adventure trip to Siberia in the offing, a week in California to meet his parents in Santa Ana. Investments, insider tips. Auctions perhaps, crypto trades, social gossip and small talk. Lily, a dutiful Chinese daughter, wondering how to buy her parents a new house. Buford explaining for the hundredth time his disdain for his superiors at the firm. His plans were tinged with a hard romanticism.

Secretly he was running up formidable debts, but these he kept to himself. It was nothing he couldn't pay off with a concerted austerity push.

The maid would arrive at nine to clear up the shambolic mess inside the house where they had often been partying all night. Then they went their separate ways. Lily took the cable car down to Wang Chai to work at her mainlander bank, and Buford departed in a tracksuit for his morning run along the pathways and staircases cut through tropical forests, where he gradually worked off the effects of the previous evening's drugs. It was on these runs that he did his best thinking, arriving after a full circuit of the Peak at a lookout over the sea, where he sat above the forests for a while reading the papers at an outdoor café and making his first call to the office at eight on the dot. His secretary, Natalie, would take this call and arrange his day. Then his driver would take him down to Sheung Wan directly from the Overthorpe and, after a morning's trading, he would lunch at midday alone at The Chairman, where his table was always reserved.

Every morning was much the same until early April, one of the first hot days when kestrels and sea-eagles had reappeared, circling the towers of the Peak. His secretary told him on the phone as he was waiting for the 8 a.m. car that the office was having a 'reorganisation' and that it would be more expedient, if he didn't mind, if he could come in a little later that day and meet Alan Fitch for lunch at The Chairman instead. The limo reservation had been altered accordingly.

'What do you mean, "reorganisation"?' he said to her.

'I think Mr Fitch will explain it to you.'

A little put out, Buford retired to his black balcony and

watched the kestrels while the maid cleaned up the takeaway cartons and the beer cans stained with lipstick from the main room. The sun had acquired its first heat of the year, and the forests all around the complex had burst into wild colour as the bushes flowered as if they had been activated overnight. There was a change in the atmosphere of some kind, a recalibration. Even his secretary's voice was not as it normally was. He thought, *My party habits got back to the big boys and they want to bust my balls about it.* In his mind, accordingly, he prepared a defiant little speech that he would deliver to Fitch over their poached urchins at lunch. He would point out that in their amoral world only results mattered, not the occasional and entirely private abuse of cocaine. How could the senior partner demur? Buford could then issue a quick reassurance that, in the circumstances, he might be able to modify his behaviour a little. But had he not brought in eight million to the firm that year?

The car came for him at eleven and on the way down he read the *Financial Times*, as he always did. The ongoing real-estate crisis in China had finally made the front page. The ghost cities of the mainland were going bankrupt and the banks in Hong Kong were growing nervous. The tremors of a distant crisis were now being felt in a city that was becoming ever closer to her wilful master. Perhaps that was the root of the change in atmosphere. He should have thought of that sooner. Gradually his collar began to feel uncomfortably constraining and he reached up to loosen it with two fingers. He caught a glimpse of his slicked blond hair in the rear-view mirror and for the first time that he could remember he noticed that his forehead was no longer suavely dry. His heart rate had quickened.

The car let him off at the corner of Aberdeen Street and Kau U Fong, the small alley in which The Chairman was located, and he walked to the restaurant without hurrying in order to calm himself down before Fitch caught sight of him. The Chairman's staff welcome was the same as usual. Buford's superior was waiting at a different table on the first floor and had already ordered a plate of crispy enoki mushrooms and a bottle of chilled mineral water. The dry sixty-year-old American did not drink and imposed this restriction on all his lunches. When Buford appeared he didn't get up or extend a hand, but merely motioned with his head that the younger man was to sit down and tuck into the mineral water. Seated, Buford turned to the waiter and asked in Cantonese for a small pitcher of lemon juice.

'What do you usually eat here?' Fitch said coolly.

'Poached urchins or the pigeon with Longjing tea.'

'The one with chrysanthemum?'

'Yes.'

Fitch ordered the pigeon immediately (without the urchins) and added a request for some Chinese buns. The two men then looked at each other. They were both wearing dark-grey suits, but Fitch's was double-breasted and exuded a slightly different heft. A gold tie seemed to fix his head in space with the monumentality of a statue.

'How old are you, Buford?'

'Thirty-seven.'

'Fine age for a man. You have a girlfriend, don't you?'

Buford nodded.

'Works in finance. Mainlander?'

'Yes.'

'Any plans for her?'

Resentfully Buford mumbled something about marriage discussions.

'Well, you know what they say, Buford.'

'No, what do they say?'

'Monogamy is staying with the person until breakfast the next morning.'

'So that's what they say.'

'It has a kernel of truth, don't you think? You should get married.'

'You mean it would look better for the firm?'

'Now that you mention it . . .'

But Buford could not foresee exactly where their conversation was going. He admitted that, all in all, settling down might not be such a bad idea. He had been with Lily for three years. It had already occurred to him that she might be the right one.

'Of course,' Fitch went on as the Chinese buns arrived, 'it's not the ideal moment to make such a significant move. I suppose you heard the news about Evergrand this morning.'

'I saw it just now in the *FT*.'

'The markets are having a conniption fit. But as I'm sure you are aware, this is long-term. It's been going on for months. We're all going to lose a lot of money.'

'Ah.'

'Not only that, but the Chinese authorities are changing their attitude. We're getting demands to show up for audits. They are taking a rather different sort of interest in our operations. You see, Buford, we are going to have to let some people go. It's not only for financial reasons, either. I know this will come as rather unwelcome news for you. You know how I feel about it, so let's not waste time with sentimental expressions. It is what it is. The firm simply has to cut back its more ostentatious appearances. The rents we are paying for staff are getting quite incredible. I'm sure you already know what I am talking about.'

'You're firing me?'

'That's a very 1950s word, Buford. I assume you have some savings, don't you? It would be preposterous if you didn't, given the bonuses you've enjoyed these last three years.'

Free rent, too, was the sour implication.

'Savings?' Buford could not quite comprehend the word since he had never employed it, even inside the privacy of his own mind.

'Leftovers,' Fitch said, fixing the pale eye upon him. 'You know, the bits you didn't spend on coke and girls and yachts. The bits, as George Best used to say, that you wasted.'

The dry laugh set the younger man on edge and he steeled himself to appear calmly nonchalant. Fitch went on to say that they would need to recuperate the town house by the end of the month. Forty thousand a month was too much to 'throw away' in the firm's changed circumstances. That gave Buford three weeks to make alternative arrangements. It was enough, was it not? Of course they would pay a separation fee. He was not sure what it would be. Not that much, his dour expression betrayed.

Arriving just as Buford's throat constricted, the tea-flavoured pigeon could not quite distract him from a quiet desperation.

'Of course,' he muttered, and wondered in a tragic moment whether this meant that his days at The Chairman were also over. He was silently calculating the relation between his remaining 'leftover' funds and the amounts needed to continue living on the Peak. There was, in fact, no relation.

BUFORD WALKED TO THE office alone, since Fitch had another appointment. On the twenty-third floor he greeted his downcast secretary, who helped him pack up a single box of belongings. She was not slow to say how sorry she was. Whispering, even though the office was half-empty as the crisis washed over it, she told him that several of his colleagues had been laid off as well. It was a bloodbath.

'Yet no blood is actually spilled,' he said with fatalism.

The box was primly pathetic in its way; he had always kept a clean and spare desk. When it was packed he called Lily and asked her to meet later that day at a sake bar called Ronin, also on Kau U Fong. It was one of the most secretive bars in Hong Kong, tucked below a wall at the end of the cul-de-sac, and he wanted to be unseen. Then he went to his gym. He cancelled the following month's membership and sat in the steam room for an hour, thinking and plotting, naked. He emerged restabilised.

Still in that morning's business suit, he walked down to Kau U Fong in the heat, threading his way through the usual hectic crowds clambering up and down Sheung Wan's steeply exhausting hillside streets. It was the hour of indecision between nature's soothing dusk and the onset of the city's excessive electric illumination. Trapped in the suit, his skin broke into a fresh sweat. When he got to Ronin he found it empty, just opened, and the barman stood there alone in his long cavern, twisting a cloth inside freshly cleaned glasses. They were familiar with each other and they shook hands.

Buford ordered a carafe of Junmai sake on ice and gulped down two glasses to steady himself. He was an hour ahead of time. Early in the summer evenings the clientele was entirely single businessmen dressed exactly like him, a lost tribe assuaging their anxieties at a silent bar. But at the same time it was his and Lily's place. They had been coming there since their first date. When she arrived at seven, Buford was still drinking alone and they had the place to themselves. Since she had no inkling of his bad news he let her down a glass first and then related the day's mournful events, including the largely uneaten pigeon with Longjing tea at The Chairman.

'They can't do that,' she blurted out at once.

'Can't?'

'You can sue them.'

'In fact, no, I can't.'

'What about separation money?'

'To be discussed. I have a feeling they won't pay it anyway. We're in a new world now. The old rules have vanished.'

In the awkward pause he lifted his glass and proposed a sarcastic toast. 'To the future!'

'What about the house?' she said almost at once.

He shrugged, reaching out for her forearm laid across the bar, the Codis Maya bracelet he had recently bought for her. He fondled the metal for a moment, then the cold skin around it. He could tell she was thinking her own thoughts and that they were racing ahead in time even faster than his own. He said, 'I'll have to move out end of the month. Or come up with psychotic rent.'

'You can move out. You don't have to pay that kind of money. Just not on the Peak.'

'It's a shame that I'm so used to it.'

'You can get unused to it. I can get unused to it.'

Can you? he thought, and yet there was a thread of sincerity in Lily's voice and he let it go. The problem was his, not hers. It was he who would be unable to get used to not having that morning run among the Indian rubber trees and not having his pool table in view of the sea. The barman brought them a second bottle and a second ice-bed. They knocked glasses and for the first time that day the idea occurred to Buford that maybe it wouldn't be so bad after all. The firm was a collection of corrupt ghouls anyway – better to be out of it. Then, without much delicacy, Lily asked him outright how much money he had saved up. He lied; $28,000 was far from what he actually had, which was in reality closer to $10,000. Not to mention the credit cards.

She said, 'I shouldn't really ask you, but maybe I can help. It's none of my business. But it's better this way, because now I can help out more. It's better to know where we stand.'

'Help?'

'I know a lot of people here, in case you didn't know. I'm going to ask around for you. You're young, you're talented. You're good-looking, you conceited asshole. I can help out.'

He took her hand and kissed it.

'It's sweet of you. But I doubt it.'

'You're not even Chinese. You don't know anything about anything here. It's me who can help you, not the other way round. And you've been sweet to *me*. I haven't forgotten anything.'

When he had met her at a finance party three years earlier, Lily had been a classic small-town rube from a place fifty miles back of Shenzhen. Heyuan, he thought the place was. He had traced it on a map. Her father was a mechanic slowly dying of lung cancer. He never asked her much about it, or them, sensing that she did not want to be asked, although she did occasionally bring up the matter of their needing a new house. Instead, they forgot about their respective pasts in order to enter the slow-moving tornado of an affair that swept them through darkened club dance floors and back rooms filled with cocaine tables, through weekend yacht trips to Lamma Island and then other weekends in Tokyo. Here and there, he had splashed out on her. But she liked Rado watches, not Jaegers, her tastes were quiet and unostentatious; she had never drained him of large amounts, for any reason. In fact she had never asked for anything. Patiently, insistently, she had won Buford over in the most important place of all, his unconscious. In that still centre of his being, she had found a secure place that could endure through a crisis.

'What friends are you talking about?' he said.

'Just friends. People who can help you out.'

They went for dinner at the Java Road markets, then passed the hours in a club they liked, dancing together as if alone, his afternoon's shock and depression gradually ebbing away to be replaced by defiance and lust. It was past one when they climbed back up to the Peak in a public taxi. Since the night was warm they slept outside on the balcony, with mosquito burners, and finished a bottle of rosé. Now he remembered that for the first time since he was at college at UCLA he didn't have to get up in the morning. It was a small upside to his predicament. In the event, however, they woke up at dawn and Buford saw that no messages had flashed up on his phone. It meant that the firm had not yet made any public announcement. He made Lily scrambled eggs and they ate together as the moon disappeared and the cruise ships turned off their lights in the harbour.

'You already look more relaxed,' she said. 'Maybe this was not a bad thing. It's a shame to give up this balcony, though.'

It's not real, he wanted to say. No mortal could afford to live in such a place. But he murmured, 'I can still find a bedsit with a view. Every dump in Hong Kong has a view.'

'You're not going to live in a dump.'

After Lily had left for work, he put on his jogging gear and headed out to the jungle paths as per his usual routine. He had already decided that he might as well benefit from the vanishing perks of his now-past life.

He took one of the colonial-era pathways, with their old British railings, and ran in solitude under the rubber trees and tropical vines until he reached one of the viewpoints where runners always rested for a few minutes to take in the view. That morning there was no one about, not even the lean bankers taking their morning constitutional. He stopped, unusually exhausted – it had been a long night of 'entertainments' – and let his weight lean into the railing to relieve his joints. His lungs sucked in air and he panted heavily, the sweat pouring off his face. Runner at college, now broken down by too many long nights and stressed by a lifestyle that no longer accorded with his advancing age. For the first time since the preceding apocalyptic day he felt disgust rising within himself. The city, as everyone now realised, was changing hands as the Communist Party asserted its control, and the future of American expat finance operators such as himself was none too bright. Once he lost his perch on the Peak he would be unlikely to recover it. The house he occupied was likely being coveted by some Party bigwig he had never heard of and his ejection from it had been carefully planned in advance. There was little he could do but acquiesce. The power structure was turning over, throwing all the little men into the void.

As he stood there, getting back his breath, he gradually became aware that the bench behind him was occupied. A middle-aged Chinese man in a blue-and-white tracksuit sat there reading the morning paper, with a plastic cup of takeaway coffee. The man was partially bald, his grey hair undyed and groomed, and his sneakers were of the expensive variety. Probably one of the bankers out for his morning run, like him. Buford half-turned and offered a Cantonese 'Good morning'. The man lowered the paper and replied in kind. He was wearing gold-wire reading glasses, his eyes merry and inquisitive. In English he told Buford that he had seen him out running early the morning before. Buford told him which house he lived in.

'Ah, I know it. Do you own it?'

'Rented.'

'Company rent then. I just come up here for the run. Can't afford even the rents.'

They chuckled. Buford turned from the railing and came to the bench. Some part of him felt a need for a conversation with someone who was a stranger. It would be a renewed contact with down-to-earth reality, with the healing power of the ordinary.

'I've never seen you up here before,' he said to the stranger.

'Melvin Hui,' the man replied, extending a dry hand.

Names exchanged, Buford decided he might as well sit down. Hui put down his paper and took off his reading glasses.

'I avoid the crowds, you know. That's why you've never seen me. I'm a ghost.'

'Of course.'

It was a pun, since the common Chinese word for a foreigner was *gwailo*, roughly translatable as 'ghost'.

'The ghost of the Peak,' Hui went on. 'Me, not you. I was going to walk to the playground around the corner. Would you like to walk with me?'

'I was going that way anyway.'

'Hopefully the nannies and kids haven't arrived yet.'

They set off at a leisurely pace and as they rounded the first bend of the mountaintop pathway Mr Hui said that he had something to admit. He did not know Buford, obviously, and Buford did not know him, but it had not been entirely by accident that he had been on the pathway at the same time as Buford and at the same spot. Hui began to smile to himself, indicating that it was something completely innocent.

'The fact is,' he said, 'I know your girlfriend, Miss Lily. She told me all about you. I hope you are not *too* surprised.'

'More than that.'

For a moment Buford stopped, shook his head and laughed.

'Wait a minute . . .'

'It's all quite ordinary really. She told me last night about your circumstances.'

'Last night?'

'She called me right away.'

'She told you about my circumstances?'

The smile from Hui was, in its way, visibly blameless.

'You must be a bit startled. Don't be. I've known Lily for years. If you must know, she has been worried about you getting fired for months. She has been thinking far ahead – more than you, it would seem.'

'How do you know Lily, again?'

'We used to be colleagues at China Construction Bank, years ago. Then I left to start my own company. Then I retired. But we stayed in touch. She helps me here and there with business things. We're both from Shenzhen, you see. I look on her as my adopted daughter.'

'But she's never mentioned you.'

'I asked her not to mention me to anyone. I prefer to keep it that way. But when she needs a favour, I am here. By the way, she didn't ask me to come here and meet you. She knows nothing about it. You'll have to promise me not to mention it to her, either.'

'Why would I do that?'

'Because if we keep it between us, Rowan, I am sure I can

help you. I might be able to help you get a new job. Though it might not be in Hong Kong. Of course I don't know if you'd be agreeable to that, but maybe we can discuss it at some point.'

Reaching the playground park, they found it empty and sat at one of the stone tables under the trees. Buford expected the visitor to now present him with a business card, but he did not. Yet there was something genially furtive about him, an impression of some kind of underhand efficacy. Hui went on. He had been looking for someone like Buford for quite some time and so he had taken it upon himself to 'leap into the breach' and seize the opportunity as soon as he could – and before Buford received a more attractive offer from another quarter. It was fortuitous for him, at the very least.

'What do you mean, someone like me?' Buford said. But he felt subtly flattered and relieved in the same moment. The very day after the catastrophe a potential opportunity had materialised.

'Why don't we discuss it over dinner tonight?' Hui offered.

'I don't know. It's a bit of whirlwind. What kind of job are you talking about?'

'It would involve you going back to the States. You might not want to go back, but I could make it comfortable for you. You could return here afterwards and I suppose, if you liked, you could resume renting the house you are in now.'

'Oh?'

'We – my company and I – have deeper pockets than Mr Fitch, if that's what you are wondering. Much deeper. I was being ironic earlier about not being able to afford the rents up here.'

Then, mutually, they both seemed to relax, and Buford looked over at a mob of jackdaws hopping from table to table, cocking their heads. One appeared to stare back at him malevolently. He shook his head as if in disbelief, then he thought, *Fuck it* and accepted the dinner invitation. Betrayed by his treacherous company, to which he had contributed so much, he no longer felt inclined to be mistrustful of a stranger, since the latter could no more harm him than the men whom he had, until yesterday, considered to be his allies. If they were all the same – strangers and allies alike – why not toss in your lot with a stranger? Relatively speaking, what were benevolence and malevolence when they both offered the same pay cheque?

'I'm very happy to hear it,' Hui said when Buford accepted his offer. 'Shall we go to Tin Lung Heen and pretend we are adults?'

'I've heard it's quite empty now.'

'Yes. That had occurred to me.'

Hui then stood up and said that he had best be on his way. They shook hands, Buford curious and bemused, and parted ways as the jackdaws scattered around them.

Buford retraced his steps to the house and spent the afternoon answering emails from colleagues and associates – the word of his firing having now got out. He decided to be flippant and offhand, as if it didn't matter to him. One gets fired, one gets re-hired. The nervous tone of his correspondents suggested that they knew otherwise, but he kept up an impeccable façade. He called Lily and told her he would be busy that night; he left it as a message on her answering service. Then he waited for dusk, playing pool by himself in his grandly austere living room, with Deep Purple on his antique jukebox. At seven, dressed in a dark pinstripe suit, he called a cab for the ride down to Kowloon and the Ritz-Carlton. He intended to be slightly and unfashionably early, and he was.

ON THE LIFT RIDE up to the restaurant on the 102nd floor Buford reflected that for the first time in his life he was skating over ice of indeterminate thickness. And he no longer cared. He made a confident entrance into the discreetly elegant restaurant and found, to his consternation, that Hui was already there, reading the same *South China Morning Post* that he had been reading earlier in the day, but now dressed in a suit almost identical to his own. Fitch the previous day, now this. At least Buford wasn't picking up the tab for either. Hui looked up calmly and welcomed him courteously. Tea for two had already been served in gold cups, abalone was on the way. Did Buford want a shot of Kaoliang *baiju*?

The American thought it would be a good idea. His stress needed a little unpacking.

Hui raised a hand and the alcohol was arranged. When the shot glasses and bottle arrived, he offered a toast: 'To semi-strangers!'

They knocked back the first shot and the bitter liquor went to Buford's head at once. The tensions of the previous twenty-four hours seemed to burst into his frontal lobes for a moment, then vanish as if for ever. Hui, relaxed and unshakable, put Buford at his ease by describing some of his background. He had grown up in Guangzhou and migrated to Hong Kong just after college. He had laboured in the storage facilities of a huge meat importer, then gradually worked his way into the real-estate business. He had worked in banks subsequently, had acquired a fortune doing business on the mainland, working as a go-between for government higher-ups. Buford knew the script. It was a familiar story. Hui had learned English in night school. Now he wanted to expand his real-estate business into the American market. Buford knew perfectly well why. The Chinese wanted to get their money out of a closed capital account like China, whose property market was going through an astonishing crisis, and get it into properties in rule-of-law countries like Canada and the US. Hui had been thinking about it for some time.

He had several contacts in California, which was where he wanted to invest, but he really needed a California native who also knew China. His idea was to send the candidate to California for six months and set him up in an attractive house with a considerable wage. From this base he could survey the landscape of opportunity, as it were, and set out to make advantageous contacts with influential Americans in that sector.

Hui himself was unsure how such things worked in America. In China you had to know politicians in order to wheel and deal in high-value property. Perhaps America was the same. He assumed it was. He could hardly go in there and do it himself. Anti-Chinese sentiment was running high, was it not?

'So I've heard,' Buford said.

'Well, that is my idea. It's a rather simple one, on the face of it. Do you think you might be interested in doing it? All I ask is six months and after that you'll have no obligations to me. All I need are contacts, ways in, people who might help me on a basis of mutual profit.'

'And what kind of property are you interested in buying?'

Hui leaned back and his eye seemed to track the illuminated tourist junks floating by below. Their red sails stood out against the violent reflections in the dark water.

'It could be anything. Nothing sensitive. Ranch land, mansions, farms maybe. I've heard the lettuce farms in the Imperial Valley turn a nice profit. Or the land around Rancho Santa Fe. Do you know it?'

'Of course. Hard to buy.'

'Then you see what I mean. What about the area around the Russian River?'

'In the north?'

'My wife says she would love to own a house there. Maybe you could choose an area and then socialise with the local bigwigs. I'd give you enough money to make that possible – you could contribute to campaigns and such. Charities. American love giving to charities, do they not?'

'It's the nicest thing about us.'

'There you are then. You could go in as a nice guy with deep pockets and impress people with your generosity and altruism. You've got the right kind of face. I think it would be surprisingly easy for you. You're a native, and everyone loves a native.'

'Do they?'

'They do, in my experience. They especially like a native

who's a donor. These are strange times. People will take money from wherever it comes. Like us, when it comes down to it. You know perfectly well you're going to have to move out of that beautiful house in three weeks and you aren't going to find a place like the one you had with Fitch. They tossed you out in a heartbeat as soon as their bottom line was threatened. That's the way it is. Look out for yourself, Rowan. Yourself.'

It was a perfect reflection of Buford's own thoughts. He had been sold out, and so all his misgivings and inhibitions had been thrown out as well. Hui was right about the house and the job prospects. A lifeline had been thrown to him and he was beginning to think he had better seize it before he drowned.

'What exactly do you want me to do?' he said. 'I don't have to pretend to be someone I'm not, do I?'

'Well, that does rather come with the territory!'

'You mean I'll have to change my name?'

'If you don't, your real history will be traceable in a minute. Think about it. It will be known, for example, that you were just fired from a company in Hong Kong. That would ruin everything. You have to do a Gatsby.'

'A Gatsby?'

'Isn't that the phrase you use? I read that book last summer. Very interesting look at American manners. I think the Chinese title might have been *Capitalist Prince*.'

Hui winked and, as if orchestrated, the abalone arrived. Only a single other table was now occupied, three young female socialites drinking bottle after bottle of champagne.

'So,' Buford ventured, 'how do I do that exactly?'

'It will all be done for you. You will enter the country under your own name and then we'll set you up somewhere under a different name. No one is going to check your new identity with Immigration because they don't have any reason to. And American bureaucracies are totally chaotic and hopeless, as I'm sure you know. Besides, you won't be doing anything illegal. On the contrary. You'll be an outstanding citizen contributing to charities.'

'I suppose you already have a list of charities that you want to get friendly with?'

'We are not entirely unprepared. I was thinking . . . I hope you don't mind me saying what has been on my mind? There's a lot of land I'd like to look at along the border. Most of it is the fifty-first congressional district. I believe the representative there is a man called Eugene Vargas. He's in his seventies, but his wife Melania is much younger. We bought a property in a place down there called Bella Lago. I don't suppose you know it?'

'Not at all.'

'It's in Chula Vista, so part of the fifty-first district. But it's out in the desert, the most expensive area in Chula Vista in fact. Some wealthy Chinese would love to live there. Buy the plots, build the dream house. You know what I mean. It's the way my clients think. They want to be away from prying eyes. *Our* prying eyes is what I mean. They want to park their money offshore and have it be invisible.'

'They want to be ghosts.'

'Ha, exactly. Very well said. Exactly so.'

'And I will be the ghost who prepares the way.'

'You could put it like that. All you would have to do is a

bit of socialising and hopefully get to meet Mrs Vargas. She supports a charity for handicapped children from the border areas, called Able Minds. It strikes me that you could make a donation when you get there and her office will get in touch with you. The rest will be up to you, and I don't think you'll have too much difficulty fitting right in with the people down there. They're not the most sophisticated, you know. You'll wow them, and that's what I want you to do. Gatsby them.'

'I don't think you understand what Gatsby—'

'No, I understand. I'm just joking. In fact we want you to be, if anything, understated, discreet. A rich young man living alone. You should avoid all your previous friends there, and even your family. Do you think you can do that?'

'Not call my parents?'

'Absolutely not. As far as everyone is concerned, you are still in Hong Kong. Let's keep it that way.'

'And what about Lily?'

'Yes, Lily. There's something to consider. If you agree to this, I think it would be better to not see her until you return. Can you manage that?'

'I'll have to tell her why I'm leaving.'

But Hui had already considered this.

'I'm her friend. I can step in here and do it tactfully. I'm sure she'll understand. To be frank, Rowan, I've already discussed it with her. I took the liberty. I told her three months and you'll be back.'

'And what did she say?'

'She said if it saved you from bankruptcy, it would be worth it.'

'Bankruptcy?' Buford snorted, feeling the muscles in his

face strain. He hoped his display of disbelief was convincing.
It was not.

'Rowan, we both know the situation you are in. You
haven't saved a dollar worth shit. You'll be broke by the time
eviction day comes. How is that going to be? I could have
told you drugs are a waste of money. But I didn't know you
six months ago. It's too late.'

You have me there, the American thought and, against
his better judgement, he bit his lower lip and glanced
downwards.

'You would talk to Lily?' he said.

'I think you should call her, but not meet. I'm afraid she
might make you change your mind. I can see you like her.'

'Yes – and she might take it badly.'

Hui called over two more glasses of Kaoliang.

'Oh, don't make a drama out of it. Six months is nothing.
I'll explain it to her at the three-month mark. Here, let's
drink to our deal. We have one, do we not?'

'I guess we do.'

They sank the second round, and Hui told him to leave
everything at the town house – his company would take care
of it all. When Buford returned it would all be exactly as he
left it and the rent would be paid up. His financial reward for
accepting the 'commission' would be enough for him to stay
there for another two years if he wanted. Or live in Hawaii
for the rest of his life. Which would be worse?

They laughed, and Buford asked when Hui expected him
to leave for California.

'I think you should leave in two days. Everything is
already set up there. You fly into Los Angeles and my team

will drive you to the house. *Your* house. You won't have to do anything but settle in. It'll be the easiest money you ever made.'

'And what about you?'

'What about me? You'll never see me again. You will tell people, if they ever ask, that you've never met me and have never heard of me. Once you return here, you'll be Rowan Buford again and you'll continue as you were before. You've been fired, remember. No one will care if you are seen around town or not. You'll say you were brooding at home.'

By now the *baiju* had overtaken his senses and Buford did not notice the time at which the meeting ended, and Mr Hui had called his driver to take him back to the Peak. They did not go down in the lift together. Hui departed first and asked Buford to wait at least fifteen minutes before he exited. The handshake was jovial. 'Good luck, and buy something nice for your girl in Beverly Hills.' Hui then rose and the staff fluttered around him like starlings.

He vanished and Buford sat for the allotted fifteen minutes, drinking more of the *baiju*. Out of curiosity, he looked it up on the menu and saw that it cost $3,000. Then, alleviating his anxiety, the staff quietly notified him that his car was waiting for him downstairs. Half-drunk, he staggered to the lifts and fell into the limousine awaiting him in front of the hotel's entrance. The driver wore a peaked cap and a black uniform and said not a word as they swept up through the jungle roads to the Peak, leaving the American to his own turbulent thoughts and fears. On his balcony he called Lily, but, as before, she did not pick up. *Hui's told her already*, he thought, and this rapid coordination did not seem quite

natural. Yet since he could not affect it either way he submit-
ted to the flow of events, which now seemed predetermined.

In the morning he went for his usual run, and upon his
return found an envelope laid by his door. It was a printout
for his flight to Los Angeles the following night with Cathay
Pacific. First-class, direct. There was a note from Mr Hui:
'Pack nothing, just yourself and a suit. Don't worry about
anything. My team will be waiting for you at LAX. Have a
good flight. Do not call anyone before you leave. I'll keep
everything in order while you are away. Good luck with your
"vacation".'

DURING THE LONG FLIGHT from Hong Kong, Buford
dreamed he was wading through a field of sugar cane while
above him, perched upon a mountain sunk in nocturnal darkness, an arsonised house burned merrily like an improvised
beacon, shooting its reflections into puddles within the wet
fields. It was a place he vaguely knew, perhaps in China
somewhere. When he woke it was dawn and they were
descending into LA, the sun on the sea, croissants on the tray
before him. He didn't even want to look at his watch. The
airport was empty. At the exit a tall Chinese man awaited
him, in the same company uniform as the driver who had
taken him home from the Ritz-Carlton. The man knew him
even from afar and raised a hand to beckon him. He took
Buford's carry-on bag and said in perfect English, 'You're on
time.'

They drove down Interstate 5 to San Diego in blue-sky
weather, the driver not talking from the far side of a heavy

tinted screen. From time to time, Buford lowered his window and let the sea air wash over him.

It was his landscape, familiar from years of visiting: the imperial palms standing in military lines and lots of ice-plant serving as architectural relish to parking lots and state beaches. They passed Trails State Beach, which he had once visited as a child, the Old Pacific Highway running parallel to it in obscurity. Now he understood what Hui had meant by the irreplaceable nature of being a native.

On the far side of San Diego they emerged to the south in Chula Vista, getting off on 54 and driving inland. Great swooping overpasses and sassafras trees and signs for Plaza Bonita. Turning south again, they came to Eastlake. Here the low brown hills were capped with static mist, despite the sunshine. The Proctor Valley with its half-hidden Spanish villas, and then the turn-off uphill into Bella Lago. It was a neighbourhood of sweeping drives and white villas at the edge of the sierra, with firs and palms set on the lawns. They moved along Coastal Hills Drive and the driver finally turned and said, 'Bella Lago. Do you like it?'

'I know it, if that's what you mean.'

They came at last to a gated development sitting at the high point and closed off with wooden gates. The driver got out and opened the gate manually, a curious arrangement. The place looked shut, uncertain of its commercial destiny and half-abandoned. On the far side of the gate there were large mansions, many of them with stickers in their windows. They looked as if they had not yet been sold, or had been sold and not yet claimed. At the far end of the development they came to the last house at the edge of the mountain terrain, from where the Otay lake could be seen, desert scrub fringing the half-finished road.

There were no cars parked outside the other units and it seemed that they were not occupied, but outside this last house a brand-new Mazda convertible was stationed. They parked behind it and got out into a cool wind sweeping up from the lake. The mountains were dark even under the sun, with great cumulus clouds rising behind them. The mansion itself was almost grand, newly finished, its arched and high windows fitted with what looked like fresh glass. The driver took Buford to the doors, opened them and then handed the same keys to him. For a moment Buford thought about his dream in the aeroplane. It could well have been this same house, seen from a great distance below. They stepped into a lofty reception area smelling of varnish and artificial air freshener. It was made of pale wood, the glass-fronted inbuilt cabinets still empty. The driver took him through the ground floor: an immense kitchen with an aisle, glass doors that opened onto a terrace, with the mountain view angled away from the other houses nearby so that one could forget them.

'Does Mr Hui own this place?' Buford asked, somewhat unnecessarily.

'He owns the whole development. But he keeps it empty for the moment.'

'Just me, then.'

'Just you. The car outside is for your use. Try not to get it scratched. The keys are in the welcome package on the kitchen table. I'll be going now. Groceries will be delivered here twice a week. You can write down requests and leave them by the fridge. The deliveries will be left in the kitchen – our staff have copy keys. It doesn't matter if you are here or not.'

The driver then shook Buford's hand and let himself out, leaving the American to wander out to the terrace and admire the distant lake below. The familiarity of the land was now undermined by the artificiality of his position within it. The house had obviously never been occupied. The paint on its surface had acquired no character, and the air-conditioning units jutting from some of the windows looked as if they had been installed the day before. A small fir tree planted at the edge of the terrace quivered in the valley wind and beyond it the sombre earth sloped steeply down into an arroyo. It was nowhere – a doll's house in nowhere. He went into the kitchen and opened the package that awaited him in a small box. It contained the expected essentials: the car's keys and papers, with a note asking him to use his own driving licence in the event of being stopped by the police. But there was also a fake licence with his photograph under the name Ralph Long, which could be used for all other purposes. There were two credit cards in the false name and a tin lockbox filled with cash in $100 notes.

Looking at the cash, he casually estimated that it must be at least $80,000. There were luxurious business cards with the name Ralph Long and a single phone number and, to match, a new iPhone registered with that same number for his use. At the bottom of the box lay a factory-new laptop.

By now, feeling tired, Buford wandered up the wooden stairwell to the first floor, where there were three bedrooms and a study with an antique desk. He placed the laptop there and went to the master bedroom, with a four-poster bed.

There was a walk-in cupboard and he soon saw that it was filled with jackets, suits and shirts. Trying on a jacket, he found that it fitted him perfectly; so they had thought of everything. A whole wardrobe cut to his size. From where had they obtained the measurements? He didn't pause too much to consider the matter, since the bed beckoned and his jetlag had caught up with him.

When he woke it was dark and a light rain whispered against the windows. He went into the bathroom and found it as fully equipped as the rest of the house: shaving utensils, bathrobes, soaps and oils, stacks of expensive towels. He took a long bath and listened to the rain. According to his instructions, he had left his own phone in Hong Kong and so there was no way to satisfy his curiosity about Lily or anyone else. Dried off, he went to the study and opened the laptop. Its programs had been customised for him and there was a Gmail account with a new password, which, he assumed, could be used to communicate with Hui's company. There was a welcome email from an unknown 'Harry' in the in-box with instructions on how to wire money to accounts in the US. It might have been a pseudonym for Hui himself. On the desktop he found files relating to the Able Minds charity in El Centro and personal details about Melania Vargas.

Activating the phone, he took it with him down to the kitchen and plundered the immense freezers, packed with steaks and legs of lamb. After defrosting one in the microwave, he made himself a T-bone and scrolled through the numbers pre-loaded onto the phone's contacts. They were mostly real-estate agents operating along the border. A private message had also appeared on a Facebook page set up for his new identity – it used his photo in the profile and displayed hundreds of 'friends' whom he had never heard of. The message, meanwhile, was simply a map of the border area east of El Centro in which lots of seemingly empty desert lay, marked out – he sensed – for acquisition. So this was the land that Hui wanted to acquire. Lots adjoining the Mexican border north of Jacumba Hot Springs, most of them bereft even of buildings or farms. Some, however, were home to lettuce and strawberry farms in the Imperial Valley and these were marked accordingly. The hint was clear enough.

After his steak and half a bottle of Ridge from the ample wine cooler he went outside into the drizzle and looked out over the dark and empty enclave now submerged in a wet mist. As he had suspected, the other mansions were totally dark, unoccupied. He had been planted in a perfectly secretive place.

He walked down to the car and ran his hand along its untarnished contours. He was beginning to think that he had landed on his feet after all, since all he had to do was buy some land for a man 4,000 miles away, with no questions asked. Obviously by this point Buford understood that in order to do that he had to ingratiate himself with the congressman's wife. There was nothing about it that was not straightforward, in theory.

THE FOLLOWING MORNING HE reached Jacumba Hot Springs near the border by 9 a.m., the 100-mile route from Chula Vista to El Centro being mostly a smooth, tedious drive through white-earth desert.

Passing creosote bushes and *chollas* with stiff yellow flowers, Buford had the feeling that he had seen them before in his dreams. The sky's clean blue glare made the road shine. He turned off onto Old Highway 80 and trundled down the sun-cracked two-lane road right into the little town of Jacumba, with the border fence to his right. He stopped several times and took photos with his new phone. The spaces north of the road were littered with flat boulders and weathered telephone poles. An abandoned railway track was half grown over with desert plants; he took snaps of it standing on a newly renovated bridge above it, where mesquite trees had come alive with desert birds.

In Jacumba he parked at Mountain Sage Market across from a line of picturesque adobe shop fronts and drank a coffee at the lone outdoor table. It was a place sunk into its own contented slumber. Mexicans and old men. On his phone he found the number of an appointment-only real-estate agent and called: Terry Gomez picked up.

Buford said, 'My name's Ralph Long. Are you taking people out to lots today?'

Gomez said that he would meet him at the Market in fifteen. From the tone of his voice Buford guessed that he had not scored a client in weeks, or even months. He continued with his coffee and waited. The shop fronts opposite showed no sign of life, not even in the newly painted 'Tattoo' joint. Perhaps it became a bar later in the day.

He examined the lots that had been indicated on the map from Hui's company and could see that they were all close by, subtending to Old Highway 80. The idea was presumably that he should select two or three that seemed propitious – to build houses. He should get their prices per lot and see if any had water supplies. Gomez's battered old Pontiac arrived just as Buford finished his coffee. A hefty man of about fifty rolled out of it, wearing a ponderous Stetson with a Navajo-style metal band studded with turquoise stones. They shook hands in the harsh sun and Buford agreed to ride with him out to a couple of plots that he might enjoy having a look at. There were in fact several lots for sale along the Highway. Numbers thirty-six and forty-one might suit. They reached number thirty-six within two minutes of driving. It was closed off with a padlocked metal gate and they got out to unlock it and take in the view. An easement road ran through it and they could see the border fence in the distance. It was $55,000 for twenty-eight acres.

'You'd have to drill your own wells,' Gomez said as the gates swung open and they wandered up the easement road, with electric poles along the edge. 'One thing is the Border Patrol use this road. They go in and out as they like. There's nothing you can do about it.'

'They can come in any time?'

'Any time. And they do and will. That's why the land is so cheap. No one wants land by the border. They're hunting illegals on it, day and night.'

Buford was already thinking ahead. So this was where the congressman's wife came in.

'Where you from anyway?' Gomez said.

'Up north. My parents are in Mendocino.'

'That's where you should buy. You can't do nothing with this land. Unless you're a smuggler.'

'Got it.'

They laughed and Buford took a few more pictures on his phone.

Gomez went on, 'The last owner wanted to make a resort here, but he gave up. He got no compensation from the Fed, either. They wanted to build a holding facility on his land. Can you imagine?'

'Do they still come through on this road?'

'Every night, far as I can tell. I might as well be upfront with you about it. Guess you probably won't want to buy now.'

'I'll have to think about it.'

'It's a beauty of a spot, don't you think?'

Buford took off his sunglasses and gazed over the low purple mountains on the Mexican side, the arroyos of cactus and sage. The easement road went down to the old railway line, followed it for 200 yards, then curved down to the border fence.

'There's a hunting club down there, the Lakeside.' Gomez pointed to the fence as it rolled east. 'Right on the border. You can go shoot there if you have a mind. Do you shoot?'

'Never tried it.'

'Well, if you come to live out here you can do that. Are you looking to build a house?'

'Was thinking of it.'

'Best stargazing there is. Maybe you won't mind the wetbacks running across your land. They'll probably leave you alone.'

'I'm thinking I like the unit. It's a good price.'

'Damn right it is. It's a giveaway. Frankly, it's the better of the two lots. The views are fine.'

They drove down the easement to the rail tracks and then closer to the fence itself. The road ran alongside the latter but they didn't follow it, returning instead to the Old Highway 80, where no cars seemed to have passed in hours.

Gomez said, 'Call me whenever you want to talk about making an offer. We haven't had many enquiries, to be honest with you. The place has a bad reputation.'

'Is it unsafe at night then?'

'I'd get a gun, if I were you. You can keep it under your bed.'

That was a fine idea. Back at his car, Buford offered to buy Gomez an early lunch, wanting to get more information from him, and they sat together at the same side-table with burritos and *agua de Jamaica* in outsized paper cups filled to the brim with crushed ice. Buford asked him about El Centro. Wasn't it a city in decline?

'Depends what you call "decline". They moved the gangs out finally and cleaned it up a little. You can always drive there on a Saturday for a little trouble.'

'What about the Vargases? Are they around in El Centro?'

'We see them now and then. The wife more.'

'What kind of person is she?'

'She was crippled in a car accident. Her husband was driving. Most of the landowners around here know them a little. They might want to know who you are.'

Now Buford understood; he needed the Vargas's backing to free the desert plot from the recurrent intrusions of the Border Patrol. Under a high sun he drove into El Centro on 98. The desert there was smooth and devoid of vegetation. A mountain dark as a pile of iron slag rose by the border, baked in the sun. Then, close to town, the beige plain suddenly turned green. Mexicans in straw hats ambled along the aisles of plants, swinging hoes, while behind them acres of solar panels were angled up to the sun. Soon he was in the town, cruising wide avenues of low bungalows, trailer parks and shaggy imperial palms, the streets paralysed in sun-shock. The shadows whittled to a minimum. He found Adam's Avenue and its trucker motels where sugar rigs spent the night, and nearby the low bungalow where Able Minds was housed, helpfully advertised by a large sign. He parked right in front of it and walked in.

He found a big single room with four desks and a lone woman behind one of them. She looked up and he turned on his hedge-fund smile. Stepping to the desk, he whipped out his card and said, 'My name's Ralph Long. I've wanted to come and see you guys for some time. I've admired your work enormously.'

The woman was too surprised to react immediately, but he continued his prepared speech. He would be honoured to make a donation to the cause.

'You know the congressman's wife is our CEO?' she said.

'Of course. It only makes the honour greater.'

The woman looked over his beautiful thick card.

'So you live in Chula Vista?'

'I've just moved down from San Francisco.'

'I'm sure Mrs Vargas would love to talk to you. She's not due in until Wednesday. But could she call you?'

'Please ask her to. I was thinking of donating a hundred thousand to you. Do you think that would be satisfactory?'

'Satisfactory?' The eyes examining him expanded for a moment. 'It's very generous of you, Mr Long. And you've simply walked in. I suppose you must have thought about it beforehand.'

'I sure have. I've thought about it for weeks.'

'Is that so? Well, how marvellous. Will you be at home tonight?'

He said that he would be.

'Are you a philanthropist then?' the woman asked, now a little more nervous.

'I'm a capitalist prince. But now I want to do some good.'

'A hundred thousand will help us a lot. A great deal.'

'That's what I'm hoping. It's a token of my respect. I don't want to take up any of your time. I know you're busy. I just wanted to pop in and show my face.'

'Oh well, I'm glad you did!'

As Buford began his courteous retreat she rose awkwardly and made to shake his hand while stepping forward, knocking over the waste-paper basket by her foot as she did.

'Mrs Vargas will call you tonight.'

'Perhaps you can give me your bank details now and I can arrange the transfer?'

'Oh yes, of course. Let's see.'

Flustered, she retrieved the details and wrote them down for him on a business card. She came with him to the door, then outside into the hot sun. *Easy*, he thought. It was never difficult to bowl over provincials. He must have been the only man in El Centro wearing a $4,000 suit. He could see it in her eyes as she walked him to the car. The dull amazement, the futile hope of seduction. He flirted just a little, flattered her tan. She took in the brand-new Mazda convertible. As he drove out of town, relieved to be leaving, he was satisfied with his performance, sure that he had made a good impression and that the assistant would relay her opinions enthusiastically to her CEO. At home again, he made another steak, put some Chris Isaak on the sound system and drank another bottle of free Ridge with his feet up on the terrace, watching clouds form and dissolve over the Otay lake. Everything was proceeding even more smoothly than he had expected.

On the laptop he sent a message to the email account already loaded onto it and wrote, 'Donation accepted. Suggest 100k.' By the time he had finished the Ridge, a reply had come back: 'Agreed. Send bank details.' He then mentioned the price of the lot on Old Highway 80 and sent his pictures.

This done, he went to the cooler and retrieved a second bottle. At 10.30 Melania Vargas called. She was with her husband in a restaurant in Hillside and the introductions were mutually tipsy. She thanked him for his offer of a donation and he told her the funds would be in their account in three days.

'So you've done it already?' she said.

The noise of the restaurant became quieter as she evidently got up and walked away from the table to a different part of the premises.

'What a wonderful thing to do, Mr Long.'

'It's the least I can do for the children.'

'Are you – I mean, do you live in San Diego?'

'I've just moved. Chula Vista.'

They talked quietly for a while, several minutes.

'I'm sorry I wasn't in El Centro to meet you,' she said. 'Daisy told me all about you. Well, not *all*.'

There was a wine-fuelled laugh and he smiled. Daisy had told her that he was a young looker.

'There's not much to tell,' he said.

He went on about his childhood, truthfully, then made up imaginary years in New York, based on what he actually had been doing in Hong Kong. He improvised and laid on the charm. At the far end of the line he could feel her bending to his warmth, intrigued and trusting.

'I have to go now,' she concluded. 'My husband is waiting for me. But shouldn't we meet for lunch so I can thank you in person?'

He gave her his email address and she suggested two days from then, a place in Rancho Santa Fe called Mille Fleurs. It was a restaurant she loved to go by herself.

'You don't have to thank me,' he said.

'I always like to meet our donors face-to-face. It's a question of respect.'

'I'll be there then.'

'I'm going to tell my husband all about you.'

When the call ended, he went to the cash box and separated $56,000 from the total and placed it in a separate envelope. The payment for the plot should be done in cash, as he had guessed at once, and he had decided that if Hui agreed, then he would drive back out to Jacumba and make the deal. It would probably take several weeks to do the legal paperwork, but it was also possible that in a place like Jacumba things would go secretively and swiftly. It was time to relax a little, let the days pass and concentrate on the Vargas wife.

HE ARRIVED EARLY AT the Mille Fleurs restaurant two days later and found, basking in the sun, an internal courtyard with an *azulejo*-tiled Mexican fountain and propane patio heaters. He was early and was shown to Mrs Vargas's reserved table next to the fountain, where he sat for twenty minutes drinking punch and eating olives.

The clientele looked exactly like him. Rancho Santa Fe was rich and exclusive and its restaurants were the same. He wondered whether he could live like this, if he ever returned to the States – at ease and respected from a distance among his fellow racials. A fountain at lunchtime, a glass of over-oaked wine, knee-high dress socks. The white upper-middle ranch-owning class enjoying their long but chilly autumn.

Before long there was a soft commotion at the doors and two Mexican waiters appeared with a small woman in a tartan two-piece suit, wielding in her left hand a rosewood cane. Unsteadily she came down two steps to the courtyards, supported by the waiters, whose familiarity with her had obviously bred respect rather than contempt. She was wearing vintage cat-eye sunglasses with green lenses, and Common Projects sneakers to help with her awkward gait. Buford remembered the car accident with her husband and rose with an impulsive gallantry that made him instantly conspicuous. The cat-eyes came off and Mrs Vargas squinted in a slanted beam of sunlight to take him in. The waiters stepped back and she lifted the cane, then placed it firmly on the paving stones in front of her, propelling herself safely forward. He was quicker, coming to her and offering his hand.

'Ralph,' he said simply.

'There you are.' She turned to the waiters and there was a mischievous delight in her eyes. '*Quisiera una michelada con hielo. Sabes.*'

'*Para servirle, señora.*'

He escorted her to the chair, the arm replacing the cane, which he took in his free hand. *Cabellero.*

When her iced-beer stein came, she proposed a toast. To socially responsible donors.

'There aren't many of you, Ralph.'

'I'm sorry to hear that. I made my money young and now I don't know what to do with it.'

'You don't have a girlfriend?'

'New York days. I came out here after a break-up.'

'Oh, I'm sorry. Me, I've been married for twenty-seven years. I suppose you're wondering about my leg.'

'It's none of my business.'

'I don't mind you knowing. My husband went off the road during a barnstormer. An argument. I suppose I made him do it. I'm grateful I can still walk.'

'You do fine.'

'Painkillers – you know how it works. I must down a pound of them every day.'

'Your husband—'

'There's a subject to fill a library. Or a landfill. He's a busy man. He's in Mexico a lot, as it happens. He has business down there.'

'I can imagine.'

'He gets *asked* down there, I should say. Did you ever go to Mexicali? Well, you're not missing much. That's our twin city across the border.'

Buford shook his head, admitting that it was unknown to him.

'But why did you move down here?' she went on. 'You could live anywhere, I'm assuming. Wouldn't you want to live somewhere glamorous – Italy, Asia?'

'I am a native son. I wanted to be in the same state as my parents. They're in Mendocino.'

'That's a quite a drive, though.'

He smiled.

'Yes. But psychologically—'

'I know what you mean. Still, Chula Vista is nice, too.'

He said he had just moved into his house in Bella Lago. It suited him for the moment. You could smell the desert there. The house was brand-new, he had commissioned it himself. Nobody had lived there before him. He was taking a breather from a formerly hectic life, thinking things over.

'Really?'

For a moment she seemed sceptical, as if unconvinced by something in his narrative, or in his delivery of it.

Sensing he ought to provide an additional reason for his sojourn in Vargas's congressional district, he said slowly, 'In reality, I have another idea that has brought me here. I've been thinking about investing in land. If you really want to know, I went to see some lots in Jacumba the same day I visited your offices. The prices are attractive. I was thinking of buying a lot and then building a hunting lodge there, or something of that sort. Am I insane?'

'Not at all. Plenty of people do exactly that. There's a lodge at Lakeside right near there. I don't know if they make any money.'

'I'm not worried about the money side of it. I just want somewhere quiet to retire to twenty years from now. Or ten.'

They ate their lobster bisque and he rambled on about Jacumba and its beautiful landscapes. It would be a fine place to be an older gent living alone. He had thought of building a Spanish-style villa with tiled fountains exactly like the one they were sitting next to now. What did she think? He didn't want to get bogged down in an unrealistic fantasy. Moreover, he wanted to get involved positively in the local community – a sickly, largely meaningless phrase, but he was sure she knew what he meant.

'Cartels?' she laughed.

'Well, not quite.'

'I'm kidding. I think you've already joined the local community through your donation. You don't need to worry about that.'

The innuendo was clear enough and he thought, with satisfaction, *Score!* He pretended to be unsure, however.

'If you say so. And it's very kind of you.'

'I told my husband about your donation and he was very impressed. I think you've made a lot of friends overnight.'

'I saw something on TV about the orphaned kids and I was moved. I thought I really had to do something for them. It isn't that difficult. The way people hang on to their money is quite depraved, when you think about it. It's so easy to make a difference.'

He could feel her sentimental side rising to the occasion. And now that he considered it, she was quite attractive in her lean, wary, half-crippled and wounded way. *She needs taking care of*, he thought.

They progressed to fruit with Kirschwasser and coconut sorbet. The flirtation grew more obvious and neither of them minded. He ordered a second glass of wine and she went along with the same. Soon they were exchanging childhood anecdotes, favourite musicians, films, political banter. He said that he liked the idea of living close to Mexico – closer than anywhere! – and to making trips south of the border to familiarise himself with its culture. In the long run, the kids he was helping could even come to his new property in Jacumba and learn desert ecology if they wished. It was something that he had in mind anyway. It would give them a taste of nature that they maybe didn't have at present. He could even set up a botany school there. Half-amused, she said she could help with that, if he was serious about it.

'Certainly I'm serious about it!'

Their lunch ran on until three o'clock and when they came back to the streets where their cars awaited them they were happily tipsy. He walked her to her car and they shook hands more warmly than a normal leave-taking would demand. As she leaned in to take his hand she said, more quietly, 'I like you. We should do this again. Here's my card with my private number. Don't disappear, now.'

'How could I?'

She lingered for a moment, about to say something, then

held off and got into her black Lexus. It was amusing to see her overcome by a sudden shyness. In the space of three hours they had become quite familiar.

On the drive home to Bella Lago he wondered how long he should wait before sending her a quiet message by email or WhatsApp. Perhaps that same night he could thank her for the lunch and slip in a suggestive comment that would make for an adventurous move. He was sure that she was ready for it. She would not rebuff him.

He suggested that they meet again in Chula Vista, if she liked. Meanwhile he sent her a picture of the lot he wanted to buy. She replied close to midnight that she wanted to see him, too. As for the lot, she knew it and she thought it was a good buy for him. He was tempted to ask her if she knew Gomez, but decided not to. He calculated that she would bring it up eventually.

FOR DAYS HE BUSIED himself with buying the lot, since Hui's people had given him the go-ahead. He drove back out to Jacumba and arranged lawyers and contracts with Gomez, giving him the required cash to seal the deal. The two were becoming friendly. Buford was coming to understand that Gomez might be a useful person to know in the desert.

This done, Buford returned alone to the plot and looked it over again, but this time in more detail. There was a small hill of boulders with an old pylon standing upon it. He climbed up to it and looked down at the border fence. This time he saw a Border Patrol SUV crawling along the easement road, its windows reflecting the sun. It stopped and the occupants seemed to be watching him, the conspicuous alien standing on his hillock. Down by the railway tracks the gate to the lot was apparently open to them. It was midday then and the desert was shadowless, yet across the lower slopes a small black dot moved, a human creeping its way from ravine to ravine.

It scampered across the easement and for a moment he thought it was a teenage girl. She ran off to the edge of the lot in the direction of Old Highway 80 and disappeared into it. He walked back to the road as well. When he arrived there he found it empty of life. The girl had either run into the wild arroyos on the far side or had been picked up on the road by someone.

That night he wrote to Hui's people that he had purchased the lot in his name, as requested, and would receive the deeds shortly. Two hours later they replied, asking about the Border Patrol. He was reassuring. Mrs Vargas would be the key, he explained, but meanwhile he could never, under any circumstances, bring this up directly with her. How then was he going to enlist her help in making sure that the property rights to privacy on the easement road would be respected? He would have to suggest it obliquely, slyly, as if it had never occurred to him previously. The best way would be pillow talk, he told Hui's people.

Several days passed before he was able to return to Jacumba and sign the deeds for the lot, and receive them. Afterwards Gomez took him to the lot himself and gave him the keys to the half-useless metal gates.

'You're one of us now,' he said. 'How do you feel about being a landowner?'

'It feels fine.'

'What are you going to do with the land?'

'I haven't decided. I'll talk to an architect or two, I guess.'

'You can build a magnificent house, for sure. Let me know if you need builders.'

'I'll do that.'

Yet Buford felt an undercurrent of mockery in Gomez's voice. Mockery or pity, he could not decide. When the agent had departed, he ruminated alone on the easement road in the desert quiet. For a moment he regretted that the land wasn't really his. It would be held in his name, but he would sign a separate agreement with Hui's American lawyers giving them the title to it. Still, at least now he could return to Hong Kong and get back into his house. That night, meanwhile, he jauntily suggested to Mrs Vargas that she come out to Bella Lago the following evening and join him for dinner at his place. He figured that he could concoct a reasonable culinary effort, with four freezers filled to the brim. It would be better, he was implying subtly, that she come there than that they be seen together in a public place. This hint did not need to be spoken overtly and she understood it, he thought, at once. She said she would come if he had any decent wine. 'Ridge,' he replied, 'a whole cooler full of it.'

HE DECKED OUT HIS terrace with tea lights and set up a table outside with heavy silverware from the kitchen drawers. The lake wind had calmed and by seven a desert moon had risen over the bare mountains around the house. The development was still a ghost town, with only the street lamps activated. When her car arrived, Buford went out to greet her. As Melania descended she looked around with a slight expression of puzzlement.

'I've heard of this place,' she said as he shook her hand rather formally. 'I thought it was owned by a Chinese company.'

'Probably.'

'Is that who you bought it from?'

'I think they were American. A company in Los Angeles.'

It was an awkward question, which he had not thought through in advance, but mercifully she didn't follow it up with a more detailed probe. He took her hand, boldly, and walked her to the edge of the property so that they faced the darkening canyons. Holding her hand was a way of taking her mind off the question of Chinese property companies. It also enabled him to relieve her of her walking stick, thus giving him an excuse to offer her his support. She let her hand stay in his. Glancing down, he saw that her face was nervous, almost tortured, and that this was not a familiar scenario for her. Her husband was in Mexico and she was taking a step in a dangerous direction with a person she didn't know. It was, then, up to him to reassure her that the adventure could pass off without a hitch. How many years, he wondered, had she been alone in the bedroom, quietly ignored by a powerful husband who could do as he pleased? It might even have been a decade or more. He thought that his instincts were good enough to tell. Moreover he could feel her moving towards him, purely physically. Soon they were embracing, kissing and he could feel her whole frame trembling with anxiety. They walked to the house and he showed her the elaborate table he had prepared.

'What a gentleman you are,' she said. 'You really go all out in the effort. Did you make baked beans on toast?'

'The gourmet version with Parmesan on top.'

Their dinner was long and conversational, made languid by the clear moon reflected in the surface of the Otay lake; and letting time go by unheeded was, to his mind, gently pulling Melania into deeper waters as she drank glass after glass of the wine. Midnight passed. She ventured the pedestrian thought that she really ought to be going home, but did not act on it. He brought out a bottle of brandy. They made a toast to Buford's 'new life'. She was clearly expecting that he might be a permanent fixture in hers. If he had been telling the truth, he might have been. She was not unattractive; she was good company as well. In other circumstances it might have been an interesting encounter. In any case, long after one in the morning he showed her around the house as they held their wine glasses and eventually they fell into his four poster bed and kicked off their shoes. She told him she had been terribly lonely for a long time and that 'fate' had tossed him into her path as a sign of some kind.

'A sign?' he said.

'A sign that my life isn't over yet.'

During their night together he kept thinking about these words. It could as easily have been the other way round. She was a sign that *his* life was not yet over. While she slept he had a desire to wake her up and confess everything to her before more damage was done.

As it was, Buford did nothing. Through the night her

body burned hot and damp as if a fire was raging inside her. When he woke it was much later than he had planned to rouse himself, and he saw at once that Melania was already up and had left the room. He threw on a dressing gown and went downstairs, thinking to make her coffee, but she had already left. He glanced at the kitchen clock: 11.45. The wine had knocked him out. He rushed outside to see that her car was, of course, gone. Yet there was a message on his phone. 'Had to leave, sorry, have a lunch in San Diego. Text me tonight.' The tone felt easy and natural. He had simply got up too late.

Since there was nothing else to do, he made himself coffee and toast and went out to the terrace to revive himself with them. A dark mood had come over him and he could not enjoy the golden flower heads cascading down from the house to the first ravine below. He was sure that all was not exactly as it appeared with Melania. She had got spooked and had fled. Perhaps the enormity of what she had done had finally come crashing through her little romantic fantasy. It was possible.

Then he noticed something peculiar. She had left her cane behind her, exactly where it had hung on the back of a chair the night before. Admittedly she didn't need it to walk, but all the same it indicated a panicked departure.

He picked it up and weighed it in his hands. Perhaps she had left it on purpose in order to be assured of a second meeting with him. Or else it meant nothing. Yet it contradicted her easy-going text.

During the rest of the day he hiked along the canyon paths surrounding the development, killing time before receiving further instructions from Hong Kong. None had come by midday. As he laboured along the mountain inclines he began to wonder if he should quietly go off-path and off-map, continue walking until he reached a small road and vanish into his own hinterland. He could call his parents and come up with a wild story to elicit their help. Of course they would help him. He had friends all over the state, though none he had talked to in years. He would forgo Hui's money, but at least he would be free. A foreboding had entered his consciousness because, he felt, it had entered Melania's mind as well during the night.

Back at the house, he was gripped by a new curiosity about it. He went through the drawers and cupboards in all the rooms, examined the walls behind the artificial-looking paintings, followed the electrical wires as they meandered throughout the house, as if they might tell him something. He had seen it all before in the movies. The lampshades, the vases, the wiretaps hidden inside light bulbs.

He sat for a long while on the bed and thought it through more calmly. He looked up at the teak fan moving above him and saw that at its centre there was something like an insect staring down at him. Hauling a chair beneath it, he leaned up and pulled the little chain to stop the motion of the blades, then reached up to touch the tiny shining black 'eye' at the centre of the contraption. But he already knew that it was a camera.

Too late, he realised that his gesture had revealed to whoever was watching that he had discovered their set-up. In the study he opened the laptop and saw, sure enough, that a message had come through for him. He was to wait outside the house at five that afternoon and meet the driver who had escorted him there on his first day. His mission was completed, and congratulations on a job well done! He wrote back immediately that he would do as requested and asked if there was anything else he needed to do. 'Nothing at all,' came the reply. 'And thank you for your hard work. You will not be disappointed with the reward.'

Closing the machine, he went downstairs, took his wallet and ventured out to the Mazda. He drove down the empty road to the gatehouse and found that the gates were locked. He probed them a little and saw that there was no way to open them. It was an electronic mechanism. He looked around at the vacant units, the deserted traffic circle on the far side of the gates. Perhaps he could walk after all. But scaling the gates was no easy matter, either. He was trapped inside, since the gatehouse was bordered by high barbed-wire walls on both sides. He got back into the car and reversed to the house, then descended and looked wildly around for an escape route through the canyons, as he had earlier in the day.

But after a minute or two he calmed down. It was likely all inside his feverish mind at that point, and he was probably concocting overly-dramatic scenarios that did not, in fact, serve his own interest. So what if they had caught Melania in a sexual blackmail? Did that concern him in any way, once he was safely on a plane back to Hong Kong and the warm embrace of Lily, about whom he cared far more? Not at all. He felt sorry for Melania, but in the end it was not he who had engineered the conditions of her life. It had nothing to do with him. None of it had anything to do with him. Moreover, he was owed a fair amount of money for his exertions and his lost time. It would be insanity to cheat himself of a small fortune just because of a sudden onset of paranoia. Relax, Buford told himself; let them deal with all the loose ends. It was a job after all, nothing more. After completing a job, one ought to be paid and then return to normality. Which for him meant a house on the Peak.

Therefore he returned to the house, packed his single bag and waited. At four, the company car made itself heard as it pulled up outside. A different man – this time an American – appeared in a black suit and with a cheerful wave. This one had a slightly military bearing and he shook Buford's hand with a reassuring vigour.

'They told me to pick you up,' he said as they stood together in the shrill sunlight, 'but I came a little early. Is it inconvenient?'

'Not at all.'

'I don't know what it's about, but they said take you to the airport. How about it?'

'Great with me.'

Buford went into the house and retrieved his small bag and returned to the company limo, which was well chilled inside. The same papers, bottles of water and a small drinks cabinet.

'Work or leisure?' the driver asked as they buckled in.

'A bit of both.'

'Always the best, eh?'

He caught Buford's eye in the rear-view mirror, and the stranger's was merry, hard and mineral-blue. Buford looked back at the house and suddenly remembered the abandoned cane.

'Wait a minute,' he was about to say.

But then he recalled that the blackmailers would love to have that cane and that abandoning it in the house was surely a plus in their eyes, as far as his own mission was concerned. He sank back into the seat and a wave of shame rolled over him. The cane, so pathetic, so incriminating for Mrs Vargas, who would probably do anything to get it back.

The door locks clicked and they departed, rolling slowly down to the gates, which were now opened with a switch. They drove out on the freeway the same way Buford had arrived, and soon he nodded off in the back seat, emotionally exhausted by the previous twenty-four hours. Curiously, he had the same dream he had had on the aeroplane coming over from Hong Kong. He was plodding through a water-logged rice-paddy, while upon a shadowed mountain a great house was on fire, sending up clouds of sparks into the night air. He stopped and observed it. Around him stood terrified water buffalo, their heads bent and their eyes turned upwards towards the conflagration. It was an hour before Buford regained consciousness, and when he did he saw that they were in open desert on a plain filled with flowering red *ocotillo*.

Before he had time to tap the glass divider, the limo began to decelerate as it glided to a halt and pulled over into a grav-elly hard shoulder. The driver turned and smiled.

'Shall we take a quick break?'

They got out simultaneously and as Buford's head began to clear, he tried to calculate where they might be, relative to Los Angeles. But there were no roadside signs there. He blinked in the low late-afternoon sun as the driver handed him a plastic cup of coffee, and saw only low mountains at the horizon already darkened as a prelude to dusk. He sipped and was aware, dully, of the driver standing behind him at a distance of a few feet. There was indeed something irrational and unbelievable about the way he had trusted everyone thus far. Comical almost. He didn't even bother to turn to verify his disbelief. There was no point anyway, he was too tired. The coffee was very sweet and he enjoyed it as the sun began to sink into the horizon in the opposite direction to the mountains. *It's the Anza-Borrego*, he thought to himself. Nowhere near Los Angeles, and in a place where no one passed. The driver was humming to himself and there lay between them a huge silence that seemed to go on for minutes. In reality it was only seconds.

ON THE PEAK, IN the house in the Overthorpe estate that had once belonged to a young American whose name no one could quite remember, Lily spent her evenings playing Patience with herself on the balcony whose floorboards had once been painted black. She had always hated the colour, and since she had taken over the house she had repainted them white, which according to her was the colour they should always have been. She passed her afternoons during the humid season swimming in the Overthorpe's awkwardly shared pool and sometimes invited a friend or two over for sunset drinks. Where in Hong Kong was better to enjoy them? One evening, however, she received a call from Mr Hui, who asked if he might stop by and see how she was doing.

Although she disliked him, she was averse to contradicting any of his demands since he was known to have little patience with insubordination. He duly arrived at six, with a bouquet of flowers for her and a gift of a cake of rare Pu'er tea wrapped in rice paper. He was dressed in a dark-grey suit with a flower in his buttonhole and addressed her politely. They sat on the balcony and he admired, with some predictability, the view of the sea sunk in its glamorous twilight.

'I see you've repainted the boards,' he said, glancing down at them. 'I must say, I agree that it's an improvement.'

'Thank you.'

She served tea made from his own gift, along with some Fortnum & Mason biscuits.

'You seem at home here,' he remarked at length. 'I'm glad. You deserve it after so many years of loyalty. We never forget loyalty.'

'And nor do I.'

'Ha, that's the spirit. You can stay here for a while, anyway. We might have something else for you to do shortly. But I'm not sure what, as of now.'

During a pause they savoured the tea and it made the mood between them jovial and easy.

'By the way,' she said at last, 'do you know what happened to Buford? I suppose he just decided not to come back.'

'You know how it is with Americans. They get homesick. They can live abroad for a while, but it never sticks. They want to go back and marry their high-school sweetheart. Why, did you get fond of him?'

'Of course not. Work is work.'

'And so it is. It's amazing how many people forget that simple truth. What's important is getting paid for it.'

'You've been very generous, Mr Hui.'

'Never mind about that. A loyal citizen does her duty to the state and gets paid accordingly. I don't see anything unusual about it.'

'Still,' she was about to say, but then decided to say nothing.

'I'd say you've scored the best house in Hong Kong,' Hui said, smiling. 'At least you couldn't have done better.'

Not knowing how to deny this, or how to better it as an observation, Lily poured the tea and they laughed between themselves. Then, reclining in the slightly ridiculous chairs that Buford had bought years before, they admired the sunset, the ships crossing the harbour with all their lights on, and the bats that had suddenly alighted from the Indian rubber trees nearby and were now circling the human world with little cries that reminded Lily of children lost in the dark.

PIG BONES

I T WAS A WINDLESS AND SHADOWLESS NOON WHEN she got off the propeller plane from Timika along with gold prospectors in Stetsons and Javan businessmen in Nehru collars, and the sun over Sentani had ascended into a cruel stillness that made the American gold men flinch for a moment as they reached for their shades. Cassidy didn't flinch from the light, however; she had come straight from the dirty rains of Jakarta with all her scholarly bags and she was glad to be in the hot light at last. The passengers walked in a silent group across the grass in the suffocating sun. Around them were silky mountains and the low buildings of the airport. The terminal had no cooling system, but she waited for her other luggage with a patient contentment. The handlers were Papuan, the officers pale Javans with anxious eyes.

It was the latter who looked her over, who asked her the questions at Immigration. There was no one waiting for her on the far side. She had just the name of a small hotel not far from the airport and the telephone number of the Seventh-Day Adventists in Jayapura who were going to help her travel into the forests of the interior with their company,

Adventist Aviation. AA for short. Her linguistic studies were taking her there, remote languages for which dictionaries did not yet exist. She gave the hotel name to the driver of a taxi and he said nothing, but he knew where it was. There was that feeling in the air: people who had never seen a woman alone before. No matter the race or the pride.

They came to a small street from where the wide skies above the airport were visible. But no planes at high noon. It was a hotel for travellers, for foreigners. A dark but wide-open ground floor with a restaurant, bare cement rooms with green shutters and doors. The girls working there were Papuan, with broad white shirts with stiff lapels. She paid for the two nights in cash and was shown to her cell. There was no window, just the sky above the open shower room. The bed was metal, like a prison bed.

She left the bags and went back out into the restaurant. All the fans were on and there was a Christian sermon on the televisions. A group of Papuans stared up at it with interest. Yet a muezzin sounded in the distance from somewhere. She got her first lunch on the island, a Javan affair with tempeh and rice crackers, and drank a beer. So beer was available in this part of town. She was the only white person, at that moment of the day at least. 'Jesus, Jesus,' the TV sang, and the group watching it swayed a little.

She had two days to spare in Jayapura while she got her papers in order. She had agreed to pay a fixer provided by the Church to handle it for her. The man arrived at three and she gave him her passport and papers. There was nothing to explain; he had been briefed. There was probably a bribe involved, but she didn't want to know. She had been told to give him the money in an envelope and she did so. *Maybe*, she thought, *it's not a bribe. Who is to say?* He was a Javan of extreme gentility and discretion. He took the papers and promised to return the following day. Her university had provided the money anyway.

The heat built up during the afternoon. The sky turned quicksilver with clouds that swirled at their edges. She wandered into the chaotic streets of Sentani, with their bitter dust and chattering barber shops. She bought a hefty supply of batteries, jars of peanut butter, toilet paper. She had been assured that on the far side there would be people to carry everything for her. It was a repugnant idea, but an unavoidable one. She wandered along a main street of some kind, stared at by Papuan schoolgirls in uniforms, the men who sat in the shade with a spectral intentness and chewed betel. It was a town in the Deep South a half-century ago. A black town with the whites living elsewhere, but aware of their subjects.

When dusk came she had a cold shower and read in her room for a while. She heard a plane take off, the only one that day. It was the first hour of true loneliness, of quiet desperation. She felt the panic come, then go. The desolate singing inside. Books were no good now. They had suddenly become pointless. She tossed aside the George Eliot she had been reading and wondered if she should leave all the novels here in Sentani and pick them up again on the way out. But the wrench was too great. Novels were life itself. They couldn't be left behind; one has to grit one's teeth and bear with them. So she resolved to pack them anyway. George Eliot, Kurt Vonnegut, Saul Bellow – the ones who stood by her in desperate hours.

Night, and she was drawn out to re-join human life. A Russian air crew had arrived in the restaurant, plump and menacingly jolly in their regulation shirts. Their table had four bottles of vodka and it was said they preferred to fly in sober and fly out drunk. Fewer crashes that way. They sang their toasts with Papuan girls in bright floral dresses on their laps. Cassidy took a table alone as far away from them as possible and ordered the same tempeh and rice crackers and a beef rendang. The Russians looked over, ascertained that she was not Russian and laughed with a sweet and unctuous contempt. Her hand shook a little. The beer was so cold it stung her throat. She was now so isolated, so exotic in her own right, that there seemed to be a halo of black space around her. It was a frontier town of the Wild East, not a place for a travelling linguist. Not a place for a secular woman on her own private road. She tried to make herself inconspicuous – it was the best policy. The hair drab and drawn back, the eyes quick to avert and withdraw. It went against her grain, but it was only for two nights while she waited for the flight into the interior.

While she ate, she read and worked on a few papers. She had a plan to calculate every astronomical event that might occur while she was in the Maukele forests far to the south. It would be a way of keeping herself sane and connected to something, and aware of time beyond the calculations of a mere watch. How flimsy a watch was going to seem out there in the forests! She drew up a list of the lunar phases and the date and time of a lunar eclipse that was due to fall during her fifth week there. Knowing its precise time would be emotionally useful and it might even impress her new friends. Though 'new friends' was an optimistic formulation.

She wrote everything on the last page of her first unused notebook. She had waterproofed the covers against the violent rains that were going to plague her, day in and day out, and she wrote with a pencil, which was going to be the only reliable instrument in extreme humidity. The risings of Venus, the eclipse, the showers of meteors that were expected. She wrote them down next to a table of dates and times. Then she got her Javan coffee and tried to delve once more into *Middlemarch*. The hours passed. The Russians disbanded with their nocturnal companions. The hotel fell into a cicada-inflected silence. The moon came out. It shone down on a wall of barbed wire, datura flowers and a stationary aeroplane parked on the grass field of the airport. There was a rumble of far-off thunder and a flash of horizontal lightning in a clear sky. She had never seen that before. How could it be? A wind came through the empty restaurant with the scent of the datura. She put down *Middlemarch* yet again, her mind clouded and tired. European humanity cast no vibrancy into this empty restaurant and into the light of this ancient and history-less moon. She didn't mind.

A REQUEST VIA THE Mission reached her while she was still in Jayapura waiting patiently for her flight to Wamena: could she please bring them a gramophone player that didn't need an electrical supply, an old wind-up model that could sometimes be found in the Muslim flea markets of the city centre and similar to the one that old Pastor Bohrs had donated to them two years earlier? 'It has worn through with damp and flies,' the letter read. 'The children would love a new one.'

Cassidy searched the flea markets until she found a 1929 model made by the British Gramophone Company itself, in virtually mint condition and sold with a slim collection of LPs of Balinese court music from the 1940s. The covers were grey cardboard with the disc centres exposed. A few discs of old jazz and swing from the Thirties were thrown in – *rich material for the jungles*, she thought drily. She took them with her on the hour-long flight to Wamena, where the Dani cultivate their sweet potatoes on terraces of liquid green, and she played Casa Loma's version of 'Sophisticated Lady' in her dollar-a-night hotel room near the airstrip, while Dani and Yali Pygmies from the highlands stood outside her door, gently heaving from foot to foot in their pig-grease second skins and moaning as if in pain – a pain leavened with a mysterious pleasure. They had never heard American old-style music and, speaking through the Javan owners of the hotel, they asked her if this was music that she knew how to create herself. 'Are they pigs singing in that music?' they asked and they touched the fine bones threaded through their ears. 'Is it pig bones they are hitting with their magic bows?'

'Yes,' she said, not knowing what else to say, and wondering if she should venture an explanation of foxtrots.

THE NEXT MORNING THEY flew through glaciers with the doors of the plane wide open so that the Dani porters could stick out their legs. Below them, as they circled Wamena, they could see terraces that reminded her of the Sacred Valley of the Incas, a place discovered only in 1941 by a passing

American plane – and yet those people had been there, building their intricately irrigated terraces, for 10,000 years. Beyond the mountains lay the forests, cloud suspended only a few yards above the ironwood trees, a static field of luminosity. At Balo there was a rectangular space cut into the sea of green. The airstrip was paid for by both the Seventh-Day Adventists and the Global Frontier Tribes Mission, who used salt as their currency with the Citak. A bag of salt a year kept the airstrip cropped.

The American family lived in a ramshackle house of tropical wood to one side of the lawn, which the Outer Citak clipped every week with iron shears donated by the missionaries. They were waiting for the plane when it came down. But the Outer Citak ran away into the forest at the sound of the engine, a sound they recognised, but to which they had not yet become accustomed.

Pastor Hollinger was there, a spindly man with a tuft of hair that made him look like an ornamental plant, along with his equally pale and spindly wife, Daisy. Both were in khakis and had a soft, impenetrable look about them, like a couple who have been together on a liferaft for years and survived by being amicable and just. They had set up a trestle table next to the airstrip at which the children, Robert and Olga, had cut up huge jackfruits with a pair of penknives. The kids were dark-haired and half-naked and they moved like animals rather than Americans. *Ten or eleven*, Cassidy thought, *and feral already.*

Hollinger came up to the plane and shook hands with the pilot, while Cassidy was greeted by the wife and kids. She stepped into the adhesive heat and was aware at once of the darkness between the trees, the orchids glittering in shadow. The children took her hands.

'You're huge,' the girl said, looking up at her and leading her towards the table where the fruit lay dismembered in a cloud of wasps.

'Did you bring the gramophone?' the boy asked.

Though they were under a pale and clear sky, there was a rumble of thunder, which turned her head. The pastor kissed her on both cheeks and watched the plane circle, restart its engine and take off again. Soon it was a mere speck on the horizon.

'Won't see them for six months,' the pastor remarked in his sing-song English, and they sat down on rickety deck-chairs to eat the jackfruit. He was slightly sarcastic in his manner, as if she had yet to prove herself.

Since Cassidy had held the boy's question in suspension, she now said, 'Yes, I did. I got it in Jayapura.'

'Wow,' he said.

'It was a business getting it into that plane.'

'Thanks,' the children said together and gave each other a knowing look.

She realised now what an event it was for this family to have her living among them. They had built a small house for her near the school room and the chapel, a half-mile away on the far side of the airstrip. The children frisked around her excitedly. The pastor absorbed her unfamiliar attractiveness, fresh from the outside world – the world of milk and honey – which was so unlike the weathered, jungle-resistant toughness of his wife. Daisy seemed to accept this alteration in her symbolic status, because it would have no consequences. The pastor would not be received hospitably by an attractive young woman like Cassidy, even if their God did let him put himself forward. Their dry love-making was assured a long future.

After a lunch of tinned-spam sandwiches, they walked over to the schoolhouse. They were followed by three or four Citak children from the village. The children were always the first to lose their fear of a new arrival. They were less thickset than the Dani children. They were slender and delicate, with little chicken feathers scattered over their heads. They had toy bows and sugar-cane arrows carved with mice teeth, the rows of barbs whitened with ground oyster shells. Their shoulders were pale with ringworm.

The white children had begun to speak Citak with them, and Cassidy's expert ear caught it at once, a language that ran with the contiguous mobility of liquid mercury, rippling and tripping and flattening its consonants. Language like silver that shines and is then turned away from the light and dulls. One of the Citak children came up and brushed a finger against Cassidy's wrist, hastily withdrawing it and then conferring with her companions.

'She says you're not cold,' Robert said. 'They touched a block of ice once, from the aeroplane.'

'Hot like a pig,' the Citak girl was saying.

'Well,' Cassidy replied, 'they can touch me as much as they want. They'll get bored of me.'

'Don't give them your pens,' Robert whispered, and the children laughed a little maliciously.

The pastor hauled the gramophone onto his shoulder. They laboured over a wide field of flowering grass in which the song of insects was deafening. The schoolhouse and the chapel stood at the edge of this dazzling field. Their roofs were pitched steeply, in a vaguely 'native' way copied from the architecture of the coast. The Citak lived in treehouses. The schoolhouse itself was open to the air, its benches made of roughly planed logs, and Cassidy's new home was little more than a cube of logs with a bark mat rolled across its floor. The evangelists apologised in their ironic way, and then the family got on their knees and prayed for 'Sister Cassidy's' happiness in the land of the Outer Citak.

'We'll leave you now,' Daisy said, touching her arm. 'Come up to the house for dinner when the sun goes down. We'll let you settle in.'

'We have an electronic clock,' the pastor put in. 'You'll hear the chime when it's dinner hour.'

'Thank you all so much.'

She lay on her sleeping bag. The heat of the afternoon declined. *Where am I?* she thought wildly. At length, after a long sleep, she heard people moving across the field, swishing their way through the waist-high grass. She emerged into an opal dusk, on the edges of which storm clouds had massed. Green lightning flashed down into the thimbok trees and by its light she could see a dozen men with bows, painted white and blue, standing at the edge of the schoolhouse clearing in an attitude of tense curiosity. They wore penis gourds made from acorns, and fibre bands around their heads. There was a languid elegance to them. Two of them had adorned themselves with bird-of-paradise feathers, turning their heads into Edwardian high-society hats, and they watched her with the attentiveness with which children will track the movement of plates of apple pie. Night fell in five minutes, but they swung bundles of dry grass from side to side, the tips of the bushels alight with a slow-burning fire that cast a dim orange light.

Cassidy walked up to the missionary house as gobs of rain began to fall. The Hollingers were accustomed to eating on their verandah, where parrots had nested and where the Citak women came at nightfall with flying foxes to sell as dinner. The pastor would sit at the piano in the main room behind them and the family would sing their hymns, which among themselves the Citak called the 'the disastrous sound of witchcraft'. The Dutch Reformed Church was the only missionary force in this part of the Maukele sago swamps, and they prided themselves on persisting where no other Christian groups even dared set foot.

That night the Hollingers had paid the Citak women to make a flying-fox stew. The pastor had some sodas delivered by the plane, cans of winter-melon tea from Java, whose pale-green exteriors caused some consternation among the women gathering around the house. They sat at the table in a European fashion, slightly stiff and formal, as if resisting the Citak tendency to informality, and the family cook brought out two saucepans of the stew, which was heavily scented with cloves. The children looked glum. *Never mind*, Cassidy thought grimly, *it won't be as bad as all that*. The pastor ladled it out into china plates, which they must have brought all the way from Holland with considerable trouble. He alone seemed genuinely gay and optimistic, as if it had been he who had dragged everyone here and it had been for his reasons and no one else's.

'We're impressed you came,' he said now as he poured them glasses of the canned winter-melon tea and gave them each a straw. 'Few people have the fortitude, unless Jesus is with them. Just as a matter of curiosity, is Jesus with *you*?'

'Sometimes,' Cassidy said, and a smile went the rounds.

The pastor was not discouraged.

'I do believe we can improve things on that front. Nothing concentrates the spirit so wonderfully as this forsaken place. It has made us all, I dare say, a little harder-working. The Citak inspire us, and I am sure they will inspire you as well.'

She nodded, with a show of agreement. She would depend on this homely family for her survival, so she didn't want to annoy them in any way. And, in a sense, she felt that he might be right.

'I can see that.'

'Well,' the pastor said, 'you'll find Him more easily here than you would in other places. We all see Him readily here. He is close by to protect us. But of course he would not be so evident if the Other were not also more evident.'

'The Other?' Cassidy said.

'His rival.'

The Devil?

'I see him every day,' the little girl said, and she pointed across the darkened airstrip to the forest.

'Who?' Cassidy asked.

'Amen,' they all said, ignoring her question completely.

'My wife has seen him twice this week. He is here all right.'

'Jesus,' the boy said quietly to Cassidy.

'Amen.'

'He is here to encourage us. Cassidy, you'll see him too.'

'I might,' she said.

'You will. The Citak see Him too.'

'Have you converted many?'

It was an innocent question, uttered without much fore-thought. But the pastor stiffened and raised his glass as if to signify that it did not require a totally honest reply. He pursed his lips and jiggled his head to suggest, *One or two, one or two*. Daisy smiled.

Forest humidity misted the shells of the oil lamps. Cassidy could taste the scent of decomposing orchids, the sweetness of fermented sago rolling across the darkness and turning her stomach. Her nostrils filled with sugary, lazy aromas that had no edge to them.

The house was lit by a single oil lamp. When they had finished, the pastor leaned down to this lamp, which sat on the floor, and said, 'Watch this.' He then lowered the flame until it was virtually invisible. Almost immediately a line of people stepped out of the facing forest and walked slowly towards the house. They carried the same burning branches, which they swung across their knees, lighting the ground with an ineffectual glow, and within a minute they had reached the verandah. The pastor went down to greet them. He brushed his great white hand against their tiny black ones and spoke to them in fluent Citak laced with English words, which they now appeared to understand. *Pool, generator, candle, don't touch, knife*. Hands were grasped more firmly then and there were grins flashed towards the new-come woman.

'He is telling them,' Daisy said to her in a whisper, 'that

you have come from outside the forest, beyond even the Great Dog. He says you come to play some music to them, from a metal dog that doesn't wag its tail. He says you are Jesus Number-One Woman, and that Jesus has put His confidence in you and that they must listen to the words you speak.'

'That's a bit of a liberty,' Cassidy blurted out.

'The gramophone?'

'I thought it was for you.'

'It's for all of us,' Daisy assured her. 'We do get terribly bored here. The children have been looking forward to it so much.'

The Citak warriors stepped gingerly onto the verandah, edging themselves forward into the alien dimension of European order. They ventured to touch the white hand of the new woman. They were eager and tender in their way. Their eyes were bloodshot and opened wide, like crude windows. Their skin was scaled with ringworm, faintly fragrant and unctuous, despite the scaling. Gesturing to the schoolhouse, they asked the pastor with an elaborate protocol if the new woman would play the dog to them right now. 'Could you?' the pastor asked hopefully, turning to her with his pale Dutch eyes. 'Play something, I mean? The children would love it, and the Citak too, it would seem.'

Cassidy walked back to her house in the rain, with a warrior whose body was covered with white spots dabbed onto his skin with the point of a stick. She took a torch with her, and as the rain whistled around them she watched with care the muscular backs of his calves and the long feathers trailing down his back. It was striking how the men and women stood so far apart at all times, never touching, never exchanging intimate words.

At the house he laid his bow on the ground and watched as she cranked the machine and placed upon its turntable the copy of 'Sophisticated Lady'. Shortly, the cracked strains of another age rose from the horn, echoing with incredible effect through the forest – the tea parlours and dance floors of 1933.

She left the disc playing and they returned to the house, where the Citak had all laid down their utensils and were sitting on the ground with their lizard-skin pipes, puffing silently among themselves. They said, quietly, 'It is a tremendous noise. Horrific. But never have we been so happy!'

Her dreams see-sawed, and rain pattered on her roof all night. A melancholy singing came through the trees, a music unlike anything she had ever heard. At dawn she was awake, with the thunder echoing. The pastor was already there in the schoolhouse with three Citak women with whom she was going to start her studies. His son was with them, as translator.

'I brought you some Nescafé,' the pastor said playfully, holding up a Thermos. 'But I thought you would turn down the fried bat.' Instead, he gave her some malted biscuits.

The women were middle-aged and their hands were broken in from handling the stone clubs with which they pulped the insides of sago palms. Their eyes were heavy, unemotional and suspicious. The lids drooped a little as they stared at the paper and pencil, which had also wilted in the humidity.

Cassidy had come to think that one had to maintain a

certain bearing at all times with such people in order to win
their respect. She wanted their respect more than anything
else. She made the boy ask them if they were suffering from
any diseases, and the responses filled the better part of an
hour. She jotted down the words for ringworm and malaria,
for headache and arthritis. She got them to tell her about
cooking, children and sago-processing. Sago was the staple
of their diet, made into a white paste that could be rolled into
balls.

Thereafter she spent her time in these three-way conver-
sations, sitting in the schoolhouse in the sunshine in the
mornings and then relaxing in the cooling downpours of the
afternoon. They ate little wild pineapples. The three women
were close friends, and one of them, Timi, had a fifteen-year-
old son whom the pastor had named Judah, who came to the
sessions sometimes in the afternoons. He was a tall boy with
close-cropped hair, which he fussily sheared every day with
a bamboo knife. He took to the white woman at once, paying
her compliments and asking to see the dog that made enormous sounds. After class, around three o'clock, he took her
with Robert to the watering hole, where the people in the
four treehouses bathed and collected water. It lay at the bottom of a long, winding path between sago swamps that
smelled of stale beer.

Its water was coloured like stagnant tea, deliciously cold.
There was a small beach of sugar-white sand. Behind it stood
a field of immense cane. While the boys pretended to turn
their backs, Cassidy sank naked into the shallow pool clogged
with leaves and washed off the sweat and mosquito-repellent
that accumulated every day.

It was during those moments in the pool that she began to find the forests less inhospitable. What struck her about the Citak was their strong sense of fear. It was a fear directed towards animals, darkness and the dead. One day one of the women told her that the dead walked about in the forest all night and that they were coloured white. They were white as capricorn larvae. It was why the people of Balo never ventured out alone after dark, and they certainly never ventured far into the forest. But, Cassidy said, the dead lived in the belly of the Great Dog, didn't they? They came out of it to wander in the forests, the woman said. But it was possible, Cassidy thought, that in the garbled translations she had not understood this correctly.

'When a person is dying,' Judah said to her on their way to the watering hole later that day, 'they can name someone as the witch who killed them. The witch has to be present as the person is dying, but he is always disguised as an animal. He can be a bird, a worm, a dog – anything. Then the relatives must find the witch, kill him and eat his insides. They must cut the body into four parts and bury each part at the edge of their territory.'

The following Sunday the pastor made a feast from roasted cassowary. The quills were given out to the Citak women who, with considerable pomp and vanity, stuck them through their noses and walked about like queens.

'You seem to be making some progress with the women,' he said to Cassidy as they carved up the strange meat on the verandah table and prepared to say prayers. 'They say you are like an infant, with all your questions.'

Daisy served her plate, and when they said grace she held

Cassidy's hand very firmly, almost too firmly. There was a cool enquiry in the Dutch woman's eye and it had to do with Judah.

'He's a strange one, don't you think? He keeps swimming in our water tank. When I tell him not to, he lurks around all day in the trees nearby. He misses his father, I suppose.'

'Perhaps,' Cassidy said, 'they don't like our religion.'

'I was hoping,' the pastor said mildly, 'that the gramophone might help us, in that respect. It introduces an element of novelty, of astonishment. I've found that those things are very important in the conversion process. Of course it's not what counts in the end. But it's a weapon in the gentle war for souls. I hope you don't mind.'

When they played 'Sophisticated Lady' that night the entire population of Balo sat on the airstrip and moaned. They swayed from side to side as they puffed at their long lizard-skin pipes and their minds filled with fantastic images derived from the strains of the Casa Loma Orchestra. Moreover, the sound carried very far in the stillness of the night, even with the background of the thunder that never seemed to stop. It echoed and seemed to spread itself over vast areas. Several miles away, in fact, at the treehouse cluster of Makelepup, the people heard those echoes rolling across the canopy, above which they sat on their bamboo platforms, gazing across the sea of green, which the lightning illumined. A woman was dying of malaria there, left alone in one of the huts on the ground, which is where the women always had to sleep while the men kept to the treetops. The men of Makelepup talked among themselves when they heard the orchestral swoons of 'Sophisticated Lady' reaching them from Balo. Sounds of derangement, of sadness, of women in strange shoes; sounds of spirits that were coming back to claim something, but who, alas, knew what? They knew the giant birds landed at Balo and that the Citak who lived there used steel axes to cut down their sago, though they hid them from the Jesus Number-One Man. Perhaps, they said to themselves, the great noise coming from Balo was a form of medicine, which could be used to heal the fevers of their sister, Natewe.

They smoked in silence, deep in thought. The boy Judah from there had come by the day before and said that it was a dog shaped like a box. 'Aha,' they cried, 'it must be connected to the Great Dog!' The Great Dog lay around the forest, with the dead in its stomach.

They dreamed on their sides as the treehouse swayed in the storm like a giant bamboo. The sound from Balo stopped. All night the woman dying of malaria writhed on her bark bed. She sweated and coughed. She dreamed that witches circled her house disguised as little birds. In her dream she was walking downhill towards Balo, where she had been once as a child, her hand held by her father.

By the second week Cassidy had annotated almost a thousand words. The grammar of Citak was beginning to crystallise in her mind and she was starting to piece together simple sentences. 'I run fast like dog', 'You like water.' But even her little sentences only approximated to the real ones, which contained inflections she could not grasp. A hundred words for every species of grass. It was a language of long compound words, of convoluted sentences, baroque ornamentation, with none of the syntactic simplicity of other languages. It was web-like, subtle in its modulations, and its words clung to the roof of her mouth like something physically sticky. A language like toffee.

The pastor sometimes took her down to the swamps to watch the men cutting down sago, and he helped her write down the words of the work songs. The women then split the trunks open and pounded the insides with their clubs, singing just as the men did. They filtered the pounded fibres with water and compacted them into a mush, working in the terrible heat like automata, with fibrous *noken* bags tied around their heads. At length, after six hours of labour, the men and women packed up their tools together and wrapped the sago in leaves. They walked back to Balo, the men carrying dead monitor lizards over their shoulders. And for all these things there were precise words, phrases and ritual descriptions, which had to be learned one by one. They formed a tapestry of meanings that needed to be pieced together with great patience. One false move and you missed the point, the tapestry fell apart.

She set up another desk in the open-air schoolhouse. It was cooler and she could think more fluently with the breezes coursing continuously through the wooden structures. They seemed to come from afar, from a deeper core of the forest that might be cooler. By now the heat no longer oppressed her as it had during her first days. She could handle the orb-weaver spiders that were apparently attracted to the wood of her house, and the sago grubs that she had to eat from time to time for their sustaining protein, their fat like runny rancid butter. In her house she set up a second work desk for the duration of the sudden and violent storms. She had brought an oil lamp with her from Wamena and a supply of oil, so that she could work after dinner, while the Hollingers sang hymns, with cups of Nescafé. She learned to work in only her underpants, and to concentrate also in bed, lying on her side under the mosquito net like an Egyptian scribe, as she thought of it. 'And to think,' she wrote to her mother, 'that I am writing the first lexicon of an entire language. Sometimes one's breath is taken away. I *cannot* put a foot wrong, can I?'

Her eye picked out the *Photinus* fireflies that danced through the trees at night. She began to love the sudden shock of starlight that could appear as the clouds parted. She was exactly on the Equator, at that point where the galaxies were most visible, although the Citak seemed to have few words for them. She wrote letters to her mother in Delaware, and to her estranged husband in San Francisco, the man who had left her for another woman. The more she did so, the more obvious it was to Cassidy that she was now alone in a permanent sense. And she could not even send the letters she wrote until the aeroplane returned after Christmas.

So she wrote in a void. She poured out her heart to Alden as if he was still there, as if he was listening to her, deep in the night, with his head against a shared pillow. It was futile. The ghost of the lover was no longer there. She told these absent loved ones about everything she did. She had to tell someone, she had to tell *them*. How the Citak women cut up the pineapples with bamboo blades. How the honey from the deep forest tasted like cold tea, and how the crocodiles, the *boya*, lay at the bottom of the pools waiting for impatient white women to slip into their element. How this world had closed in around her 'like treacle'. How the butterflies were black as powdered coal. 'How the Citak have no word for us,' she wrote. 'They have no idea *what* we are. Not who, but what. They thought at first that we were *kakua* – witches. But the pastor heals their cuts with Bactine swabs and they changed their minds. Now we are just people-from-outside-the-forest.'

In the third week of December a new suffocating heat descended from the east. The men lay in their treehouses trying desperately to catch a breeze. The women complained as they cooked at the edge of the swamp. The Hollingers went butterfly-collecting and invited Cassidy to come along. They knew a trail that the hunters used, which wound along a creek with slippery mud banks. If you sat still in this place the butterflies would come and alight on your head, attracted by the heat of your hair. As they were walking slowly along this trail, the children skipping ahead of them with their empty nets, Judah appeared, walking with a determined gravity towards Balo, as if he had come from far away.

He was profusely decorated with bundles of small orchids and he looked a little stoned. When the pastor stopped him and asked him where he'd been, Judah became slightly insolent. He waved a hand towards Makelepup and said that his cousin lived there. The pastor had not heard of this cousin, so he asked about her. She was dying of malaria, Judah said, and the traditional remedies were doing nothing. The pastor turned to Cassidy and Daisy. 'No surprise there. I suppose they'll want me to go up there with the Larium. I can use the occasion to preach the Word a little.'

'They are all talking about the metal dog that cries,' Judah said secretively, covering his mouth with his hand for a moment. 'They want to know if it's the voice of Jesus.'

'Casa Lomanot?' Daisy laughed.

But the pastor suddenly grew serious, as if a terrific idea had just occurred to him.

'Judah,' he said. 'Go back to Makalepup and say to them that what they are hearing at night is indeed the voice of Jesus. Tell them I have been waiting a long time to bring it to them. I know it's why they never believed me when I told them that Jesus had a voice like music. But now they can hear it every night, because Jesus is among us.'

Inspired, the pastor winked at his wife. Before long Judah had agreed to escort Cassidy to Makalepup the following morning.

'It'll be interesting for you,' the pastor said on the way down, and not for the first time she glimpsed the cruel, duplicitous side of him. 'They are two degrees more remote than the people of Balo, and so they have some words that I suspect the Balo lot have forgotten. In any case, you'll be doing us an enormous favour, and you'll be doing the Lord a favour as well. If you don't want to go, of course—'

'No, no. It will be interesting, as you say.'

The butterflies that the children had captured were spiked onto large cork boards in the main room. Supper that night was chicken soup from Campbell's cans and unmouldy crackers from plastic sachets. Daisy made it pretty, adorning the plates with leaves and petals, and they filled a pitcher with Rose's lime cordial, which was chilled in the small fridge that the generator could nourish for an hour a day. The Citak, as

always, watched them eating from afar, noticeable only by
the reflections of their eyes.

'I must say,' Daisy remarked as they were eating, 'the ruse
with the gramophone was pretty unethical, Daniel. I am sure
I have read of missionaries doing that in Africa. Cassidy
must think we are idiots.'

'It was a spontaneous inspiration,' her husband replied
indifferently. 'A the-spur-of-the-moment thing. One always
has to be open to the spontaneous, in our line of work. I think
it will work well enough. I know it's a trick, but one shouldn't
get bogged down in the idea of respect, no matter what. I am
trying to save the Citak first. After we've saved them, we can
worry about respecting them.'

Because then, his tone implied, it would be worth it.

The next morning they got up early. The boys loaded the
gramophone onto a bamboo palette that they could carry on
their shoulders. It rained heavily, and the sago swamps were
hard-going. They balanced their way along rotting tree trunks
laid across the marsh, the boys singing their marching chant,
the gramophone teetering under a canvas wrap. It was a six-
hour walk to Makelepup. At the beginning of the afternoon
they came to an imposing cane field, at the edge of which two
men stood with elegant bows. The white woman and the
gramophone were shown to them, and their origins explained.
The men sat down in the cane and smoked their pipes.

Makelepup was built on higher ground, so that the cane
field led up to it by degrees. The two large treehouses were
constructed on top of ironwood trees, and their walls
were decorated with painted shields to ward off witches, who
were known to roam these woods. Slender notched ladders

connected them to the ground. An intruding witch would easily snap them and fall. A low gabled hut at ground level sheltered a dozen women and snotty children, who peered out at the newcomers through a sheet of rain. Thick smoke drifted across the burnt ground, heavy with animal fat. Dozens of charred tree stumps littered the rolling surface.

As Cassidy came lumbering into its shelter, dripping wet and exhausted, the children scattered behind, hanging *noken* bags between which they could peer at her. She put down her equipment and the women were introduced to her. There was a sullen hostility about these pot-bellied, short-haired matrons with their bushy sago-fibre skirts and harried eyes. They did not cluster around her, like the women at Balo, but rather hung back and waited to be told to shake her hand. They asked no questions of her, either. The party from Balo sat and were given something hot to eat. After some discussions, the warriors pointed to the two huts standing next to the main longhouse and said that the dying woman was in one of these. They had told her that, as a last resort, they had requested the voice of Jesus to come here and make her better.

During the afternoon the gramophone was transported to the sick woman's hut, and Cassidy went with it. Inside, the hut was plunged in darkness. Pieces of animal bone were threaded to the ceiling: tibias and femurs of lizards, small pigs and rodents, and tiny simian skulls knocked together in the breezes that swept up from the gaps between the bamboo slats. They asked her to sit next to the woman, so that the dying one could see who it was that had come to rescue her. It was a woman of about forty – in advanced old age, in Citak terms — and she lay swaddled in charms and flowers on a piece of tree bark. Her wasted form was immobilised by the last stages of encephalitic malaria. Her eyes seemed to be held open by invisible threads, and they never blinked as they tracked the tall white woman invading her miserable death scene. Judah, meanwhile, was allowed to enter so that he could translate into Bahasa.

Cassidy was as gentle as she could be. She asked the woman her name, and what came back, garbled by Judah, was something like 'Kasop'.

'Why are you white?' Kasop asked. 'Are you dead?'

'I am alive.'

'She is from beyond the Great Dog,' Judah said quietly.

'So she is dead,' Kasop said to him. She appeared unsurprised.

The woman was going to die later that night. Her eyes were already wild, lost. Cassidy opened her basic medical kit and took the Larium pills in her hand to offer. She opened the wet lid of the gramophone player. The family gathered around as the machine was cranked into life, the needle lowering slowly onto the vinyl, which was already distending a little in the heat. Kasop swallowed the pills of the white sorcerers. She lay waiting for the sound of the dog, which she had been hearing every night from her bed, and which she could not forget or stop thinking about.

Now it was inside her own room and the sound was proportionately more immense. She lay wild-eyed, listening to 'Sophisticated Lady'. A light foam began to form upon her lips. Cassidy prepared an injection with a disposable syringe that she knew how to prepare, a sedative that would help. As she flicked its tip, she wondered what the pastor had wanted her to do here. Save the woman? That was obviously not possible. Save her soul? That was still possible. Cassidy was an atheist. Her mind was a scientist's. But what mattered to the pastor was the influence he might exert in the coming months. If the dying woman gave him her soul to save, it would be a sensation for years to come, let alone months. It would bring the Citak over to him in a single stroke. He was right. It was brilliant, and time-tested. A simple adjustment – the tipping of a lever – changed everything.

She sat by the woman's bed. They listened to the foxtrot while Cassidy held her hand and rain thundered in the mangosteen groves behind the hut. Death here was wretched and raw. There was no alleviation. They died without ceremony. Yet the woman seemed alive with blunt curiosity.

'They say the white men eat Jesus every week. Is it true?'

Cassidy had to choose between a yes and a no.

'Yes,' she murmured, unsurely. 'In a way.'

'Is Jesus the owner of the Dutch man at Balo?'

'Yes. He talks through him.'

'I am going to have a dream tonight. It will be my last night. Perhaps I will eat some Jesus, too.'

It was sometimes hard to hear above the noise of the rain. Faces peered through the cracks in the walls, through the open door. The children were curious. After a little while the woman turned her face towards Cassidy and said that by this time tomorrow night she would be living in the forest with the other ghosts.

A fire burned in the longhouse and the men lay around it. Judah told ridiculous tall stories to keep them awake. Between tales they sang, mournfully and idly. They smoked their lizard-skin pipes. They were wary of the white woman, alien and untouchable on two counts, but they let her sit by herself while she read by the light of her battery torch. They would have preferred that she sleep with the sick woman, but they assumed that she was afraid. Whereas Cassidy was not. She was merely apprehensive about the effect of the morphine. Fear was not the emotion that gripped her.

As the night wore on, the men fell asleep. She was left alone in her wakefulness. The rain did not ease. Barbed vines dripped in the dark. It was then that a voice rose from inside the hut, and she went over quickly to see the sick woman turning painfully on her side and sticking out her tongue. Another old woman sat with her, listening intently as Kasop talked. She said that the pastor's dog was inside her and was eating her insides. Cassidy didn't understand what they were saying, but she could tell that things had taken a wrong turn. She heard the word *kakua*. They both looked up at the white woman standing there with her torch and there was some indecision in their expression. The other woman stood up and walked towards Cassidy. She said, very calmly, 'The owner of the little metal dog that sings is the witch who has made Kasop die. Its singing is inside her and is making her die.' Kasop raised a finger and pointed at the gramophone.

She died an hour later. The journey back to Balo was wordless, weighed down by the heavy rain and the mood of unease created by the death. They stopped halfway, by the edge of a pineapple glade, and the boys quietly washed their hands in the brackish pools. Cassidy sat by the gramophone and let the water drip off the rim of her waterproof hat, trying to dispel the sadness that had now taken hold of her. The whole episode had seemed like a pathetic charade with no ostensible outcome. There was something ignoble about it. Her grasp of the language was still so tenuous that she had no clear idea what their feelings had been, and if she had known them, what would she have done with them? Warned them against Jesus Number-One Man, as they called the implacable Dutchman? The idea that the pastor was trying to communicate to them was too complex to be communicable at all. She watched the boys at their ablutions, slow and serious in their movements. She was convinced that in some spontaneous way she had been used. They knew it, too. She had been used. They looked in her direction with puzzled pity. She was not as strange and formidable as she looked. She was, like them, the tool of a superior, more organised will.

The pastor was not at all surprised by the turn of events. Secretly, he congratulated himself on his grasp of native psychology. The slow decline of the Maukele mission was about to be reversed.

He had set the dinner table outside, for Cassidy's sorry return, protecting it with a ring of mosquito coils. The smell of pyrethrin hung across the verandah, repelling the ever-curious Citak, just as he intended (they held their noses with two fingers and kept their distance). The family prayed at twilight with the candles lit, while Cassidy washed in the outside shower, nourished by a full cistern. The sky above the shower burned indigo for a while, with the stars spread out.

Daisy served them spam and garden lettuce and sago fritters cooked in their own corn coil, which made them crispy-black at the edges. They said grace with interlocked hands, and Cassidy's wet hair dripped onto the verandah floor, a circle of dark stains that drew the children's gaze. They ate the revolting food with a humorous stoicism, a relish for difficulties endured for the sake of the Lord.

The pastor heard out her account of the death of Kasop, which sounded even worse in the retelling by candlelight. 'Remarkable,' he said, appealing to his wife's cool eyes. He went on, 'I've heard a lot about that woman, as it happens. I've heard that she was a malevolent type, through and through. A gossip. They were all afraid of her up there.'

'I got her soul anyway.'

The pastor laughed very loud.

'I hope you're giving it to me for safekeeping.'

A dark scruple suddenly moved him, and he pushed his own jollity away. He wanted to know if Cassidy had, in all seriousness, received Kasop's conversion. Naturally, he said, between them, Cassidy did not have the authority to receive it, but up there in the cane fields they didn't know that. The important thing was that the others heard Kasop convert on her deathbed. Had they?

She said, honestly, that she didn't really know. It had seemed that way. Over the next few days she kept to herself in her house. She walked across to the schoolhouse at first light with an umbrella. The women were more morose and tight-lipped, although they would not reveal why. News of the death of Kasop had come down to the lower forests, and an unpleasant rumour had attended it. The children came down at lunchtime to join in lessons, and the boy whispered to her what the Citak children were saying. A *kakua* had killed Kasop.

'Who is the *kakua*?' she asked him.

He shrugged, and there was a delicate, quivering fear in his eye.

Me? she thought uneasily. A witch had to be male. But perhaps they had misunderstood.

'They say it was the music.'

'They probably saw me give the injection,' she said softly, stroking his hair to reassure him. 'It's a mistake.'

In the heat of the day, as the flowers blazed around the crudely cropped runway, she saw the pastor talking earnestly with Citak men in the shade of the verandah. Puffs of smoke rose above the sago fronds. When she had finished her work she walked around the edge of the clearings that the missionaries had made. The musky smell of vanilla orchids attacked her, and she felt a tremendous claustrophobia building up inside her. The sheer darkness of the interior jungle, with its smell of pools and decaying bark, tempted her in, yet she could sense eyes watching her from its depth, a constant surveillance. She never dared to step inwards, away from the sun.

Soon Cassidy heard the pastor calling her name and she came up to the house through the tall weeds, with the fetid sun beating on her head. The Citak had disappeared and the pastor sat alone on the verandah in his rocking chair, smoking a pipe. The children, too, had gone off somewhere with their mother. The pastor rose and shot her a slyly knowing smile. He offered her a glass of lemonade made from syrup and sterilised water. As they drank together, she noticed how

empty the village appeared. They were all off in the forest
cutting down sago and processing it, the pastor said. It was
one of the rituals that demanded everyone's presence. His
wife always took the children. It was, he said, one of the few
entertaining things for them.

He had her sit on the floor on cushions and he sat with her,
as if in solidarity.

'The people of Makelepup are in quite a stir,' he said. 'You
made a real impression on them.'

'I hope they don't think I was the cause of her death.'

'Oh, they jump to all kinds of conclusions. Some of the
men were just here. I calmed them down. They wanted an
explanation. You can see their point of view.'

'Yes, I can.'

She avoided his searching blue eye, now filled with a curious ambivalence. He said his wife and children would be
away until dark. The villagers sought the succulent sago of a
quite distant part of the forest, and it took the men the better
part of an hour to cut down a single tree with their stone axes.
The sago parties always came back late, singing to allay their
terror of the forest. She saw the tall ironwood waving slowly
above the sag-thatch of the huts, which now stood temporarily empty. She felt the pastor draw a little closer, testing her
out inch by inch, slow and probing. She recoiled just as
slowly, hesitant. The syrupy drink coated her teeth and she
felt faint.

'Still,' he was saying, his eyes boring into the shape of her
breasts, clearly visible through her soaked shirt, 'I would feel
happier if you stayed in your house during daylight for the
time being. Some of them are hotheads.'

'What do you mean?'

'I mean they may have come too swiftly to some unwarranted assumptions.'

'I gave her an injection, that's all.'

'You did nothing wrong. Nothing at all. They're superstitious and we have to work with that.'

'Like children?'

'Yes, like children.' He smiled and tilted his eyes. 'It's not an insult to call them children. Children are the preferred of God.'

'I don't think of them as children.'

'You're an anthropologist. Strange creatures, anthropologists. I have tried explaining your profession to the Citak. They were not amused.'

'I don't care if they were amused or not—'

He seemed about to reach out and touch her, without a reason for doing so, just like that. But before he could, she visibly shifted away from him and her hostility was unmistakable.

'Ah,' he let slip, and his look was ironic, almost contemptuous.

She got up brusquely and lingered, because she wanted to speak her mind truthfully.

'That was a low trick you pulled on them with the gramophone,' she said icily. 'You're playing with their heads.'

'Yes,' he said. 'You are.'

'What do you mean, me?'

'It was you who played it for them.'

Now she understood. *You gangster*.

Cassidy walked off without a word, knowing that she was

now trapped in a low-key antagonism with the only man who could get her out of there in one piece. She walked furiously into the white-flowering weeds and the crickets buzzing away from her in great singing arcs, sparkling in the sun for a moment. The shadows of the taller trees were changing their angles on the low-cut grass around the schoolhouse, and she could feel the pastor watching her intently as she strode into its welcome shade. She had a splitting headache and wanted to lie down and sleep, to forget the whole thing. She sat instead on one of the benches and caught her breath. She suddenly felt tremendously alone.

The afternoon dimmed and the butterflies came out. They fussed around the edges of the pineapple glades, around the lips of the ceraceous orchids, whose flesh was beginning to brown. Once again there was the distant rumble of thunder from a perfectly clear sky. She went to her house and lay on her hard pallet with the sleeping bag. She wept and her tears were of pure, bright anger.

The pastor, meanwhile, lit his pipe again and relished the hours of solitude that were upon him. No wife, no children, no snotty Citaks to bother with. He smelled the fragrance of the Woodbine and looked across at the shack where the succulent white woman was lying down. What if he dropped all shame and went over there and forced the matter? There was nothing she could do. The Citak were on his side, not hers. That fact had been agreeably impressed upon him by the delegation from Makelepup. They had been so comically grave and upset, so desirous of accurate information, for which they regarded him as the official source. That woman, they said, killed Kasop with her musical dog and her little witchcraft dagger. They had come to the pastor to hear what he had to say.

'Well,' he had said in his quite-fluent Citak, 'Jesus works with opposites. There are angels and there are demons. Ministers like me and *kakua*. One reveals the other.'

They did not understand. They listened, sitting cross-legged on the verandah, smoking thoughtfully. It was an absurd argument, they thought to themselves, but the pastor knew what she was, and not they. They listened. It was entirely possible, the pastor said, that the white woman had practised magic upon Kasop. How could he say? He did not know her. Perhaps he and his wife had harboured a witch without knowing it. But if that was so, he could prove the good faith of Jesus Number-One Man by letting them hunt down the witch herself. It would, he knew, make a tremendous impression on them. Even better, however, would be to assure them that he would deal with the matter himself. They were incredulous, and then moved to awe. The pastor was not a man to trifle with. He regulated even his own people.

They agreed that this was undeniable proof of the pastor's integrity. They said they were sorry to disrupt his life at Balo in this way, and when there had been enough talk and enough PG Tips, they extinguished their pipes, tucked their weed into their armbands and gently, quietly dispersed into the forest, where they were going to wait until the moment of sundown.

The pastor waited for it as well. He felt an almost sexual anticipation as the light began to drain away from the maddening panorama of high trees. The insects shrilled with new intensity, as if sensing the approach of a storm. He leaned back in his rocking chair. Then, when he was sure that the people had gone to rest in their huts, he crept down to visit Cassidy. He shook her awake and placed a finger in front of his mouth to indicate that she should say nothing. When she realised who it was, she uttered a little cry of alarm and then felt the hand tighten around her throat. Then, just as suddenly, it loosened and she felt his mouth press down upon hers. He was talking very quietly close to her ear, saying that the villagers wanted to kill her and only he could save her. Something in the way he said it made her believe him, in spite of herself. Now, in any case, she could not move and she had to wait for him to exhaust himself – a matter of minutes in the draining heat. When he had done so, unable to complete the act, he rolled away from her and took his hand from her mouth. Barely able to control his voice, he told her that it would be better if she came with him to the house and stayed there. She raised one hand to strike him, but he caught it and glared at her.

'Make a noise and they will be roused, they'll come for you. Keep quiet.'

He then pulled her up by her hand and pushed her out of the hut into the grassy field, luminous in some way, as it always was at night, and continued to drag her silently towards the unlit house where the family, who had quietly returned without fanfare, were already asleep. When Cassidy tried to twist away, the pastor held her more fiercely until her arm began to ache and the energy drained out of her.

They stumbled up onto the porch and there he released her arm and pushed open the door into the front room. He went to the rail and peered out, over the airstrip and into the leafy edge of the village, where he was sure the witch-hunters were watching them all night. But had they caught sight of Cassidy being dragged into the house? He had to take that risk. Closing the door behind them, he took her to the spare room with a bunk bed and told her to stay there until the plane arrived to take her back to Wamena in the morning.

'So *now* I have to leave,' she spat at him.

Wiping the sweat off his face, he became conciliatory.

'They've designated you a witch. I'm going to call the Adventists now on the transmitter and request a plane for the morning, if they can do it. Otherwise they're going to hunt you down and kill you.'

'Because of that old lady?'

'Who the hell knows why. I'm not a mind-reader. I can save their souls, but I can't read them.'

'How convenient. What a man of God you are.'

'It is,' he struggled to say quietly, 'what it is. Your best bet is to lie low until the plane arrives. I'm sorry about my behaviour just now – I lost control, I don't know – I gave in to Satan.'

'Like fuck you did.'

'I did, he came and entered me. I know it.'

She looked away, disgusted. 'Shall we tell that to your wife? Will she buy it?'

'She'll pray for me. But better not do that. You need me to get you out of here, remember. Without me, you're on your own with the witch-hunters.'

When she was alone in the room Cassidy lay on the bunk and tried to sleep through her terror. The pastor, for his part, did not seem to sleep at all. She heard him start up the transmitter and talk to the mission in Wamena. Then he wandered out by himself to the porch, where the rocking chair began to creak. Gradually the sounds of the forest engulfed him and helped her to forget everything as she lapsed into sleep. It must have been only for five hours.

When her eyes opened it was first light and the dawn chorus was so loud that for a moment she could not collect her thoughts. Her body was wretchedly dirty and sticky, and yet she didn't want to douse herself with the stale water from the rain tank. Instead she went out tentatively to the porch and immediately saw, as if by some miracle, a Cessna light aircraft parked on the runway, with a fat little missionary smoking a cigar on its landing steps. He looked up, sensing her presence, and smiled, taking the cigar out of his mouth.

'Cassidy?'

'Where are the family?'

'Oh, they took off an hour ago with the villagers. They went on some sort of hunt – I hear it's a monthly game of theirs.'

'Took off?'

'Yeah, the pastor and his wife said to say goodbye and all that. There's no one here now but you and me.'

Then she saw her bag packed and waiting by the porch steps. It had all been done for her.

'Shall I take that?' the pilot asked, seeing it as well.

'No, I've got it.'

The great ironwoods were motionless, wrapped in wet mist, and the pineapple glades below them glistened as if damp. The villagers had been lured away by the devious pastor, and so had his wife and children. He had done it on purpose. She picked up the bag and strode over to the plane. It had disgorged bags of sugar, which had been left in the shade of the house. She clambered into the suffocating little hold and slumped into one of the threadbare seats, trying to remember if it was the same plane that she had flown in on. She couldn't recall. The pilot lost no time joining her and setting the front propeller in motion.

'Where to, Miss? Rio de Janeiro, New York, Paris or Wamena?'

'Wamena today.'

'Wamena it is, then. Funnily enough, I just came from there.'

The Cessna lifted off over the ironwoods and turned at a steep angle as it made its course for the hour-long flight to Wamena. She looked down through the open door and saw bursts of flowers through the ragged mist and then a smattering of treehouses, with their painted shields pinned to the bamboo walls. Only then did she begin to choke on her emotions, unable to cry, dry inside and out, her sense of failure mitigated by the knowledge that nothing that had gone wrong had been her fault. She regretted only, in fact, that she had left the gramophone and its records behind.

DAYS LATER A HEAD was found suspended in a *noken* bag nailed to the underside of an abandoned treehouse five miles to the south. The flies buzzed around it for a few days, then lost interest. The mothers of Balo told their children not to go there, not to go near that festering head. The pastor alone knew that it was a pig's head, which he had procured secretly by himself and had severed, placing it in the *noken* bag and carrying it into the jungle while no one watched. Since no one would dare approach it now, his secret was safe. Among the villagers, meanwhile, his reputation for sanctity soared. The prospect of numerous new converts justified, in his own eyes, his deception, and as a symbolic act he laid the gramophone underneath the *noken* so that there might be no ambiguity as to the meaning of the head's 'burial'. The machine's confusing sound would never be heard again.

To his own children, the pastor patiently explained that Cassidy had suddenly left on a new assignment in South America. Aside from that, the forest, he said, had got to her and she had decided that enough was enough. She wasn't cut out for it. They nodded meekly, and nothing more was said. The pastor never went to see the head, but the elders told him that it had not been removed by anyone. They carried the memory of it for as long as they lived, although they refrained from mentioning it to the pastor ever again, in case that mercurial man found it to be upsetting.

BLOOD ECLIPSE

AT NIGHTFALL, AFTER DISEMBARKING FROM THE
train, the visiting therapist was taken to a bed-and-breakfast
a mile out of Hathersage, where the hospital authorities had
reserved her a room. It was run by an old couple who managed
the organic dairy farm in which the B&B sat. They had built a
wood-fired sauna and hot tub for their guests, which were both
forever closed. The old man took Beth up to the room, already
aware that she was a therapist from the Big Smoke, and from
inside the other locked rooms the therapist thought she could
hear clocks ticking in the dark, mechanical cuckoos waiting to
explode at dawn, people turning in their sleep and clucking as
their nightmares came for them. The owner's name was
Aldiss – thirty years older than her thirty-five.

'Tell me,' he said as they went into the room and he turned
on the heater for his guest, 'did you see the blood eclipse last
night?'

'I was in London.'

'Didn't you know about it?'

She said it was the first she'd heard of an eclipse.

Aldiss continued, 'We had a view from the patio. The
wife and I had a hot toddy while it went on. Aye, grand

enough. Never seen a better one. There was also a fine one back in April, though.'

Her arrival in the Derwent village on 9 October 2014 had been met with cosmic fanfare then. A moon reddened by an effect known as the Rayleigh scattering.

'I thought there was a storm here last night,' she said.

'Not that we saw. But that may have been later on. There won't be another one until next year.'

'Another storm?'

'An eclipse.'

He looked down at her shoes, or so she thought. Common Projects trainers, too trendy for both her and the village.

She said, 'I'll be sure to look out for that one, I promise.'

'It's a fine thing to see before you die.'

Aldiss handed her the key and there was a moment of awkwardness. There was a tiny plastic bra attached to it. The suite was called 'Brassiere', a little local joke from the 1970s.

He quickly said, 'Will you be eating here tonight?'

'I thought I would. I have a guest coming.'

'A gentleman friend?'

She laughed. 'Yes, and a doctor. Doctors are very picky eaters.'

'My wife makes a fine potato lasagne.'

'It's Dr Milliner from the big hospital in Leeds. Do you know him?'

'Aye, that quack. We know him. Are you come to replace him?'

'No. I'm here to help him with a case.'

She looked at her watch and saw that it was 6.30 p.m. Dr Milliner would be downstairs in ten minutes.

'On second thoughts, I'll come back down with you. Maybe I could get a shot of coffee while I wait?'

'My wife makes the best coffee in Hathersage. Well, that's not saying much.' He exaggerated the local accent, by way of a moment of comedy. 'I'll 'ave nowt myself but coffee.'

They went down to the front room where there was a bar in the corner and a log fire spitting sparks up into a filthy chimney. At the far end of the room a few empty tables stood next to a high window spattered with rain; above them a TV was raised on the wall. One of the tables was set with a chequered tablecloth and plates for two, as if her meeting had already been anticipated. She sat down at the table, and Aldiss poured her a shot of Dalwhinnie. She was off the booze these days, she said, but he insisted, not seeming to accept this lackadaisical explanation. And, wanting to be polite, she pretended to take a sip.

A few minutes later Milliner arrived and the house-dogs began to bark. She had never met him before, but they had been corresponding for a few weeks about a patient of his in the village. A teenage girl called Maude Blythe, who had presented with severe symptoms of an unknown personality disorder and whom he had been unable to treat. In truth, he had not been able to diagnose her accurately. 'In my opinion it is not schizophrenia,' he had written to her, 'but possibly something else. Her parents are farmers and say her moods have become extreme. I ruled out illicit use of marijuana.'

Milliner was her father's age. He leaned in and twisted slightly. His eyes were lovely shells of their former selves. They sat by the windows as the rain came down in cold waves, and out in the garden two gnomes suffered silently.

'I'm relieved you're finally here,' he said. 'I hear the potato lasagne is rather good.'

Beth leaned in as well and put on the local accent: 'There's nowt else.'

While they ate he went over the case of Maude Blythe, a bright girl doing well at St Teresa Academy, a local sixth-form school. Her parents were farmers who sold, among other more basic items, renowned hydroponic cucumbers to Manchester markets.

'They came to me just after Easter, as you know. We gave her Risperidone injections when the other treatments had no effect. But I don't see any result from that, or from the Haloperidol we also tried. I feel we've come to a dead end with her. She sleeps all the time and has ceased to participate in all school activities. But she still attends punctually. It's bizarre; she still seems to pay attention in class, but at the end all her notebooks turn out to be empty. And then she hands in essays that are remarkably brilliant. No one can make head or tail of it.'

'She didn't have any trauma that you know of?'

'Nothing. No accidents, no illnesses. It's purely psychological. Perhaps something happened at school.'

'Bullying?'

'None that we can detect. It's more a sort of amnesia, a kind of mental drifting. She doesn't seem to remember anything – sometimes from minute to minute.'

'What do her parents say?'

'They're stumped. As you can imagine.'

Beth put down her fork and wondered about the glass of whisky that was still in front of her. Should she?

'It's as if,' he went on, 'Maude has in a very real sense lost her mind, as they say. As in, mislaid it somewhere. Or had it mislaid for her.'

'Maybe she has a hidden infection.'

'We ran all the usual blood tests. Nothing. In fact, it's the other way round. She is extraordinarily healthy.'

'How so?'

'Her blood is like a newborn's. Her body composition is well-nigh perfect. I know she's sixteen and all, but apparently she was a little on the stout side before.'

'So she went on a diet?'

'No. Her diet is disgusting. That's the strange thing. She ate healthily before, her parents say, and now she eats like a pig.'

Finally Beth reached for the glass and took the fatal sip. It was akin to an electric shock, with nostalgic pleasure at the end of it.

'First drink in a while?' Milliner smiled, noticing the look on her face. 'It must be good to be out of London,' he added.

'I shouldn't,' she muttered. 'But it's cold and I'm tired.'

'Then I'll let you sleep. Shall I take you out to the Blythe farm tomorrow or would you prefer to go alone?'

'I'll go alone. They're expecting me, aren't they?'

'That's an understatement. They're praying for you to come.' He went on, 'We can put you up in your own cottage. We have a place kept aside for you. If you don't mind living alone, that is. You can take it for three months. The local council will pay.'

She looked up, distracted. On the TV an image of the moon had appeared, the colour of pink champagne. It looked as if the eclipse that Aldiss had so laboriously mentioned had been recorded somewhere in the Sahara. Men in djellabas stopped to look at it on dirt tracks, beside mud walls with crenellations. The moon here was setting. Then there were other recordings of the same eclipse from the Americas – over the skyline of Los Angeles.

'So there it is,' she said to Milliner, 'the eclipse from last night.'

He hadn't noticed it, either.

'By the way,' he said, as if it didn't matter in the slightest, 'I want you to know that no one here has breathed a word about your little difficulty in London last year. I make no judgement about it. These things happen.'

She grimaced. 'Thank you. No charges were filed. And it was just a misunderstanding anyway.'

In her bed in the cold room later that evening she thought over the implausibility of his statement about the Blythes praying for her arrival, however much she would have liked it to be true. She had not talked to the parents, either by phone or by email, and she was not sure how they would actually receive her when it came to it. Did they really understand what a therapist was, even one who specialised in issues arising from puberty? Even if they understood, would they consider what she did legitimate? But then again, she had no doubt that Milliner had convinced them thoroughly that her skills were needed. But they would probably be wary of the whole arrangement. It was desperation that had driven them to accept it.

EARLY THE NEXT MORNING, after calling ahead, she drove down to the Blythe farm on the far side of Abney in her Hertz rental car. The road wound through low wooded hills, the fields tilting against the line of the horizon. Parts of it plunged through dense copses of oak saplings and fir trees, and on the far hillsides drystone walls cut the land geometrically into wide squares. On both sides of the road stood massive, shaggy trees that could have been elements from the Domesday Book, and which had taken on the sullen greyness of the clouds that swept down to shadow them.

Abney was little more than a road with farms and restored stone houses along it. The Blythe farm stood at a small crossroads framed by wet stone walls and fields sparkling with ice in the half-light. A signpost by the side of the road pointed to four different villages. At the edge of the copse a weather-beaten woman stood with a hoe, staring up at the intruder. She was in gumboots and a tattered macintosh, her hair swept up under a plastic shower cap. The veins in her eyes had burst long ago and there was no mending them. Mrs Blythe had been waiting for her.

She explained, as they walked up to the house, that her husband and daughter were expecting Beth inside. Before they went in she paused and looked up at the sky. 'Ey up, it's going to flinker again, look.'

Mr Blythe was sitting by the fire with teacups, a farmer of about fifty with the same tired eyes as his wife. He got up to shake Beth's hand. As she sat she looked around at the china animals and the black beams, the blackened iron dogs by the fire and the polished kettles. The girl was upstairs. They wanted a word alone with the therapist.

Had Beth ever come across a similar case in recent years – a teenager with comparable symptoms? Beth said she couldn't be sure without meeting Maude.

'It's all we can do to keep her at the school,' Mrs Blythe said.

'So, as I understand it,' Beth said, 'the issue isn't academic?'

'Nay. I wish it was. All kids that age have academic problems. It's something else.'

The mother: 'She's all alone now. No one will touch her.'

'How so?'

'None of her friends will go near her. She has no friends any more. She had all these friends before, but now they avoid her.'

'She must have done something . . .'

'Nay. It's not something's been *done*. It's the hormones, is what I think.'

'It might well be,' Beth said. Puberty would play some kind of role, of course. But what kind of a role?

'Has she been violent?' she asked.

'Not to us.'

Beth frowned. 'I'm sorry?'

'She goes out in the field,' the father said, 'and lies down to look at the sky. I hear her crying out there.'

'Well, that's hardly "violence".'

'It sounds like violence.'

An enigmatic remark, but Beth let it go.

It was probably, she said to them, following her own line of thought, a crisis of puberty of some kind.

'Aye,' the mother began, glancing at her husband, 'but . . .'

She turned instinctively to her husband, as if she had to obtain permission from him to continue her sentence.

'It's like she's not there any more,' he finished with

resignation. 'For the last five months or so, it's like Maude upped and walked off out of her own life, you could say. She's still the same person and yet she's not the same. I don't know how to describe it.'

'What do her teachers say?'

'They've noticed the same thing. She refuses to play games. She won't sing in the choir any more. She has no interest in any of that.'

'I see. Should I have a chat with her now?'

He turned his head to the wall, as if to shout through it, and called out, 'Maude! Come down here and meet the therapist lady.'

Beth drank her sugared tea as Maude, still out of sight, clomped her way down the stairs. As she came into the kitchen, in jeans and a strawberry cardigan, chopped blonde hair tucked behind her ears, Beth stilled: the girl was far more beautiful and more frail than she had anticipated. So this was the case that Milliner had been unable to crack.

But there was nothing hard-boiled about Maude. She was in darned socks, smiling shyly, and her skin was glowing, as if she had just come from a steam bath. Beth stood to shake her cold hand, and the eyes were mild, grey and steady as they looked back at her. Intelligent but unengaged. The therapist observed at once what Milliner had already discovered: a subtle dissociation between body and mind. She had come across this dissociation many times before. But in this girl it was not, in some way, usual. Beth could not put her finger on why.

They sat together and there was a faux-merry interlude of ten minutes during which the parents did their best to make everything seem normal and hospitable. The girl watched Beth archly as her parents went through their pantomime and there was the hint of a sardonic smile on her lips. Eventually the father suggested that Beth and Maude should talk by themselves while the elders worked outside.

Beth decided to go very gently and slowly with the girl.

'I hope you don't feel awkward,' she said. 'You know why I'm here. I'm sorry it's like this. Maybe you're wondering who I am?'

'They told me about you. It's all right.'

'Is it? I hope so. I'm only going to be here to help. It's what I do – help people.'

'I know. I'm grateful.'

'Dr Milliner has explained everything to me. Of course I'm not saying he knows everything.'

'Who is Dr Milliner?'

The grey eyes came down upon Beth and she faltered a little.

'He's the man from the hospital who gave you injections. You remember, don't you?'

'Oh, him. Sort of.'

'He's rather nice, isn't he?'

'Nice?' The girl smiled and her hands clasped her knees.

'In his way,' Beth suggested. 'He's nice in his way.'

'I can't really remember anything about him. Do my parents know him?'

'They do, yes.'

'Did my parents ask you to come here?'

'They did. Do you mind that they did?'

'They can do what they want. What did they tell you?'

'That you're having problems at school. Social problems, I mean. Not academic ones apparently.'

'Problems?'

'They said there were problems.'

'I don't know what they mean. What kind of "problems"?'

'As I said, social ones – friendship problems, maybe.'

'Friendship problems?'

'Yes, friendships with other girls is what they meant, I suppose.'

'Well, I don't have a boyfriend, if that's what you're asking. It's an all-girls school.'

'Yes, so I gathered.'

'I can't say I like it there.'

'Maybe that's the problem, then. Maybe you're going through a difficult time about things that have nothing to do with the school.'

'Oh?'

'It could be anything. You can tell me – eventually. Not today.'

'Are you going back to London today?'

'No, I think I'll be here for a week at least.'

'Only a week . . .'

The girl leaned back and smiled at her more broadly.

'It's very boring up here. There's nothing to do. There's even nowt to do. Fuck-all nowt.'

'It can't all be boring.'

'Oh yes, it certainly can all be boring. It *is*.'

Well, Beth thought, *I'm not going to sum up my report by telling the hospital that you're bored.*

'I'm sure you find some fun somewhere,' she said heroically.

The girl's return glance was, if anything, pitying.

'It's not the centre of the universe, Beth. Can I call you Beth?'

'I'd prefer it if you did.' *Click*, Beth thought. *I'm in.* 'You know,' she went on, 'this is a slightly unusual situation. I haven't done something like this before. Usually I have my clinic and people come to me. So bear with me. Where shall we meet? What about three times a week after school?'

'There's a balti restaurant in Hathersage.'

'Indian food?'

'Suits me. I don't care where we meet. You can come here if you like.'

'I think it might be better if it's away from your parents. I'm getting a cottage of my own the day after tomorrow. You can come there, too.'

'Aye?'

Then it struck Beth: the girl didn't speak with a local accent. When she did, she was putting it on for sarcastic purposes, just as other people sometimes did. That was a curious detail. She must have made an effort to unlearn it in her regular speech in order to employ it ironically. She resolved to ask Mrs Blythe about it before she left.

Mrs Blythe walked her down to the car afterwards and the two of them had a moment in the flinkering snow.

'I wanted to ask you,' Beth said. 'Why does Maude not speak like you and your husband?'

'She used to, aye. But a few months back her accent changed.'

'Did it happen overnight?'

'Aye, it did. She woke up the next day talking different.'

Beth asked the mother if anything had happened back then that might have triggered such an odd change.

'Nowt as I can think.'

'But can you remember which month it happened?'

The woman tensed slightly, a note of hostility rising into the voice.

'Why do you ask?'

'It's relevant, I think. I need to have all the information. Five months back, was it? That would be April or so.'

'I suppose it would.'

Beth drove to Hathersage and had lunch alone at Sangams Balti on the Main Road, before calling Milliner and agreeing to take the cottage for three months. Could she move in later that day? She had nothing but a small suitcase and her computer. Since it was a guest house for visiting specialists, it was comfortably equipped and she picked up the keys that afternoon. It lay on the road between Hathersage and Grindleford, a house alone in the forests and surrounded by the same low drystone walls that she was beginning to find familiar. The early snow had stopped by the time she arrived. The night trees soughed all round the house, massive chestnuts whose red-and-gold leaves made the sound of waves drawing on shingle. She unpacked her suitcase and sat on a high bed, next to which stood a radio clock and a small lamp with a pink shade, attractive to autumn moths. The interior design evoked the Laura Ashley mode of the 1980s, and the previous occupant had left an oral thermometer on the bedside table. On the far side of the lonely road outside, a river flowed under the moon, with the trees along its edges. It was a place of solace and solitude after her recent months of tumult and uncertainty, and Beth was already wondering if she could get them to extend the lease to a year.

In the morning it was a drive of a few miles to Bakewell and the outskirts of the village where the St Teresa Academy stood. The headmistress was under forty, cordial and curiously eager to talk. She corroborated much of what Beth already knew: Milliner had made a clumsy foray into the girl's well-being, but Maude had found him unsympathetic. He had not made much progress. Ms Ashford was herself a local woman via an Oxford detour, like Beth, and they swapped college gossip – St Hilda's, dreadful food! – for a few minutes to establish the ground between them.

The school was the best in the area. It was housed in handsome old nineteenth-century granite buildings with lush playing fields bracketed by calming scenery. From a high window in the main building, as they had a pot of Earl Grey with some scones, they could see the morning's PE group doing their Jumping Jacks and heard a distant cry of 'One, two! One, two!' It was a little jarring to think that Maude was in the same building right then, opening a text-book somewhere, the other girls sniggering behind her back. Beth asked the headmistress about Maude's behaviour over the last few weeks. She said she had a feeling that the parents were not telling her the whole story.

'Of course they aren't,' Ms Ashford said. 'I've long thought it was *they* who are the problem.'

'How so?'

'They come in at the end of every term, for the usual

meetings with us. But they're a strange couple, I find. They don't have a good reputation hereabouts.'

'Well,' Beth smiled, 'you'll have to fill me in on that. It's the first I've heard of it.'

'The father is a churchgoer and has a group of men he hangs out with. They go hunting up near Barber Booth, or so I've heard. Nothing wrong with that, of course. Nothing wrong with being a churchgoer, either, for that matter. It's just that I find him a bit, I don't know, *repellent*. I'm sorry, it's a strong word.'

Beth nodded calmly, encouraging Ms Ashford to go on.

'A year ago Maude was coming in with bruises on her neck and face. They were arguing, she and her parents. I don't know what went on, but one can guess. She was acting up, maybe. Girls do at that age. Staying out, smoking and whatnot. Or worse. I don't know if that's true of Maude.'

'Is it true she changed in some way over the last six months or so?'

'Her academic work soared, yes, and completely out of the blue. It's not like anything I've ever seen. She's top of her class in every subject. And yet we can't see that she does any work.'

'You mean in class?'

'Anywhere. She was bad at maths before, and now she is faster than her teacher. It's like she had a brain accident that turned her into a genius overnight – like some of those Oliver Sacks cases. Do you know his work?'

'Do I know his work?'

'Sorry, of course you do. But what do you think?'

'I can't have an opinion yet. Sometimes teenagers turn a

corner of some kind. They become motivated and passionate about their studies. They can do this quite secretively. Maybe there's a hormonal reason behind it. Puberty, in other words. It depends on the individual.'

'I'm sure it does. But if I may say, I don't think it's hormonal in this case. I've observed a lot of students in my time. A lot. There are patterns. We know about puberty, of course. This doesn't follow any of the patterns.'

'So you mean there are more unusual patterns of behaviour?'

'Her erratic outbursts. Don't listen to her parents when they say she hasn't been violent. It began when she assaulted a fellow player on the netball team. I don't know what it was about. Some idiotic teenage dispute. But Maude broke another girl's collarbone. We had to hush it up, to keep her at the school. I mean, she is going to be a spectacular asset to us academically. I want to keep her. But she broke the girl's collarbone, for goodness' sake.'

'How on earth did she do that?'

'One punch. Afterwards Maude didn't remember doing it. Or she pretended not to remember. Who can tell?'

'But,' Beth objected, 'she doesn't seem particularly physically strong to me. She's rather delicate, isn't she?'

'She does seem so. Maybe it's willpower more than physical strength . . .'

'Did the girl's parents want to prosecute?'

'They did. But the Blythes went and "calmed them down". You have to remember that up here everybody knows everybody. Disputes get solved that way. The Blythes may have paid them off.'

'Do you think they did?'

'I do. But I can't prove it.'

Increased intelligence, an increased propensity for violence.

'And the social problems?' Beth asked.

'She has dropped out of everything. The others are teasing her, but they keep it low-key because they're afraid of her. I keep hearing stories. There's a girl who studies in her maths class. She says Maude knows what the week's maths problems are going to be before the teacher's even set them. Completely accurate every week.'

'That could be inspired guessing . . .'

'*Inspired* is the word.'

'And how do you feel yourself when you're around her?'

The headmistress shifted in her office chair and her eyes shied away from Beth's, finding refuge in the windows and the view of dark-green meadows rolling away to the horizon. The girl made her uncomfortable, she couldn't deny it. Maude had a way with her that was 'disarming'. Always cool and self-contained, dressed carefully as if continuously prepared for something. She could see her in ten years' time as a world-famous mathematician. It would probably come to pass. Or else Maude would make a mistake and fall from grace.

They walked around the grounds afterwards and Ms Ashford showed Beth the facilities, the classrooms in which Maude spent most of her days. There was nothing unusual about any of it – no aura of unnecessary discipline or regulation. It seemed, to Beth's eye, like a slightly down-at-heel provincial school in a sparsely populated region filled with local girls with blue Viking eyes. Against all this Maude was clearly rebelling, and rebellions are always seen as a sign of mental eccentricity and instability. There was nothing remarkable about it, yet. She would have to see when she got to know Maude better.

THEY MET AT THE balti in the Main Road the following Saturday, a day of merry gales, and sat in one of the deserted booths, framed by dark wooden pillars like an old New York steakhouse. There was a bar with fairy lights, but no drinkers. Maude came dressed in jeans and a fur-lined parka with hiking boots. It was, as it turned out, the perfect place to begin their chats. To Beth's surprise, Maude was not in the slightest bit reluctant to talk about herself. On the contrary, she seemed to have been waiting for such an opportunity. Beth told her straight away that she had been to the school to meet the headmistress; she admitted they had discussed the incident on the netball court.

'Did something happen there?' Maude asked.

'You don't remember?'

'I'm not sure what you mean. Should I remember something?'

Beth decided to go easy on her.

'It's nothing. If you don't remember, it's not important.'

'Why won't you tell me what it was?'

'It doesn't matter now. I'd rather talk about school in general. They say you love maths.'

'I do?'

'Well you're very good at it.'

'I don't know about "very good". I just "see" the

problems, if you know what I mean. I see through them. I don't know why.'

'Were you always good at it?'

'I don't remember.'

'What about when you were younger? Like, when you were ten or eleven?'

The girl looked puzzled for a moment.

'That's a long time ago. I can't think that far back.'

'What about before April, say?'

'That's far back as well. Why do you ask?'

'Your dad says that's when you had a change of some sort.'

'Does he now? Well, he can think what he likes, can't he?'

The girl brimmed with a confident, quiet defiance, eating her naan and rogan josh at twice the rate of the older woman. It was as if she hadn't eaten all week. Beth continued asking her gentle questions.

What about her friends, her hobbies? Why did she like being alone so much? The girl genuinely didn't know. Something occurred to Beth. Maude could not remember anything prior to 15 April. It was a curious quirk. Meanwhile she was describing her relationship with her father. He was a stern man of faith. In fact Mr Blythe was a follower of the American evangelist minister John Hagee.

Beth admitted that she had never heard of him.

'He has a worldwide following, Beth. You're missing out. He leads the Cornerstone Church in Texas. My mother adores him too. They both pray every day with the TV on. There's a special channel on cable.'

'And what about you?'

'That's the main problem with my dad. I was brought up believing it all and praying with them. But lately – I don't know – I've sort of fallen out with it.'

'Does that bother them?'

' "Bother" is not the word. It makes them furious. That's why they've invented all this nonsense about me having "problems". I don't have any problems. I just don't want to pray on my knees in front of the TV every night.'

'I don't blame you.'

'That's why I'm so glad you came up here, Beth. I *knew* you'd understand. It's useless trying to tell anyone at school about it. They already think my parents are nutters. It's fair enough, I suppose. They *are* nutters.'

Maude's hands moved together on the surface of the table. The fingers intertwined and then clenched.

'So it's merely that they're angry at you?'

'Yes. In my opinion. They've said all kinds of outrageous things about me. Horrible things. They're trying to bring me back to the Church.'

The girl had leaned forward on those two intermeshed hands, her eyes wide and perfectly reflecting the rainswept street beyond the windows.

'In the end, it's why you're here as well. They want to use you to force me back to praying every evening. I thought it was better to tell you that at the beginning, so you know what you're up against.'

'And you didn't tell that to Dr Milliner?'

'Why should I? He's an idiot and a busybody. I was never going to tell him anything. I'll only tell you because you're smart and I like you.'

A small heat rose in Beth's cheeks and she felt herself slip into a moment's giddiness. She was forced to think back to her illicit affair with one of her patients the year before, the source of all her professional aggravations and complications. The trial by committee, the furious, vengeful parents. The near-destruction of her entire career.

'That's very sweet of you to say.'

'It's only what I think is true.'

'Is it?' Maude reached out and tapped the back of Beth's hand with a finger.

'Yes. I'm only a liar half the time.'

'Then I'll say thank you.'

'Where are we going after lunch?'

'After?'

'Shouldn't I show you around, since you're the tourist? You have a car.'

'That's right.'

'Well then. Let's go a-rambling,' she said in her best northern accent.

THEY DROVE UP TO Bradfield Dale on Mortimer Road. They rose past twisted trees and walls sunk in moss, the first of the moors edged with hibernating bronze ferns. On the way back they stopped at a pub on the road. Maude was underage, but she told Beth that everybody there knew her and she always drank at the pubs. They would be reluctant, but they would serve her.

The place was traditional, with an air of quiet triumph dating back to the Battle of Britain, an atmosphere illustrated and confirmed by many photographs of the establishment's long-dead former owner in goggles and leathers, posed next to the wheels of a Spitfire. Carefully placed in time. They sat privately by the fire. Beth looked around the room. There were a few locals eyeing them with sneers. So they knew the Blythe girl and didn't like her, and now they were wondering what the London woman was doing with her. *The pale swines*, Beth thought, *the nudging and winking judgers*. A formless rage was always simmering inside her, held down and made mute by a need to show calm to her peers. Now, however, it surged and almost burst out. It was proximity to the girl that did it.

Beth went to the bar and insolently ordered two ciders from the woman operating the pumps.

'How about the girl?' the latter said.

'What about her?'

'Is she of age?'

'If I say so, yes. I'm a doctor.'

She got the drinks and brought them back to the table.

'Fuck them,' Beth said suddenly.

'Aye.'

They knocked drinks and sipped, sharing a mutual smile over the edges of their glasses. Now Beth unwound, free-talking for the first time in years. She had a confidante. Maude wanted to know about psychiatry. Beth told her about a psychiatric doctor she knew from Israel who treated Jews who insisted they were characters from the Old Testament.

'It wouldn't be so bad,' she said, now a little tipsy, 'if it weren't for the fact that they insist the authorities provide them with driving licences dated to the tenth century BC and marked "Ezekiel". They end up in various Israeli clinics because the authorities are exasperated. But their doctors can't persuade them that in the end they are not, in fact, from the Old Testament. When they try to do so, these people look at them as if it's the doctors who are mad and demand their proof. It's quite difficult to find proof that the person sitting in front of you is not Nehemiah. You get caught up in their unfalsifiable claims and eventually you fall down over a small mistake that you make.' She laughed, making the room take notice of her. 'That's how the insane get the upper hand. They do their research.'

'I haven't met too many insane Jews,' Maude said. 'Plenty of insane English people, though.'

'Oh, we're rats in a cage.'

'But is the Old Testament any saner?'

'Your father would say so.'

They laughed together, and Maude went to the bar and got two more ciders. She was served with a kind of knowing reluctance. The woman looked Maude over with disdain, and the girl decided to return the disdain with an equivalent icy stare.

'Does your father believe in Judgement Day then?'

'He lives for it. He believes in the End Days.'

'So he's a hardliner then.'

'They genuinely believe in it. Hagee believes it's in a few months' time – or a few years' anyway.'

Maude emptied her glass and let her grey eyes wander.

'Look at them all,' she murmured. 'And they call me "possessed". They believe any rumour that enters their heads. It's pathetic.'

'People are sheep. Never mind them. Never mind anyone for the time being.'

But Beth had caught the word 'possessed' and was rolling it around in her mind. It didn't seem improbable that people like the Blythes, if their daughter was to be believed, would employ such a word to describe her.

On their way back to Abney, Maude asked her to stop the car along a stretch of road thick with oaks. There the trees shone gold under a pearl-grey sky. With the engine killed, they could hear the leaves crackling as the wind cut through them. They got out and Maude pulled Beth over a stone wall and into a wet field filled with decayed ferns. She said it was a spot she often visited to be alone. There was a lull in the wind and yet suddenly all the leaves on the oaks began to fall like a golden snow, simultaneously, as if at a given signal. The girl turned to her with a look of delight. Over the last two days everything had changed. The earth itself had changed. Maude wanted the leaves to fall, and so they fell.

'Don't be silly,' Beth said, but she couldn't raise the necessary coldness in her voice to dampen the adolescent mysticism.

Maude said, 'I'm just saying that's how it feels to me. *Fall, leaves, fall; die, flowers, away.*' It was someone's poem.

'Is that what you were thinking?'

'It's what I was saying to myself.'

Back at the family farm, Maude made Beth stop out of sight of the house and got out by herself. She leaned in for a last word.

'It's better they don't see you dropping me off. It's all right, but they'll start asking questions about what we talked

of. Let's go for another drive tomorrow. We can go to the
lake at Howden Clough.'

'Wherever you like. It's Sunday.'

Maude stepped closely for a moment and, out of nowhere,
brushed Beth's cheek with a gossamer kiss. Then she skipped
off, hair blowing golden in the wind, leaving the older woman
stunned.

BETH PASSED THE EVENING reading and writing postcards
to a few friends. They would be surprised to receive them.
For a while she googled the words Maude had uttered about
the leaves falling. It was Emily Brontë. She fell asleep at the
front-room desk at around nine and woke again just after
midnight with a start. All around the cottage the trees had
begun to seethe, like forests of kelp distorted by ocean currents, the leaves and small branches raining down on the roof
and hitting the casements. The chestnuts surrounding the
house appeared to be bending to the point of breaking.

She went outside. The sky was starlit, quiet. And yet little
tornadoes of detached leaves swirled across the empty road
and into the half-frozen mud beyond it. It was all in her mind,
obviously, but that in itself was reason enough to observe the
apparently physical commotion coolly. She was in a state of
quiet tumult that was nevertheless intensely pleasurable. If
the girl could make leaves fall merely by wishing it, then why
couldn't her own moods externalise themselves in those same
trees? She sat on the stone wall and gulped in the gritty wind
and the smell of the moors. She had been given a stern lecture by her superiors about interacting with her patients, in

the months after her crisis, and she had herself seen a therapist to make sure she adhered to their advice. She had done so willingly, anxious to reform. But now that she was away from London and its neurotic social disciplines, the months of pent-up resentment and frustrations were ready to boil over. No one watched over her here. She was freer than she had been in years.

And why, she thought bitterly, *shouldn't I interact with my own patients? How else am I supposed to get to know them?*

Yet for the rest of the night she couldn't sleep. In the morning she drove into Grindleford and went for a coffee at the café by the station.

The railway tracks were covered with mist, the tops of the majestic trees around the station café invisible, like a suffocating corner of the Papuan jungle visited by unprecedented cold. After the coffee Beth went outside onto the small bridge and stared down at the tracks and the tunnel's entrance opposite.

As she sat there brooding, a man walked past her, tossing out a word. It was 'Bitch', loud and clear. She turned angrily and saw a ragged tweed back and a pair of tracksuit bottoms making off along the lane with a limp. She swung her legs round and thought about pursuing him. But she was the stranger here, not him, and she decided it would be unwise. Still, she tried calling him out. The man turned on his heel and grinned back at her. 'I saw you,' he called out, moving backwards without missing a beat, 'you and her. I saw you.'

Later in the day she picked up Maude from Hathersage, as the girl had asked. This time Maude had two pairs of

Craghoppers boots for both of them. They were her mother's, apparently.

They drove up to Mortimer Road and saw that the dales were beginning to sink under a light cover of cloud where the rain had begun. Near a pub called the Strines Inn they came to the Foulstone Road path and parked the car by the gate. From there they walked. After a few hundred yards the road turned into a waterlogged moorland path, with the grouse butts around them. It was lonelier and more ominous than Beth had expected, the land rolling away into penumbra, with misshapen rocks making the moors look like bone-yards. They walked for a mile and a half and then sat down in their waterproof capes, opening the box of sandwiches Beth had bought in the Main Road, along with a Thermos of hot coffee. It was about three or four miles to Howden Clough. After their rest, however, they made good time and the walk was not difficult. The clouds pressed down.

They reached the pine woods overlooking a finger of dark-grey water. The rough grass at its edges appeared exhausted after the first weeks of autumn. They sat down again, eating the rest of the sandwiches with the coffee. The silence was so great that, for a while, talking felt like sacrilege.

'Do you think anyone ever comes here?' Beth said eventually.

'Not now it's colder.'

'What did your father say to you last night?'

'They were out at the pub until ten. When they came back they gave me a hard time.'

'About me?'

'No. Just in general. It got a bit rough, though.'

'What do you mean, "rough"?'

'Dad takes out his belt sometimes. It's a family tradition.'

'He hits you?'

'Always has. It's the Lord's whip!'

'Why didn't you tell Milliner that – or someone at school?'

'For what?'

'You mean it happens often?'

Maude shrugged. 'So what? It's the way it is.'

'No, I don't accept that.'

A wave of rage broke over the older woman. *The filthy swine*, she thought. 'You can't let him do that. *We* can't let him.'

'But we do.'

Beth thought about the girl's body under her clothes. It must be covered with bruises that she would never show to anyone.

'You know, if you ever need a place to stay, you can knock on my door any time.'

The girl smiled sarcastically: 'Oh aye?'

ON THE WALK BACK to the road Beth felt the girl's quiet and unexpected magnetism overwhelm her. She wanted to take her hand, but didn't have the guts to do it. But at least she could talk. Talking was what she did best. She knew not to press the issue about her father's beating, so she steered the conversation towards Maude. But the girl was no longer interested in talking about herself. She was more curious about Beth. And so Beth's strategy was turned back on her and she reluctantly found herself talking about her own problems. She became gradually incoherent. By the time they had regained the car she had divulged the ugly details of her professionally unforgivable trespass with another girl.

They went to the Strines Inn nearby and ate biscuits by the fire while doing crosswords from that day's *Times*. Beth wanted to know how fast the girl's mind really was. She read out the questions and the girl answered them without hesitating. 'Economies upset firm producing wall-covering.' *Stucco*. 'Brown jelly having zero fruit'? *Tangelo*. Maude went through the entire puzzle in minutes. For the first time it occurred to Beth that Maude must have a form of autism. Why had she not thought of this earlier? It was certainly the most likely explanation at this point. Asperger's or something close to it on the spectrum. That would explain why her parents couldn't understand her. Though why it had not manifested itself prior to April of that year was a puzzle she could not yet solve. An external trigger must have set in motion a chain of inner events that had culminated in a shift of some kind.

Then there was the crossword. How did her mind read the clues so easily? For Maude, they were like panes of glass one could look through with no effort.

'I think this is boring for you. I should have brought some maths problems with me.'

'Even more boring.'

'Is anything difficult *and* interesting?'

Maude, seated in a rocking chair, leaned back and the grey eyes seemed to have acquired a subtle new colour – a very pale sage. When Beth looked into them, they made her think of small silvery fish frozen in clear ice.

'I'm trying to figure out the sky.'

'Oh?'

'I lie outdoors at night and try to figure it out.'

'Well, the greatest minds haven't figured it out.'

'No. That's a funny thought. You know what I think? I have this feeling that I came from up there. The rest of you are just humans.'

'Just humans?'

'*Mere* humans. No insult to you, Beth. I like some humans. Most of them are simply pigs, of course. Inferior material. But I like you.'

'It's good to know I'm inferior material.'

'You can't help being what you are. Nor can I. It's the cards we've been dealt.'

Beth couldn't help a short laugh. 'You can say that again.'

The calm certitude of the girl's insolence was rather wonderful, childlike and world-weary all at once.

'If the situation was different,' Maude went on, 'I would hope that you would still like me. But the others – they're generally not worth talking to.'

'But you *have* to talk to them, Maude.'

'I talk to them in my own mind. I think that's enough.'

'No,' Beth insisted gently, 'it isn't enough.'

'It's enough for me,' Maude pushed back. 'It's calmer that way. And more truthful.'

'But it's not more truthful. You have to engage—'

'Engage?' Maude's tone implied that engagement with inferior material was hardly anything to aspire to. 'I can engage with you. That's enough for me.'

Beth could not reply. It was exactly what she had wanted to hear.

As before, she left the girl at the top of her drive and watched her trudge down to her gate, pause for a second to offer a parting wave and disappear inside. By that point the rain was coming down heavily and the dales around them were submerged in the ever-recurring vapours. She drove home feeling strangely disconsolate. On the way she stopped at an off-licence and bought herself a consolation bottle of Royal Stag.

THAT NIGHT SHE RESEARCHED the cult of Reverend Hagee. He was a remarkable figure, if unknown to her. His books sold millions of copies around the world. His face appeared on the Trinity Broadcasting Network and the Inspiration network. People in villages in Africa and remote parts of Asia could watch him weekly. He preached the End of Times and the Second Coming, the imminent invasion of Israel by Russia and the Islamic states, and the destruction of the latter by a vigilant God. He was a hero to the Zionist Organization of America and a nemesis for Catholics and Muslims. For these two were reserved, at various times, the phrase 'a Godless theology of hate'. His earliest published book, in 1973, was *The Invasion of Demons*; his latest, in 2013, was *Four Blood Moons: Something is About to Change*. The latter was a global bestseller and it immediately made Beth think back to the eclipse on the day preceding her arrival. Within five minutes she had confirmed an astonishing connection.

Hagee had written a series of prophecies based on the Tetrad of Blood Eclipses, which occurred and would occur between April 2014 and September 2015. The four dates of the eclipses were 15 April 2014, 8 October 2014, 4 April 2015 and 28 September 2015, with a solar eclipse amid the four on 15 March 2015. The four eclipses coincided, in the prophecies' view, with Jewish holidays and presaged an End of Times, such as those described in the Book of Joel, Acts and Revelations.

The red colour of these eclipses, however, was not due to Jehovah's propensity for human and animal blood, but to the Rayleigh scattering, named after the British scientist Lord Rayleigh, one John William Strutt. The minister, of course, was not concerned with such a mundane explanation. For him, the colour was of the highest significance and derived precisely from the Deity's obscure intentions. Which would be fulfilled, come the end of 2015.

The End Times were so close; 150 million people might be watching Hagee or reading these same words at that very moment, in dozens of both impoverished and developed countries, and people would be waiting for the next blood eclipse on mountaintops and rivers' edges with a glassy faith that the dimming of the moon must mean something that their own minds couldn't grasp. Out of the jumble of cut-and-pasted biblical quotes would emerge a vague premonition of vengeance, a movement towards chaos and violence. Millions of people quietly and secretly sick in the depths of their own minds: it was an epidemic of the mind, if you chose to look at it that way.

For Beth's purposes, the only thing that really mattered was that 15 April had been significant to the Blythe family, and especially to the parents. For them it must have been a portent, with more to follow.

Having internalised this superstitious nonsense, they had inflicted it – knowingly or unknowingly – upon their helpless daughter. Maude had absorbed its monstrous hysteria herself and it had caused unpredictable effects within her. Who could know what their demented family dinners were like, with the three of them holding hands while saying grace, with John Hagee on satellite TV behind them. Families were the incubators of neuroses, were they not? A dangerous idea could spread like an infection, moving from one unconscious to another, like a pathogen. This was unquestionably what had happened here. Maude was the victim of a mental and emotional infection based on the idea of eclipses bringing escalating crises. Little wonder that the pedestrian Milliner had been unable to detect it, or even to conceptualise it. It was a pathogen of the mass-media age. For satellite TV was the least of it. Hagee was all over social media. His message saturated it, if you knew where to look.

But in that case, what new crisis had been precipitated by the blood eclipse close to the day of Beth's own arrival? Herself, obviously: she was the crisis.

This gave her pause. The Blythes could not have orchestrated such a thing. Nor could anyone, for that matter. It was pure coincidence. Yet it could not be. The timing was too perfect – so perfect in fact that she felt duped by it. Someone must have known. Perhaps Mr Blythe had manipulated Milliner in some extraordinarily cunning way. The question bothered her over the next few days, during which time she was unable to find a solution to it. Meanwhile the two of them texted each other furtively and constantly. Maude agreed to meet her the following weekend, and Beth wondered if it was a question she could raise with the teenager directly.

She drove to the balti in Hathersage the next Saturday to meet Maude, as usual. But the girl did not show up. Beth texted her a little frantically, but there was no reply. After an hour she gave up and drove back home, quietly enraged but also concerned. For the rest of the day she sat fuming at her desk while the wind turned yet again to rain and the trees around the house grew still. The monotonous downpour began to silence the little road outside. The river still moved, with its obstinate music. *Surely*, some part of her unconscious said, *it was unacceptable for her patient simply not to show up*. She called repeatedly until it grew dark and then she reluctantly gave up.

She went out to the stone wall at dusk and looked down at the swollen, slightly threatening river. Suddenly she felt the claustrophobic weight of isolation descending upon her. It was as if a malicious spell had been cast on her cottage. She was alone, in a landscape hostile to her.

A little later, as she was writing in the main room, she heard thunder rolling across the moors, and the trees outside her tiny window flickered into visibility as the lightning preceded it. Miserably she lay down on the sofa, watched television for an hour and then fell asleep. Three shots of Royal Stag helped her on her way. Half-tipsy, she slept until two, when wind beating on the windows woke her again and she fumbled for her phone, thinking it was ringing. Instead, it was a knocking on the door that had roused her.

She opened it to see Maude standing on the porch, wet to her skin, dressed in nothing but a tank top and cotton trousers with trainers. She looked as if she had walked all the way from Abney in the rain.

Pulling her inside and slamming the door behind her, Beth sat the girl down and went to the bathroom for towels.

'You didn't walk all the way from yours, did you?'

Maude nodded stoically. 'Can you make some tea?'

So it would be a long story. Beth made a pot and then dried the girl's hair with a towel, rubbing it vigorously until its shine returned.

As she did so, the girl began to talk.

Maude had had, predictably, an altercation with her mother. Not about anything specific, needless to say. It had escalated and her father had fallen upon her with the belt. But this time she had fought back and managed to get the belt off him. She had struck him in the face and her mother had called the neighbours. At that point Maude had run out of the house and into the road, simply to escape. She had nowhere to go except Beth's cottage. A walk of several miles in horizontal rain, but she had no choice. Soon they would come looking for her. She begged Beth to hide her.

'I can't hide you. That would get me fired. I'll negotiate with them.'

'They'll send the police, I know they will.'

'It's all right. They'll understand.'

The police would arrive at the sensible conclusion that Maude had come there for refuge, but as Beth contemplated the arrival of suspicious officers at her door at that hour, her old nightmare of professional disgrace returned to her mind. They would not believe her, given her prior history. She would not be able to talk her way out of it.

'I'll explain everything,' Beth said quietly, 'when they come to find you.'

'But don't let them take me. Let me stay here.'

Beth hesitated, then gave way. 'I promise. I'll keep you here tonight, don't worry.'

'What about afterwards?'

'Well, afterwards I can't say.'

The girl drank her tea morosely and Beth thought about the knock at the door that would inevitably come. But when?

Exhaustion laid the girl out on the sofa and she fell asleep. Beth went out onto the porch and listened to the road. But there was no sign of an approaching car. She locked the door and turned off the lights.

It occurred to her that this might dissuade anyone from intruding until the following day. She went into her damp bedroom and lay down to think, but the wind had only grown louder and now it drowned out her own thoughts. There was just Maude and the dark rooms.

Restless, Beth got up again and crept back into the front room. The girl was now asleep on her side in a foetal position. The two cups and their spoons stood cold on the coffee table with the empty teapot. Yet now the room felt warm, even stifling. She sat at the foot of the sofa and laid a reassuring hand on the girl's calf. Maude didn't stir, so deep was her sleep. A kind of parallel drowsiness came upon Beth as well, subtly maddened by the movement of the fir branches beyond the windows. She leaned back and felt the objects around her blur. As she did so, she cast an idle glance at the teacups and noticed that one of the spoons had shifted its position without her having disturbed it. Before she had time to think, the spoon rose away from the cup and hovered above it. There it turned slowly on its axis, rotating while she observed it in disbelief, the metal shaft shining each time it turned. She watched it, spellbound and disbelieving: she must be dreaming it. She closed her eyes to banish it from her mind. *Sleep, then, and make it go away.*

It was several hours before she woke, but when she did she was curled by the kitchen door without remembering how she had got there. It was a fist hammering on the door that had woken her, and it continued to shatter the silence as she regained consciousness. She sat up in terror and saw at once that the girl was no longer on the sofa. She called out her name quietly, but she could tell that Maude was gone. She went to the door.

It was dawn and a policewoman stood on the porch, shivering and blowing into her cupped hands. There was nothing malevolent about her. The police car stood on the water-covered verges. Its lights were turned off. The woman, middle-aged and dutiful, wanted to know if she was Beth and if this was her house. Could she come in for a moment?

'Of course,' Beth said; there was no refusing. They sat by the same coffee table with the same cups and spoons.

'Looks like you slept on the sofa,' the woman observed.

'I must have fallen asleep without realising it.'

'Aye well. Did you have company?'

The awkward questions came rather gently. Rashly, Beth said that she had been alone. *Skating on thin ice*, she thought to herself as the policewoman's eye performed its verifications of the room. Not a stray sock or shoe, not a golden hair on the cushions. Two cups, two spoons, however.

'Two cups?' the policewoman remarked.

'I made two pots,' Beth said calmly. 'I always use a clean cup.'

'Oh aye?'

'It's an old habit.'

The policewoman smiled and accepted it for the time being. She knew that Beth was lying but didn't want to capsize a precarious boat. Instead, she suggested that Beth contact them if Maude ever showed up.

'So she ran away?' Beth said.

'It's not the first time. Did she not tell you that?'

Beth shook her head. 'Patients don't tell us everything.'

'Same with us.'

'What did her father say?'

The woman shrugged. 'He says she attacked him with a golf club.'

'Well, that's a lie, obviously.'

'Is it? You've only been here a few weeks, Beth. We've had these situations before with the family.'

'Maude runs away?'

'Yes, but she comes back after a couple of days.'

'Where does she go?'

'She hides out in the woods, as far as we can tell. We put teams out to search for her, but we never find her. She comes back of her own accord.'

'Why did no one tell me, I wonder?'

'That's a good question.' The woman got up, wearily. 'I do hope you're telling the truth, Beth. It would be very awkward if you weren't.'

'I always tell the truth.'

When she had gone Beth went outside and stood by the road. The mist rolled in and covered her completely. She called out to Maude. Within minutes the girl appeared, slipping out from among the trees, her hair soaked and spread across her shoulders. She came down to the wall and stood a few feet from Beth. She said that she had hidden in the woods and waited. She had heard the car approaching while Beth slept. She wasn't ready to go back with the police just yet.

'You can't stay here another night.'

'Who says?'

'They'll be back.'

'No, they'll wait a while. I'll text my dad. They'll know I'm alive. They won't care where I am.'

'That seems unlikely.'

But the girl was calmly adamant. She said, 'You know it's the best thing for us both. It won't cost you anything.'

Beth had begun to tremble and her will ebbed. She went back inside and the girl followed her. She locked all the windows and the doors and told the girl to stay in her bedroom for a while. She wanted to make a few enquiries, but in the end she only contacted Milliner. She wanted to know what she should do.

'Are you completely insane?' was his response.

HE INSISTED THAT SHE meet him in Hathersage during the afternoon and he drove out from Leeds without telling anyone that he was doing so. They met at the balti, and Beth began by saying that she had never been anything less than completely honest with him.

'With *me*,' he burst out at once, 'but what about with the family?'

'Oh, them. They are the ones who are insane, as you put it.'

She was so sure of this fact that she didn't feel the need to ask him what his opinion of them actually was.

'Are they?' he retorted. 'You know nothing about them.'

'I know what they do to her. I know about their religious beliefs.'

'Their what?'

'You didn't know they follow some crazy American televangelist?'

'They do what?'

'You didn't follow up,' she said, proudly defying him. 'It's psychological torture on their part, and you didn't follow up.'

'Of course I followed up.'

'Well?'

'Well, nothing. They're just ordinary farmers.'

'So naturally they didn't mention anything about their belief in blood eclipses.'

He scoffed.

'They kept it from you,' she almost shouted.

'I've no idea what you're talking about. Blood eclipses?'

She explained it in a few garbled sentences, the words falling helplessly over themselves until his eyes hardened.

'Where did you get all this bloody nonsense?'

'She told me everything.'

'Who, Maude?'

'Who else?'

'I can't believe you could be so naïve, Beth. It's not like you don't have something to prove here. People are asking questions.'

'Oh?'

'About you. About your dismissal last year. That was a teenage girl too, wasn't it?'

The blood rose to her cheeks and she stammered.

'What does that have to do with this? Can't you see the girl is being practically tortured by her parents because she doesn't believe what they believe? Her father—'

Milliner began to chuckle grimly.

'Yeah, go on. The father . . .'

'He thinks his daughter is possessed because of the blood eclipses. Don't you see? It's a prophecy about demons. He has inflicted it upon her. There's nothing wrong with her. Nothing at all. It's all in his head.'

'Or yours.'

'Mine?'

'Or the girl's. I can't decide. Maybe all three of you are beyond reason. But I have to deal with you first. You're supposed to be the sane one, remember, not them. You've read the report on Maude. She's a compulsive liar. She's probably schizophrenic. You can't trust anything she says.'

'I didn't say anything about blindly trusting—'

'But that's exactly what you're doing.' He lowered his voice and removed the sarcasm from it. 'A lot of people think you are compulsive, that you can't be trusted with a patient like this. I stood up for you. I gave you a second chance. Now this. You have to give me your word.'

'About what?'

'About you and Maude. You haven't crossed the line again, have you?'

'Crossed what bloody line?'

'I don't have to spell it out. You can't sleep with your patients – not twice. And she's underage. Surely you don't have to be reminded of that?'

Beth insisted that she had not seen Maude since that morning, that the girl had wandered off, probably to go home. Silently she promised herself that she would not surrender Maude so easily, not to people who didn't understand the danger she was in, and certainly not to her parents. The two parted with mutually distrusted promises. Beth went shopping in the village for enough supplies to hunker down for a few days and drove home, realising slowly that she was following a course of action that would inevitably doom her. Yet she could see no other way to protect Maude, even if only temporarily.

When she returned, she found the girl asleep in her own bed and decided to let her be, while she barricaded the cottage. She drew the curtains, locked all the windows and doors and turned off all the lights, bar one in the front room. She laid out plates and wine glasses on the dinner table and some candlesticks. Then she whiled away the afternoon reading on the sofa and listening for visitors along the road. To her satisfaction, none came. She calculated that there would soon be an uproar. The school, the indignant parents, Milliner himself would all come together to form a little perfect storm. But before they did, she would at least enjoy a cosy dinner of crab ravioli with Maude by candlelight.

When darkness fell she lit the two candles and roused

Maude from her sleep. The girl hardly remembered where she was. They put on some Handel, and Beth poured out the Portuguese wine. They sat at opposite ends of the dinner table and giggled as they drank.

'I'm not legal,' Maude said.

'You're not. But I'm not telling your father.'

'I should thank you, I suppose.'

'*Salute.*'

'What's that?'

'Italian for cheers.'

They touched glasses.

'You know,' Maude said, 'I've decided to quit school. Don't look so surprised. There's no point to it now.'

'But you can't do that.'

'I can. I want to go travelling.'

'What?'

'Yes. I want to go to India.'

'Of all places. How can you do that?'

'Oh, I can do it. I have some cash saved up.'

'Where is it?'

'I have it in a safe place. I can do what I want with it.'

'I think we should talk about it, don't you?'

'If you want, but I've decided anyway.'

Beth felt a sudden grief, a realisation that Maude would soon disappear for her own reasons and there would be nothing she could do about it. She let the subject drop for the time being.

Soon a becalmed atmosphere took over the table. They got drunk. The candles melted down but seemed to glow brighter. Beth felt herself begin to relax. Maude raised her shirt and showed Beth the welt marks from her father's assault. Yet she was cheerful about it. The old fool could only hit her one time out of three. He was usually too drunk and incapacitated to inflict much damage. Beth thought – or rather she was sure – that the girl was flirting with her, but in an ambiguous way. 'Don't you prefer being here?' she said boldly, holding Maude's eye. '*I* prefer you being here.'

'I love it here.'

'Do you?'

'I don't want to go home ever again.'

'Then . . . then, you don't have to.'

'So we'll live here, just the two of us?'

Why not? Beth thought, but she could not bring herself to say something so absurd.

Right then the candles guttered for a moment. There was the hum of a car moving along the road, slowly, and without thinking twice she reached out, licked her fingers and snuffed out the two candles. The car came to a halt and someone stepped out into the wet grass. Footsteps came up to the door. Beth put her finger to her lips.

Trying not to smile too much herself, she rose quietly and crept to the door. She leaned her ear to its surface, but as she did so the handle turned and to her horror the door began to open inwards. As it opened further she inserted herself protectively into the gap. She looked down at the exterior handle and realised that it had not been pushed. And yet there was a man standing just beyond the porch light, which she now turned on.

It was not a person she recognised. Protected by a long raincoat and wearing a brimmed hat dripping with rain, he

had come to a standstill like a train that has had its power supply cut, his hands resting inside his pockets and his face
frozen in a look of now-purposeless determination. He
looked like another farmer, a local, maybe a friend of the
Blythes who had been sent out to look for Maude. There was
something malevolent and stubborn about his face, which
had nevertheless been rendered impotent.

Timidly, Beth asked him what he wanted. But there was
no reply. He stood in the rain as if in a trance. Closing the
door again, she bolted it and went back to the table.

'Who is it?' Maude asked.

'It looks like a farmer from around here.'

'It's probably Mr Arnold. My dad will have asked him to
go looking for me.'

'Why him and not your father himself?'

The room was so dark now that Maude's face could only
be seen by the light of watery reflections cast by the
windows.

'It's a long story. Listen, though.'

They heard the man turn round and walk back down to
the car. The engine started up, the vehicle moved on, the crisis seemingly past. They burst out laughing and the candles
remained unlit.

'What was that?' Beth said.

'What was what?'

'He didn't even knock. He just turned round.'

'Yes. People are peculiar, aren't they?'

Merry eyes, Beth thought, looking at Maude's. *Too merry
not to know*. But, for that matter, she didn't care, either. During the night they slept together, clothed but in the same bed.

Beth stroked Maude's wild hair and let her sleep. But she wondered about the visitor. Some force had thrown him into a hypnotic spell that she had never witnessed before.

Very early, she went out again and drove into Hathersage to buy some eggs and milk to make pancakes for them both. It would be her morning surprise. In the little supermarket there was a hush as she entered and while she wandered the aisles the hush became a loud mutter. She realised with each turning head that it was about her. When she came to the cashier, open suspicion was written on the woman's face. Beth almost confronted her, but held herself back. She walked to her car with her bags and as she struggled to open the door, with the rain in her face, something flew past her head and exploded on the road behind her. Then another missile detonated on the back of her head: a cold egg from the supermarket. For a moment she remembered the man who had sneered at her as he walked across the railway bridge. But when she turned, she saw it was not him. Instead it was a young woman whom she had seen in the shop only moments before. She had a twelve-pack of eggs and was using them as ammunition.

'What's it to you?' she shouted at Beth.

This time, Beth cracked. She flung her own bags into the car and there was an altercation. A second egg hit her in the face, and soon she heard another person across the street, erupting into laughter. The people in the shop had come out to watch.

'You just fuck off!' the woman was shouting now. 'There's worse than eggs, if you like it.'

'Look at that,' another woman in the doorway of the shop muttered. 'She's covered in yolks. Look at her hair!'

Beth retreated in confusion and slammed the car door behind her. She drove off in a frenzied storm and was still shaking by the time she reached the cottage. She didn't want Maude to see her in that degraded state and went straight to the bathroom and took a long, hot bath. She lay in the scalding water for an hour, until her rage had calmed and the egg had dissolved away from her hair and skin. So the little village bigots had had their moment. But she had sensed that it was Maude whom they hated most. They hated Beth because they hated the Blythe girl, and perhaps the Blythes in general. Only now was she beginning to realise what a peculiar reputation they enjoyed. The villagers had taken their superstitions out on Beth and what they imagined to be her sexual predation of a minor.

When she came out of the bath the house was still. She went to the kitchen and made the pancakes, as she had planned. When they were ready she went to the door of the bedroom and peered inside. Maude was not there. She realised at once what had happened: the girl had slipped out at last. She might not even have gone home, but had simply disappeared somewhere else – gone 'walkabout' like the Aborigines, taken a bus to nowhere for the sake of going nowhere. All the theories were equally valid and equally idiotic. Maude had walked out on her without a backward glance.

Beth texted her, but got no reply. Left with a pile of pancakes, she sat down and ate them mindlessly, until tears began to roll down her face and dripped onto the plate.

Gorged and drained of tears, she then lay down in the still-warm bed and let herself drift into unconsciousness.

What did it matter? She knew already that her time was up and she would likely be fired that very same day. Word of the egg fusillade would get back to Milliner within an hour. She was finished. When his call did come, early in the evening, she was too drowsy to put up any real resistance. She only wanted to know what had happened to Maude.

'Obviously,' he said, 'she went back home. It was just a game with her parents. Surely that was obvious to someone of your experience?'

'I must have lost focus. I'm sorry.'

'I'll say. I think it's best if you come off this case and go back to London. We need things to settle down a little. They'll calm down if you're not there. We'll have to review your situation again, I'm afraid. There's one other thing. It's really best if you have no communication with Maude from now on. We'll have to assign someone else to her. She played you far too easily. I can't understand how you could have been so easily fooled. Well, I think we both know. But all the same. You knew the risks.'

After a long pause she said, 'That I admit.'

'Take a few weeks off and we'll see where we are by the New Year. How does that sound?'

Suddenly her spirits collapsed, and wearily Beth agreed, since there was no alternative.

Although she packed that very night she remained at the cottage for a few more days. She drove around the country-side aimlessly, hoping against hope that she might stumble upon Maude and be able to speak to her alone.

The land now brimmed with meaning. The stone houses like tombs waiting patiently for future centuries. The dales sunk in torpor as winter moved in upon them. Around the roads, the trees a psychedelic yellow and tall as those of a rainforest. One day she went for a hike near the Kinder River about eight miles from Hathersage. She climbed early in the morning up from the small road to a crop of tumble-down grey rocks with tough blond grass growing between them, some flat on their tops and darkened green by moss. There she lay with her Thermos, with the crooked reservoir shining in the distance, and at 9.30 a.m. the sun began to disappear into a storm. She watched the shadow cover the fells. She felt paralysed, as if it was yet another eclipse, the grass seething around her in a spiteful wind, and the mad dreams of previous nights suddenly resurfacing with intent. Her hands clutched at the grass and tore out clumps until her fingers were bruised. Then, almost as suddenly as the pseudo-eclipse had begun, it ended and a burst of sunlight hit the distant water and the great slabs of mossy rock became green again.

She crawled to one of the shallow pools formed into the depressions that pitted these immense surfaces and scooped up some cold water to dash on her face. There was no one there, but all the same she felt a need to turn quickly and look behind her. She was sure that for a twinkling moment Maude had appeared in some supernatural way, watching over her. When she thought about it more calmly, she knew that the spinning spoon had been a dream, and so had the trance of the unknown visitor, and yet of course she didn't believe any of this, in a deeper stratum of herself. No. The eye does not lie, not even when it is otherwise enchanted. Regardless, for a while she was sure that she was being watched and that nothing she did escaped an unseen eye that followed her. It noted her trembling left hand, her maddened expressions that unfolded like a slideshow, her teeth biting into her lower lip as she had lost herself in a grief that felt like vertigo. But she could not know to whom that watching eye belonged.

THE BOATMAN

THE BOATMAN

FOR SEVERAL YEARS HILAL RAN A BOAT HIRE OUT OF Qantab beach, taking rich Saudis and Qataris to the remote coves that lay along the coast on either side of Al Bustan. He slept in a trailer and conducted his business entirely by mobile burner phones that he discarded every three months. His boat was forty years old and yet he painted it anew every few weeks to keep his customers impressed, an almond eye on either side of the prow. From time to time, when the season was slow, he was approached by the men who traded black-market items in and out of Muscat and was asked to take them to the same remote coves where goods were dropped off and picked up.

He never asked them their names or who they worked for. When the agents of state security came round, as they some-times did, to ask a few questions of the men running boats, he shook his head every time and said that all he did was service tourists – may God praise them and their offspring. But the agents knew better. They told Hilal, intending to threaten him, that he was well known among the traffickers, who called him 'Stray Dog'. *Kalbon dalon.* The agents wanted to know why they called him that.

It was an insult he could explain. But Stray Dog, who already knew what the traffickers called him, protested that he had never heard such an insult applied to him. He was not a stray and certainly not a dog. He had a trailer parked behind the beach and a robust business. He walked over to the Qantab village mosque every day for his ablutions and paid his bills. By God, no man had the right to call him a stray dog, or even just a dog. His reputation among the families who drove down from the Emirates every season was such that he had no need to advertise his boat trips: they were famous by word of mouth. Such a man would never have to defend his honour, even to the Jahaz al Amn al Dakhly state security.

Yet he did keep watch on the sea. He was there night and day, every day of every month. He prided himself on being the sea's eyes. Boats passed in the night without lights, smugglers making their way along the rugged coastline with their cargoes. He had heard that human beings were sometimes in their holds. The men who owned freelance boats in Qantab, a village of low white structures set again desert hills, all knew each other; as far as Hilal could gather, they all skimmed a little profit from the secretive trades when they were on offer. Yet no one talked about it, not even when they were drinking their sugared coffee together under the trees. Their main business was the tourists. Those wayward, fickle animals.

Sitting outside his trailer in front of his beached boat, he scanned the wide sands trapped between headlands. The telltale chaos of spoiled and fattened families were his prey. It was like crab-fishing. The ones who knew of him beforehand called ahead and made their demands. Picnics on the sea, transport to the isolated coves. Usually he would collect them at dusk and ferry them back to Qantab beach. He was sure that the women, secluded for the whole day, took off their niqabs and danced naked on the beaches out of view of the world. It was said that they did. Omar from Sifa once passed on a boat at midday and saw them for himself. Saudi women naked and screaming with joy. It was a lie, but it was an enjoyable lie.

Then, on a windless day three days after the New Year of the unfaithful, a young couple appeared on Qantab beach looking for a boat hire to take them to those same coves, and Stray Dog was the only man among the boatmen up at nine in the morning and available for hire. He could tell at once that the girl was an Arab; a Lebanese, he would have said, and probably a Christian.

The boy was a Canadian, but he could not have guessed just by looking at him. They were about twenty-five, in shorts and linen shirts, wearing straw hats and carrying water bottles and a little light scuba gear. Perfect prey and not even sunburnt yet. They must have flown in for New Year's and ventured out for some mild adventure.

Stray Dog waved until they noticed him.

'You want a boat, I can see you want a boat. I am Hilal. This is my beauty.'

He spoke in Arabic and the girl replied, 'It's your boat?'

'God willing. For fifty US, it's yours. Take you to a cove and bring you back at sundown.'

They came forward and the boy's eyes were naïve and tender, but the girl's, being attuned to his own language, were not. This was unfortunate and he would lose ten dollars on the transaction.

'Thirty,' she said.

'By God, I cannot lose money on the round trip. Have mercy. Forty-five.'

'Thirty-five.'

'Forty. Forty is theft, but since it's quiet this morning I can consider it. Coffee?'

They sat on his folding chairs and exchanged their names. The girl was Isra, the boy was Clive. They were junior lawyers living in London. They had driven to Qantab from the Al Bustan resort a few miles up the road in a rental car from Muscat airport. It was the staff at the reception there who had recommended Qantab for a hired boat. Those admirable men could utter no falsehood.

'You want to scuba, I see. I know just the cove for you. Where the water is very quiet and clear. Believe me, you are not the first.'

The boy was enjoying his coffee and thinking to himself that Hilal the boatman was the sort of con man you can generally trust. The man's hands were worn down by the sea and, by the looks of them, by a few fist fights over the years. His eyes were cynical but also weary – it was a good sign. Doing something bad to them would take a lot of effort. Clive decided he liked Hilal. But for the duration of the coffee it was amusing to watch his girl from Beirut haggle with him. She was asking for an ice-box with cans of Coke. The boatman threw up an exasperated hand. '*Habibi*,' he groaned, going Lebanese on her, 'you want me to walk across this wide beach and get you Cokes?' But in the end he relented by making a call to one of the vendors, who came over with the cans. They stacked them in one of Hilal's ancient ice-boxes and carried it down to the boat. The visitors threw in their scuba gear and climbed in. They sat down at the prow, while Halil fiddled with the outboard motor and Isra took Clive's arm for a moment. 'How easy was that?' she said.

Clive looked up at the granite cliffs with their striations and grooves, then out onto an empty dark-green sea where the rollers were far out. The desert wind had dried out his nose and he felt cleansed, invigorated. After a claustrophobic winter in London, the blueness of the sky was a beautiful shock. Women in black stood in the shallows eating frozen lollipops and there was about them a gentle quietness, a delicate contentedness. He had had his doubts earlier that morning about venturing to a practically uninhabited place, but Isra had supplied the confidence that he himself lacked.

When they pushed off, it was like saying adieu to all the prior days, which had been stressful. Especially trying to score a decent bottle of champagne on New Year's in a dry city. *We found a jolly pirate*, Clive thought to himself. *Although he probably found us*.

They passed the bare headlands they had spotted from the car driving down from Al Bustan, the ranges of dark burnt-coke ophiolites rising behind them with their primeval jagged profiles. They moved around a large promontory as dolphins came up behind them, cautiously curious. The boatman cut the engine a little and they took it easy as they came round the promontory and its boiling rocks. On the north side were grotesque outcrops of wind-torn rock with hermetically sealed-off beaches between them. They could pick any one they wanted. No one could approach them unless it was by sea. The formations behind each beach represented a long and difficult climb, and Hilal assured them that nobody ever attempted it. They chose one randomly and the decision was set. Hilal guided his boat gently up to the beach of a cove a hundred yards wide, framed on both sides by immense igneous cliffs and divided by a stream cutting across the sand.

They pulled the craft half up onto the sand together and then offloaded the scuba equipment and the ice-box, now also filled with the sandwiches and apples they had brought with them from the hotel. These they hauled into the shade of the cliffs before Halil shook their hands, took the money and promised that he would return at five to take them back to Qantab.

'If you need me before then, you can call me. Maybe the phone will work. Sometimes it does not. You have to be easy-going about that.'

'All right,' Clive said, breaking into the Arabic conversation, 'we'll see you at five. Are you punctual?'

'Is sky blue?' Halil replied in his own language.

They watched him move off from the sun-hot beach, the boat circling in the tiny bay and leaving them to while away the whole day. Hilal turned only once to give them his affirmative thumb and within seconds he was gone.

Nothing moved but the warm water of the stream flowing around their feet. They stripped off naked without delay and plunged into the surf. They swam just out of their depth, then returned to the beach and lay naked in the sun until the light became too much for them and they retreated to the shadows thrown down by the cliffs. Above them, the dusty crags were pathless, covered with scrub, and the iron in the rock gave it a dark glossiness here and there. Behind the beach the flat, coarse sand looked like a desert wadi. *So many hours*, Clive thought, *and nothing to do but vegetate*. He reflected on the last four days and especially their night out on the town for New Year's, a disaster that had culminated in a row in a booze-free Yemeni restaurant after hours of driving around in the seaside neighbourhood called Qurum Heights, where they had tried the Crowne Plaza for an advertised champagne dinner and found it booked out by a vast Lebanese party. They had driven along Qurum Beach among hundreds of honking cars.

At the end of it, the Intercontinental, also miserably booked out even at $300 a head for Moët & Chandon at midnight. Eventually they had asked people; a Yemeni place could do their midnight celebration, but without champagne. They had got there at ten to midnight, angry, lost, arguing, and found a vast garden of hanging lanterns.

A silent meal after a muted midnight toast. 'I shouldn't have trusted you to find champagne,' she said. The bad mood had lasted into the following days, until in fact the very moment they had pushed off from Qantab beach. Isra had finally lost her simmering disappointment and had returned to normal.

CLIVE TURNED ON THE affection now to cement the new mood into place. He stroked her faintly sunburnt arm and then her hair. Against the current of their mutual mood, they found themselves aroused. Glancing up at the cliffs she registered a moment's doubt but then cast it aside. An hour later, while he dozed, she started awake again and, still half-conscious, untangled herself from his sandy limbs. Across the blinding sand dozens of tiny crabs were scurrying down to the water. Wanting to be alone for a while, she quietly got up and walked down to the far end of the beach, where a grim wall of rocks broke up the currents. She dipped into the sea then lay in the sun waiting for the heat to overpower her. Strangely, she had only known Clive for about a month. They were relative strangers to each other. They worked at the same London firm and so had seen each other at a distance for longer than that. But they had only spoken privately for the last four weeks. And then, out of the blue, it had been her idea to take off for New Year's, after they had been sleeping together for only a couple of weeks. A risk that had perhaps not paid off. She should have waited, but she had not. Sometimes the dice are worth rolling and sometimes not. Now she was beginning to feel the first pangs of regret.

They were not, perhaps, as compatible as she had at first assumed. The physical attraction was not maturing into something better, not even incrementally. Isra wondered what it would have been like to have been here alone. Better, surely. Richer. She had made a mistake, but it was not an enormous one. In a few days, after all, they would drive to Dubai, whence they had come, and board the same aeroplane they had taken on the way out. Back in London, they would disengage with good manners, and life would go back to what it had been before. They would remain pointless friends. Life would go on.

They spent the afternoon exploring the cove. There was a path that led up to one of the cliffs and from there they could watch boats passing at a distance. While they were there, sitting among the burning stones, she was suddenly seized by unease. This place was not as lifeless as they had thought.

'I can hear insects,' she said quietly, looking over at him. 'Can't you hear them?'

'Grasshoppers?'

'No, buzzing. I know what it is.'

'I can't hear anything.'

Clive couldn't understand why she was being so stand-offish since they had had sex. Had he done something wrong?

Abruptly, as if not listening to him, she got up and dusted her legs. But she did it with a sharp impatience or, as became clearer, with alarm.

'What is it?'

'I can hear something. Like I said, buzzing.'

He laughed and defiantly relaxed himself, refusing to go along with her mood.

'Don't be ridiculous.'

She picked up her towel and snapped it around her as if warding off something. He could see that she was genuinely agitated, but there were no insects there.

'It's a bee,' she hissed.

'No, honey. Calm down.'

'Don't call me "honey". And don't condescend. I said it's a bee. I can hear it.'

'No, you can't.'

Since it was useless to argue with him, Isra swore as if to

herself and moved off, taking the path back down to the beach.

Clive perked up. 'Come on, honey, you're exaggerating.'

'Get lost. It's after me, not you.'

Within moments she was within shouting rather than talking distance.

'What do you mean, you?'

She waved an angry hand and stumbled. He laughed again, but this time with a little more malice. She was heading down to the sea to escape the imaginary bee. So she was apiphobic – in a place with no insects at all. One had to marvel at the unexpected things you discover about someone.

He watched her run onto the beach, throw off her shorts and jump into the surf where the pursuing insect could not attack her. When she had calmed down they stared at each other.

'Sharks!' he shouted down.

Maybe she heard him because a moment later she rushed out of the water, glaring behind her. She stood lit by the sun, enraged, confused, caught between the dangers of land and sea. He waved to her in mockery. He was sure his laughter must have rolled down the cliff-face to reach her. The cove was an echo chamber. She gave him the finger, then seemed to relent a little. Maybe she had overreacted and there would be a truce. He waved again, shrugging theatrically, and she paused as she was putting her beach shorts back on. Changing her mind, she tossed them aside and began to run up the beach and then back down again. *Better*, he thought. *No bees after you now*. Then she stopped, her back to the sea, and began to do a little dance, Scheherazade-like, for her own pleasure. He was suddenly astonished at how magnificent she was, her body still oiled even after the dip, her hair now curled and salty as it whipped around her. He sat back and admired the performance, which must have been purely a release of tension.

As Clive sat there, pacified and meek, he sensed something move behind him. Before he could turn a bee flew past his ear and zigzagged down the path she had taken. He smiled to himself. If it wanted to try and kill her, it would. But in any case something else had caught his eye. Across the open sea a fishing boat had appeared, lazily trawling its way across the view, and three men lounging on its deck were watching the Lebanese girl dancing naked on the beach as if she was alone without a companion. Even at a fair distance, he could see the looks on their faces. The boat slowed, rocking in the swells, and still Isra didn't notice them. Within a minute they had moved on and he was alone with her again. He walked lazily back down to the beach.

'That was quite a dance.'

'It's my anti-bee dance. It always works.'

'Well, I told you there weren't any bees here.'

He reached out to spool her in and give her a quick kiss. He felt a little guilty for a humiliation that he had not caused. Momentarily he wondered where the vagrant bee was.

It must have flown off without even noticing her. He took her hand and they walked back to the scuba gear, which they had not even used. Perhaps now was the moment? But the sun was waning and the high heat had begun to decline; the water was less inviting. Instead Clive suggested they drink the cold Coke and wait for Halil to return. He would be there in an hour.

'I don't know why we brought all that stuff,' she said. 'We could just have brought our trunks and a bottle of vodka.'

'Vodka, here? They'd kill us.'

They lay on the sand waiting and five o'clock came and went. Clive called Halil, but the line was engaged. Repeated calls produced the same result. Soon the shadows projected by the cliffs engulfed most of the beach and the sea turned darker. The appointment had obviously been missed.

At six they began to fret. When night fell they would be stranded. To his surprise, Isra didn't get overheated about it. Clive said he was sure Halil would show up, that he was late because something had come up at the last minute. Sure, that was it. It wouldn't be in his interest to abandon them there. They'd go online and write bad reviews about him.

'He doesn't give a shit about that,' she said grimly.

And she was right, he probably didn't.

'All the same,' he said, 'he'll be here.'

The scuba gear was laid up among the rocks and was too heavy to move, but she suggested they take their light shoulder bags and return to the cliff where they had been earlier in the day. From there they would be able to see everything on the sea more clearly. If need be, they could flag down a passing boat and get a ride back to Qantab.

'Flag down?' he said with his utmost sarcasm.

Isra looked up at the sky, still bright at the edges, now filled with stars at the zenith, and didn't bother to answer him. For the next hour they would be visible. They could shout.

Reluctantly, internally unconvinced, he agreed and they started to make their way back up the cliff in the dark. When they reached the top they sat in the same spot they had occupied previously and ate some biscuits. There was an unspoken agreement between them that climbing to this vantage point was safer than remaining on the beach. But why it was safer could somehow not be mentioned. Neither of them knew whether they were thinking the same thing. Hilal had not returned as he had promised, and they were now no longer protected by him. The wind picked up. A moon embedded in blue ice rose above the desert. They fell silent. It felt as if hours had passed before a light finally appeared out at sea.

Moving slowly, it approached their beach and soon a beam shot low across the waves. Clive impatiently stood up and raised his hands, about to shout out to the boat coming towards them. But Isra pulled him down violently and told him to shut up and wait. They had no idea whose boat it was.

'What does it matter?' he barked at her. 'It's a boat, isn't it?'

'It matters.'

She held him down and put a finger to her lips as if warning a child. And as she did so, the slim, dark form of the boat slid up to the beach and three men dropped silently into the water.

In the light of the beam they waded ashore and Hilal, they could tell even from a distance, was not among them. The men followed the beam inland towards the scuba gear, still piled against the rocks. One of the men, in a *dishdasha*, swept up to the rocks and passed an eye over the gear, ran a hand over it and then called back to his companions. The other two returned to the boat and dragged out a fourth man, whom they threw into the water and then dragged up onto the beach. *Hilal*, Clive thought. They shoved him onto the dry sand and left him there while they looked along the beach and then up towards the cliffs. One of them turned on a powerful torch and walked with it down the length of the beach, swinging the beam from side to side with the motion of a minesweeper. Reaching the cliff, he stopped and then swung the beam up at the cliff itself. There was nothing to see.

Retreating back to the group, he switched off the torch and knelt by the man, prostrate on the sand with his hands tied behind his back. They talked softly. Then, stooping down towards him, one of the men raised his hand and let fall a blow to Hilal's head. The prone man shuddered and half-rolled onto his back. The others paused and sat back on their haunches. Isra made a sign to Clive: they should leave, creeping up the rocky hill behind them, away from the beach. It was cowardice, Clive thought, to leave Hilal to his fate, but there was nothing else to do. They crept away, their heads lowered, and disappeared into the pathless hillside, making their way almost by touch.

As they escaped the roar of the surf, they heard a cry. It was an animal's guttural shriek. By now they were upright and walking normally, and Clive stopped and looked back. But Isra was behind him, pushing. 'It's none of our business.' She was right. He let himself be pushed onwards.

Such things probably happened from time to time and it was best to roll with it, to let it go and escape as peacefully as one could. Behind the coastal cliffs, as they had seen on a map, a road ran that passed by their own resort two or three miles to the south. They soldiered on until they reached it, a road without street lamps that curved across the hills just in sight of the sea. It was near a place called Haramil. They trudged quietly away from the village and towards a larger main road that swept north to south out of Muscat and towards Al Bustan. Here the spherical lights burned in majestic rows, but the road itself was deserted.

They walked without much effort for about two hours until they came to a small public park to the side of the road. They went in and lay down under the darkened palms, now alive with dawn birds.

It was cool enough for them to recover their composure and talk again after the silence of the road. In the end, one could say, nothing had happened. It was not even certain that their scuba equipment had been stolen. They had to admit that they hadn't understood what they had seen. Their car was still at Qantab and Isra suggested that they ask one of the staff to go down there and recover it for them. A tip of $50 would do it, since by car it was only a few minutes away. It was better that they didn't go back there themselves.

'Halil's ice-box,' he murmured.

'He knows how to get it back. He knows where it is.' It was true, she thought. And yet it had surely been him grovelling on the sand with his hands tied behind his back.

Above the park rose a small mountain like a heap of slag, its turrets like all the black turrets of the ophiolites around them. Gradually it came more into view as the sky lightened. Isra felt refreshed as the moist grass around them extended its coolness to their bodies. Not a single car had passed and therefore no one had seen them. The incident on the beach had only been witnessed by the two of them. She could sense that Clive had begun to relax as daylight returned, and by the time they had regained the highway he was almost chirpy. From there it was a quick mile's walk back to the Al Bustan resort and the cluster of serene government buildings that lay behind it. They came into the lobby as breakfast service was starting in the restaurant. They were the first ones there.

While Clive was pushing croissants into his mouth, Isra went back to the imposing mosque-like lobby with its cascading glass and marble and walked up to reception to ask the boys about retrieving their car. Hearing the Lebanese accent, they instantly relaxed with her.

'What happened?'

'We took a boat and got dropped off somewhere. We slept on the beach. It was wonderful. But, you know, Qantab is in the opposite direction . . .'

'Ah, we understand.' The money and the car keys had been pushed across the counter and further explanations were not needed.

'You can just leave it in the parking lot. It's kind of you. Thank you.'

'*Afwan.*'

She went back to breakfast overlooking the Bustan beach, where gnarled headlands were coming back into view. They ate without speaking, gratified by the cornucopia, gulping down iced kiwi juice and mandarin sorbet. When they were sated, they went up to their room and crashed on the bed with the shutters closed and slept until well into the afternoon. It was Isra who woke first, just as she had at the beach the day before.

She heard the sea and the vacuum cleaners of maids in the

empty rooms around them. *The car*, she thought at once, *they must have brought back the car already*. Feeling a quiet unease, she dressed again and went back down to the lobby to ask them about it. Yes, they said, they had brought back the car for them, and the keys were returned to her.

'About half an hour after we brought it back,' the boy went on, 'a man came down here to ask about it. He said he had seen the car at Qantab overnight and wanted to make sure it had been returned to the correct owner.'

'Who was that?'

'He didn't say. He stayed for a while, then he left. Do you know him?'

'Was his name Hilal?'

'We forgot to ask him, I'm sorry.'

The boy then described a man who was clearly not Hilal. Something in his voice made him seem wary – was it someone the hotel knew?

'Where did he go?'

'He went back to the parking lot. Maybe he's still there.'

A do-gooder from Qantab. It did not seem likely. She took the keys and walked out to the parking lot, feeling defiant. It was now about four in the afternoon and the air was crisp with salt. She looked around the lot, but saw no one waiting for her, not even a car that might look as if it didn't belong at a five-star resort. She went to their own car and opened it up. It was filled with loose sand from Qantab and she suspected that the doors had been opened during their absence. Had Hilal tried to rifle through their vehicle during their day-long absence? No one would have stopped him if he had wanted to do that. She flipped open the glove compartment and checked that the maps were still there. In fact there was little worth stealing in the car. She slammed the doors shut and walked back down to the lobby.

'The man who came up from the beach. Was he young or old?'

'Young, about twenty-eight.'

'Was he alone?'

'He came to the lobby alone. Whether he came alone from Qantab we cannot say.'

'I see. Can I just confirm that the room has been paid for in advance and that there's nothing outstanding?'

'Did you take anything from the minibar?'

She shook her head and they confirmed that, in that case, everything was in order. What about the couple's scuba gear? they asked. Would they like someone to go back down to Qantab that evening and pick it up for them as well? So they had noticed its absence.

She said, 'No, that's fine. We prefer to leave it there. It's annoying to haul it back and forth every day. But thank you.'

'*Afwan.*'

Returning to the room, she felt something dreamlike in the way she was behaving, as if extraordinary things were happening over which she had no control and which she could observe coldly from a distance. In the lift she thought about Hilal. What kind of man was he? Was he a dangerous man or just a man? The latter could sometimes be almost as perilous to know. In the room, Clive was drinking tea in a bathrobe and reading the news online. He was sure there would be something about an incident on Qantab beach, but thus far his search had proved inconsequential. He asked Isra instead if the car had been returned correctly.

'They brought it back in one piece.'

'Well, that's something. There's nothing on the news meanwhile.'

He rolled onto his back. A crossroads had appeared in both their minds at the same time. They could stay and wait it out, whatever 'it' was, or they could go into flight mode. What would they be running from, though – a mirage, a misunderstood dispute? Maybe they had imagined something that had not actually happened. He said so, to see how she would react.

'No, they were going to kill him,' she said.

'I think they were looking for us. For you. There was something that happened earlier, which I didn't tell you about.'

'Oh?'

And he related the appearance of the fishing boat during her dance on the beach.

'You bastard!'

'Well, there was no point telling you at the time.'

'You let me make a fool of myself?'

'You were doing it anyway. It was too late to stop you – or them.'

'So that was it. They came looking for a sexual kill?'

He shrugged, as if to suggest that he didn't really believe it. 'Who knows? You know how fishermen are. Horny and violent.'

'I've never met any.'

'Well, I have, and they are horny and violent. I was afraid they would come in to shore, just looking at you.'

'Were you really?'

He laughed and shook his head weakly.

Then she said, 'Shouldn't we leave tonight? I mean, go back to the Emirates. I don't feel quite right here now.'

'Leave?'

'Yes, we're all paid up front. We can walk out the door right now. I'd feel safer. I know it's a bit absurd, but that's how I feel.'

'What about the scuba gear?'

'I don't want to get it back. I don't want to see that man again. We can write it off, and if the hotel gets it back later, they can send it on.'

'But that's a brand-new Ocean Reef mask!'

'It hardly matters now, does it? We'll get it back later. Let's just drive to the border. We can be there in a few hours.'

Do it for me, she was thinking, *and don't make a contrarian fuss*. But Clive's face had clouded.

'Ah, and I was getting to like this hotel.'

They talked it out until he had agreed; she said she was adamant and that her instincts were in 'flight mode'. It was simple. They would pack their two small bags and simply walk to the car and be gone, without saying a word to the staff.

Raising small objections, he gave way. They showered together and re-found their playfulness. They couldn't believe that anything drastic would happen. It was only Isra who thought, *We were witnesses. Witnesses are inconvenient.*

It was dusk when they emerged with their bags and walked

unobtrusively up to the parking lot, without stopping in the lobby. The air was filled with darting swallows. The car was where she had left it, and no one had touched it. They drove up to the empty main road in silence and passed along the same scenes through which they had walked the previous night: the little park, frozen under its now-active lamps – a soccer game going on beneath the rock formations – and the turn-off to the village of Haramil, plunged in dusty gloom. Soon they were speeding past the lights of the Sultan Qaboos Port on the edge of the capital. They reached the place in the port called Fish Roundabout, which Isra remembered from the outward drive; the urban buzz around them calmed her. They were around people again, they were immune, anonymous.

From there the road looped through industrial suburbs and into Muscat, slicing through the city without obstruction. The Omani capital was not unlike Los Angeles, a city of freeways and overpasses and impossible knots of slick roads that formed cat's-cradle junctions. But because of this very confusion they could pass through it quickly without entering it. On the far side of the urban sprawl the desert reappeared and they drove up along the coast with its little resorts and clusters of houses, the light sparkling against a violet sea. They drove for an hour until they had subdued their unease; she called ahead to the Four Points in Dubai and told them that they would be there around midnight, provided that the border was not closed when they arrived at Hatta in the mountains, where it lay. Then she rolled down her window to breathe in the sea and said that she was hungry. Could they not stop for half an hour just off the road before they turned inland towards the border?

Here and there signs for establishments pointed to the small roads that ran down to the sea. Clive turned off when they saw the very next one. It was a family place set at the edge of a hamlet, surrounded by low acacia trees. Because the outdoor tables were set on a small rise they could see the sea and the dusty track running down to it among the low, rectangular walls of houses and pale-grey trees. In a high wind, the lights rattled and they had to rouse the owner. Isra ordered fish and soup, and they sat at one of the tables wrapping their heads with a *mussar* and a *lihaf* they had bought on the first day at the tourist souk in Muscat. Filled with sand, the wind burned their hands. Yet the moon and the fresh air made it worth sitting outside and enduring it. Their holiday was ruined but there were worse things than a ruined holiday.

'We could even come back again later,' he said, smiling his lawyer smile.

'And try again?'

'Yeah, and try again.'

'I'm going to the bathroom. I hope it's immaculate.'

She entered the restaurant's main building and found two women inside, manning the stoves. They greeted her in Arabic. A radio was on at a high volume, loud enough to be heard above the sizzling of the saucepans. The toilet was adjacent and it was, as she had half-expected, immaculate.

She didn't lock the door this time, keeping it slightly ajar. She was curious about the conversation of the women. On the radio there was an account of Changing of the Guard at Buckingham Palace. Being a direct descendant of the Prophet, the Queen of England was revered in Oman and

Changing of the Guard was often screened in outdoor public places. In this safe, wealthy and law-abiding country it was an appropriate entertainment. Isra listened to it, and to the women gossiping about their children. Then there was a burst of radio news. Oil prices, a state visit and, lastly, a man found dead on a remote beach near Qantab. Two tourists sought for questioning. She reached up and was about to lock the door, but it was merely a pointless reflex. The women commented on the news item, then went back to their gossip. Isra waited for the King's Life Guard to return to the airwaves then walked back to the garden, where Clive was already devouring a plate of pickled carrots.

For a moment she considered telling him what she had heard. But then, moved by an obscure foreboding, she elected not to. She had to think by herself for a while. Surely now the border was out of the question, but if she told him why, he would disagree and would insist precisely on going there and giving themselves up – to be safe. Yet the road from there to Hatta was a wild one. It passed through the black peaks of the Hoggar. Between the coastal road and the remote border station anything could happen.

She had begun to think that they could have been followed all the way from the Al Bustan. Slowly, over the course of the day, this premonition had hardened and become more certain. When she sat down Isra said, seeing the fish that had arrived and the bowls of flatbread, 'I'm feeling nauseous, Clive. I don't think I'm going to eat. I don't think I can. I need to lie down somewhere.'

It was a good act and he bought it.

'What kind of nauseous?'

'I might have eaten something earlier. I'm not sure I want to go on to Hatta tonight. Can't we find somewhere to crash for the night?'

'Here?'

'I can ask the owners. They'll know somewhere nearby.'

'Are you sure?' He glanced officiously at his watch. 'We could be in Dubai in three hours.'

'I know we could. But I'm feeling totally wasted. Besides, what if there is a delay at the border?'

He was furious, but he kept his emotion under control.

'All right. Ask her then. But nowhere crummy, please. We have a nice room waiting for us in Dubai.'

She got up and went back to the kitchen. The two women looked at her sceptically. So she was Lebanese?

'You want a hotel for tonight? There's one on the beach down there. My husband and his brother own it. There's a room.'

'Can we take it?'

'I'll call my husband. We've had a lot of truck drivers staying over the last few days.'

Of course, Isra thought, *it's on the main road to Dubai, an hour from the border. Truck drivers.*

She asked, 'Is it, you know, comfortable?'

'It has TV and air con. That's comfortable.'

Isra went back to Clive and reported that there was a comfortable place down the road.

'Really? Is there a pool?'

'It's on the sea. You don't need a pool.'

He smirked and gave her the eye: 'A pool is a sign of standards. It's not that I need it.'

'I just want to crash.'

But annoyed and wanting to punish her, Clive let the meal drag on, ordering fruit smoothies and pestering them for *arak*.

'They don't have *arak*, Clive. It's not Lebanon. Stop asking for it. We're right next to Saudi Arabia.'

'I know where we are. I'll bet they have some *arak* under the floorboards somewhere. Come on. Ask them nicely in Arabic. Since I agreed to waste a bloody night out here.'

One of the women, in any case, had come out to settle the matter of the hotel and Isra thanked her for the reservation.

'By the way,' she added, 'please do not serve any alcohol beverages to my companion. Not even *arak*.'

'We do not serve alcohol to anyone.'

'It's as I thought.'

But Clive had picked out the word *arak* and his eyes brightened.

'See? They *do* have it.'

'Not in a thousand years, you idiot.'

'Another lonely night, then, in the lands of Allah's mercy.'

'You'd be lucky to get some mercy.'

The owner lit candles for then. As if for the first time, they could hear the sea, distant and close at the same time. Reassuring and unnerving at the same time. Under the single lamp illuminating the nearby dirt road, a cloud of moths weaved a ball in the air. Clive ate as languorously as he could. It delighted him that it irritated Isra so inordinately. *A coming rupture*, was all he thought, and marvelled at what a new emotion it was. It had arrived only within the previous fifteen minutes.

When at last things had been concluded, he felt an immense weariness at the thought of the unknown little hotel at the bottom of the road. He was sure it was some sort of scam set up by the devious owners. Nevertheless he went along with it since, when all was considered, he didn't have much choice in the matter. The owner came with them as they drove there. It was a real hotel, however, with a little illuminated sign in Arabic and a small lot of palms, right across from the beach. The reception was closed, but the mistress of the establishment had the keys. She said her husband would be by later to check their passports.

'Is it really necessary?' Isra said almost at once.

'It is. But there's no hurry. Why?'

'I'm just exhausted and need to sleep.'

'We can do it in the morning.'

'Thank you.'

She took them up to a fairly large room filled with suffocating heat, even though the air outside was cool. Isra stepped to the windows and threw them open. The sea's roar, the brusque wind, gave her a moment's delight, which she kept to herself. Clive had paid for the room while her back was turned. The owner told them how to make tea with the electric kettle. For a moment they stood together under the tacky miniature chandelier, with the ants scurrying around them, and the owner gave them a top-to-bottom look-down. As if there was something off about the two foreigners who seemed not to like each other very much. Then she bade them goodnight and turned to go.

Hamming it up a bit, Clive locked the door after her with a flourish and threw himself mournfully onto the awful bed.

'Swimming pool, my arse,' he said, staring up at the mosquito blood-stains on the papered wall.

But Isra didn't mind. She just wanted to turn off the lights and let everything settle down. As before, she needed to think.

'I wonder,' Clive said when they were lying peaceably side-by-side in the dark with the windows still open, 'what happened to Halil? I don't suppose you have a theory.'

'None.'

'Nor me. We probably panicked for no reason.'

'It's often like that.'

'Tomorrow we'll be in Dubai, downing Margaritas.'

She had expected a conversation, but within minutes he had fallen asleep. She lay still for a long time before getting up and going into the bathroom to take a cold shower. She didn't know what she was going to do or how long she was going to take doing it. Returning to the room re-dressed, she stepped to the windows and stood for a while surveying the empty beach, where no doubt no one ever came at this season, or any season. Something came to her from far away, a message delivered on the airwaves. She could feel what it said to her. It was a command to leave the hotel at once by herself and walk away without the car. The car was what identified them. It might as well have been a message from the spirits, from the other world, quiet but deserving of respect. Then she recalled how the owner had looked at them. Of course she had heard the news on the radio as well. But it would not be her who called the police; it would not be the police who came.

Closing the door behind her as quietly as she could, Isra

crept down the hotel's stairwell with her bag loaded onto her shoulder and walked out onto the dirt track, which was lit only by the hotel's single light. She went up it for a while on foot, and rested here and there under the low trees where the insects had not stopped shrilling. She passed the painted walls of houses where people already slept, past fruit trees with ladders stacked against them and finally a cemetery laid out under the gloom of dusty acacias.

She waited there for a while, hidden from the road, and at length a black car came creeping downwards with its lights turned off, feeling its way towards the sea. When it had passed on its way to the hotel, she turned into the groves of trees on the far side of the cemetery and made her way over open ground towards the lights of the highway, where the international trucks sometimes pulled over for a rest. She had determined to get a lift from one of them, using all her charms and her dollars. The vanity of men, after all, knew no bounds. The vanity of Clive and of Hilal was not at all dissimilar, though the two men had nothing to do with each other. It was generic, and therefore consequential. Even by the glare of the highway lamps, she could see how the men behind the windshields looked at her as she sauntered up to them with her smile. Dogs to the last, and in a way that was an insult to dogs.

CAMINO REAL

H E GOT OFF THE BUS FROM PLACITA AT THE END OF the afternoon, just as the mine sirens were echoing across the hills, and walked from the terminal into town with his bag shouldered and his boots falling apart. The *cantinas* were long abandoned, and the factory that had sustained them had closed the year before. The gas station did business with long-distance truckers and its neon sign rose above the salt-white desert, the first three letters of the word Pemex. The square that once had irrigated grass had turned to dust, and its edges were burned brown like old paper.

He already looked far older than his twenty-eight years. Two years wandering the deserts, drifting from job to job, had turned his skin a darkened copper and made his eyes both harder and more wounded. A year he had worked on the border at a gas station on the Arizona side, sleeping under the freeway sidings in a trailer moored at the bottom of a sand hill. He had waited for something to come along that straight American road and nothing had come. Nothing had improved his lot until the day he came to blows with the owner and walked off south back into the desert from where he had come. Someone at the station had told him that carpenters were needed in the mining town.

He walked to the beginning of Cardenas and turned right into the last occupied street. The hardware store still lived, a *cantina* called Lagrima and a Western Union bathed in white light. At its far end he could see the salt-white again and the beginning of another road leading to the mines. The sirens echoed down the valley and reached the *taquerias* where the old men sat outside with domed plastic cups of *agua de Jamaica* stuffed with ice and penetrated by transparent straws.

He went into the last hotel at the end of the street and procured a room. He was taken upstairs by the maid. It was at the top of the building with a view of the street and the fairy lights of the electrical company, which still maintained a line here. Fifteen by fifteen, and a crucifix. He lay on the bed and took off his hat and lit up a Cubano. He crossed his boots and blew the smoke across them, then did his peso calculations. He had enough for dinner and the bus the following day to La Mira, with some extra for lunch if he didn't get too many beers tonight. It was enough for twenty-four hours. He smoked half the Cubano, then decided to save the rest. He shaved, had a depressing and oily bath and then went back down into the street to eat five tacos. Now the lights – all seven of them – were on and the dusk-light behind the canyons had become a fine steel blue. He ate from his good hand and then strolled into Lagrima, where the music was up and a few retired miners sat under posters of Jennifer Lopez. He went up to the metal bar and put his left hand onto the plates of the *Electrocudador*.

'It's one free shot per shock,' the barman said.

'I know how it works.'

'Sixty volts a shot of mescal. Eighty, a tequila. One hundred for a Sauza.'

'Tequila.'

The miners looked up as he took the shock, received his free shot and demanded another.

'Too many will damage your ear hairs,' the barman said.

'It's fine. Shake me up.'

It hurt a little more the second time and he bolted down the tequila in one go. He went up to 100 for the Sauza. After four shots he wiped his mouth and walked out, not a peso the lighter. A stiffer wind now shot down the street and half the lights had been shut off. It was about eight o'clock. He walked down towards the neon of the gas station, which shone ever more brightly, and crossed over the rectangle of desert grass that separated it from the edge of the town. Long-distance rigs stood here, their grilles covered with plastic dolls, Virgins of Guadalupe and lengths of bronze tinsel, and the drivers stood at the edge of the light, smoking with cans of Tecate.

He walked past them until he could smell the open desert with its faint whiff of urine-like salt. Far off, a few dim lights speckled the horizon, but they were not trucks. He walked along the road a little while with the spidery *ocotillos* trembling in the wind. The stiff red flowers were out. *Chollas* at ground level were also blooming, the white spines shining by the light of the gas station and the yellow blossoms shivering.

Back in the room he checked his phone, but there was no missed call. He closed the shutters and stood by the window, looking down through the slats at the swinging doors of the *cantina*, through which fat little men were rolling like billiard balls. The dirt in front of it was peppered with bottle tops. There was a fight of some kind going on inside it, and soon bloodied men would be rolling out with colourful phrases, swinging their arms and spitting their recent meals among the husks. How many of them were left? He drew the curtains shut and then went to lie down, throwing his straw hat across the room like a Frisbee. The sirens from the mine died down and there was a sound of trucks moving across the desert. Their horns occasionally echoed across the emptiness.

He didn't take off his clothes. He smoked for some time, the Cubano proving its worth as it burned down slowly and richly, and then he lay awake with the lights off, listening to the nocturnal events. It was his habit. The laughter of women coming from far off, from the gas station. So that was their whorehouse.

He woke at first light. It might have been a sound like thunder that disturbed him, but in reality it was only the clatter of rubbish wheeling down the street. He went downstairs gingerly in his peeling boots, his mouth dry and aching. The lobby had an electric coffee maker on standby and he drank down half the glass pot with a stale donut from the plastic container.

A man was sitting there leaning against the wall, an ancient and flamboyant figure in tooled boots, beautifully polished. He was in a crumpled pale-grey sharkskin suit, Sixties variety, with a windowpane shirt underneath it and a dark-gold neckerchief. He was about halfway through his seventies but with no residual youthfulness, no smooth patches in his sun-damaged skin, but the white beard and chops were trimmed and dapper. Señor Patrick Mendes was drinking a cup of black coffee by himself in anticipation of dawn and its fiery flies. He was alone with the hotel cuckoo clock, and now he had Angel for company.

'*Buenas dias*,' he said, raising his brimmed hat. 'Have a coffee with me.'

The room was hot, and for once it was cooler outside. They went and sat on the steps and watched the windsocks coming into sight as the night receded. The older man looked Angel over carefully.

'On the road?' he asked.

'Yeah, just travelling and looking for work.'

'For work? You must be mad. This is a dead place. You aren't going to find any work here. No one finds work here unless they're a miner.'

'I ain't a miner.'

'You don't look like a miner. You look like a houseboy on the run. What's your line of business?'

'This and that.'

'This and that? Swell. Well, that'll get you far up here. This and that.' Mendes had a rough, charming laugh.

'What about you?' Angel said.

'I'm on the road to sell some properties up north. It's bad days for real estate in these parts. The cartels are ruining everything.'

'They must be.'

'Sure they are. They're fucking us good. They're hanging people from the bridges in Chihuahua. *La chingada*.'

'Yeah, they are.'

'Everyone's selling. I'm offloading most of my portfolio up north. No one wants to live with the threat of death at every moment of every day.'

'No, sir.'

'The towns are emptying out. Did you find any this and that?'

'So far, nothing.'

'That's how it is, boy. It's a desert in all senses now. You'll be getting nowhere fast. Are you waiting for the morning bus?'

'Guess I am. Nothing doing in this dump.'

'I have a car. I'll drive you.'

'You do?'

'Yes, I do. You think in my line of work I'd be riding around on a stinking bus?'

'I guess not.'

'Where are you headed?'

Angel shrugged.

'I see. Let's get some *huevos rancheros* first. I always eat hard and fast in the morning.'

They went to a place two blocks down from the hotel. The windows looked over a gully filled with wild flowers and the back of an abandoned slaughterhouse. Mendes ordered for both of them. He could see Angel was broke and mangy. They ate eggs and salsa and *churros* caked in castor sugar and *café de olla* in metal pots, with the cinnamon sticks poking through the lids. It was the best breakfast Angel had consumed in a while. His clarity returned and his muscles began to hum.

'So,' he said, 'you've driving south now?'

'Yes, I'm driving home. I am disgusted with my portfolio and flying home. I cannot wait.'

'Are you going to see any properties on the way?'

'As a matter of fact, I am. Just one.'

Angel cut the fried tortilla under his eggs with the edge of his fork. He was feeling a little pushy and insolent.

'Mind me asking where?'

'What's it to you, my boy? You think I could give you a job?'

'Wasn't thinking that, señor.'

'It's all right.' Mendes lit a shaggy cigarette and didn't offer one to his new friend. 'I can see how a man thinks when he's on the rocks. He casts about – that's what he does. I don't take it the wrong way, kid.'

'I would be up for a job,' Angel said nonchalantly. 'I can do most things.'

'We'll talk about it in the car. Have another *café de olla*.'

The sun rose as they walked to a surprisingly clean Pontiac on the same street as the gas station. A fine, gritty dust blew off the arroyos where the *ocotillos* shimmered, the ostentatious red of Christmas crackers.

Angel threw his bag in the back and sat next to Mendes in the front. The desert burst into golden light as they moved out, passing the old tanneries and the two motels that had once, long ago, flourished in morbid splendour. The road was straight now, earnest and unbending and to the point, and they sailed along it in solitude, passed only by long rigs bound for the north. At the distant foot of the mountains to the right there were pylons, white shacks, and to the left the empty plain of dark-grey sand and *cholla* cactus that stretched as far as Angel could see to the pretty hills of Hell.

'I'd say,' Mendes went on cheerfully, 'that from the looks of you, you were a drifter. But you're not, are you?'

'I'm just moving around.'

'Ah yes. Sometimes one has to move around. It's the law of life. Times are bad and you have to move around.'

'That's about it.'

'When I was your age, I moved around. Yes, sir. Then I discovered this highway. You could buy and sell properties along this highway as easy as buying and selling tacos. It was a silver mine. I called it the *camino real*. We all called it the *camino real* – that was the term for it. Those were the days, now that I look back on them. A fortune in easy commissions. *La chingada*. It's all done for now.'

Here and there, on either side of the road, stood what looked like ruined and forsaken ranches. No greenery could be seen, no grazing land, no crops, no animals, no tractors or other vehicles. Only the old water towers rusting in the heat and the bleached fences decaying year by year, or perhaps month by month. The forgiving lushness of the Tropic of Cancer was still far off. Mendes told a few tall stories of the old days, by which he might have meant merely the previous decade, and by midday they were in open desert, shining with salt and yet more yellow *cholla* flowers.

The land, however, was changing. In the high heat of the day they came to a half-dried river, an astonishing sight, with low jacarandas in full bloom around it. Here white horses were tethered in the pebbled shallows, their backs coloured mauve by the trees. The stream ran pure and

transparent across a bed that descended in shallow terraces.
Women knelt there washing shirts, their dresses tied around
their hips. They stopped and Mendes rolled out of the car
good-humouredly.

'What asses!' he cried to the women, who were not at all
annoyed. They turned their heads with no concern and took
this brutal compliment in their stride. 'Can I drink?' he
laughed, running down to the water's edge. 'It's so fucking
hot in this country. Angel, come down.'

But Angel stood on the bridge spanning the river, looking
down at the docile, tenderly hued horses. The sweat dimmed
his eyes and he had to wipe them. The heat and the light were
no longer separable. On slightly higher ground he could see
dried coral trees withered in the same element, their dark-red
blooms scattered around the earth.

Mendes knelt in the shallows and thrust his shaggy head
into the water. The women giggled and shook their butts.
'*Cabeza hueca*,' one of them teased him. It was clear that they
had seen him before, that he was part of this shrill, blinding
landscape. What role he occupied in it was not clear. Buf-
foon, interloper, genie?

He seemed to know the river intimately, wading into it up
to his shins and basking in the jacaranda shade. He looked
back up at Angel standing on the bridge and squinted. The
drifter didn't care for a fresh river.

They drove on into featureless hills. Aerial masts and
pylons stood stark next to the low shells of abandoned
houses. They went through pueblos baking in their hopeless heat; past Pemex stations alive with Christmas tinsel,
and bars shaded by painted trees where the men sat outside

in *jipijapa* hats with plates of radishes and bottles of Noche Buena. Mendes drove a little faster now, his hands light on the red-leather wheel. He smoked with a slow deliberateness and looked frequently in the rear-view mirror to inspect the road behind them. The sweat was now loose and free on his dark temples. He talked about the property he was on his way to visit. Perhaps Angel could visit it with him. They would soon be there. So it was, so to speak, 'on the way'.

'A lovely house on the plain, not far from the road. We had to evict the family. They didn't pay the rent.'

'Did they leave?'

'We are about to see, *hombre*. We are about to see. To tell you the truth, I don't want to go into that house. It was a guy from Morelia, a bad-news kind of guy. I never wanted to give it to him. But sometimes you don't listen to the gut instinct. You get into hot water.'

'Who is he?'

'Some guy. He did time a while back. Probably a drug-runner once upon a time. You know the type.'

Like me, Angel thought.

'But I don't want to run into that *pendejo*. I have been thinking. Maybe you would like to earn a little cash.'

Angel perked up.

'Sure I would.'

'I thought so. What if you'd go into that house for me and look around? It should be empty. They are supposed to have left a few weeks ago.'

'But one never knows, eh?'

Mendes turned cynically and gave him a wink.

'Money is never for nothing, *hombre*. I said I didn't want to do it. It'll be nothing, though. It'll just be an empty house.'

'What if it's not empty then?'

'Well, you would have to deal with it.'

'*Hombre?*'

'They might have left some animals in there. A dog or a cat.'

'So that's why you don't want to go in?'

'Exactly. I hate animals. I'd pay you to clean them up.'

'Take them out?'

'Kill them, I mean. What's the point of taking them out? What the fuck are we going to do with them?'

'I don't know.'

'Yeah, you don't know. We're not going to do nothing with them. Pests have to be put down. It's part of the job.'

'You've done it before?'

'Sure I have. How do you think the properties get cleaned up?'

'Shit, man, I don't know. Kill a cat?'

Mendes laughed out loud.

'Come on, boy. For five hundred dollars you won't kill a pussy cat?'

Angel felt his head go light.

'Five hundred?'

'That's what I said. Five hundred. Five hundred not enough?'

The tone was so sarcastic that Angel had to contradict it at once; he agreed quickly to whatever it was Mendes wanted.

'All right, it's fine. What do you want me to do?'

'Go through the house and make sure it's fit for repossession. I want you to go through it carefully, though. Animals get into cupboards and behind sofas. You'll have to look through it inch by inch. Can you do that?'

'Sure I can.'

'Good. We have a deal?'

They shook hands and Mendes rolled down the window. They had come to a flat, scorching plain with dust-whitened trees standing along the tracks, the walls painted cream and dotted with bullfighting posters.

Angel thought. A cat would be a dismal task, and a dog would be worse. But then Mendes had said there would probably be nothing. It was a spin of the roulette wheel, and Mendes was paying him to accept the spin. A bet was a bet, and a bet could pay handsomely precisely because it was a bet. One had to roll or bail out. Bailing out got you nothing – and if he had to kill a pet, it was worth $500. It was worth a lot less than that. He would have done it for 100. Somewhere between fifty and 100 he would have baulked, but Mendes didn't know that. Even he wasn't used to Angel's level of desperation. For all Angel knew, however, 500 was the going rate for pest clearance.

'There's just one condition,' Mendes said, 'and listen to me good. When I say I want the house cleaned, I mean I want it cleaned. I want everything living inside that house cleaned out. Flies, cats, mice – everything. Is that clear? I don't care what it is. Every living thing.'

'Mice?'

'Whatever the fuck it is, I don't care. I don't want no mice in there – no ticks, no horses, nothing. That's the deal. You liquidate whatever is in there for your five hundred. If you leave one thing alive, you'll have broken the contract.'

'We don't have a contract.'

'*La chingada*. Of course we have a contract. It's written in our heads. Or do you want to stop at a lawyer's?'

'All right, we have a contract.'

'That we do. And if you break it, I'll come for you. You can depend on that. I don't give my money away freely.'

They broke open two Modelos from Mendes's ice-box on the back seat and drank to their agreement. The car seemed to speed up and soon the walls of crazed pipestem cactus, the fields of walnut trees and the abandoned motels sped by faster, with less consequence. Angel felt like sleeping, but Mendes turned on the radio and the mariachi kept them awake.

By five they were at a wide, shallow river spanned by a metal bridge, and on the far side of it were what looked like railway cars parked in gardens of wild cactus and converted into slum homes. Sure enough, they drove over old tracks. On the far side was an older surfaced road, which swerved upwards towards sharp-tipped volcanic mountains whose lower slopes were dusted with the pale green of irrigated fruit trees. They tore up it nonchalantly, the radio blaring, and they saw the shadows lengthening from the base of the trees when they were among them.

As the mountain road rose and the earth grew more bare, they came to the house that Mendes intended to visit. It was a ranch-style villa set within high walls crenellated with broken bottle glass. A driveway led to an adobe gateway with fancy iron scrollwork. Mendes stopped the car by the arterial road, however, and suggested that Angel should walk up to the gate so as not to make too much noise. He should, if at all possible, slip into the house quietly. Mendes gave him the code to the outer gate and the key to the house itself.

'I use my bare hands then?' Angel snorted as he got out of the car. The sun hit him directly and he felt his knees weaken.

'I can give you a small axe I have in the back, if that'll help.'

'An axe?'

'Yes, a small one for chopping wood. It'll serve, no?'

Mendes got it out for him, and they stood for a moment in the baking sun, blinking at each other. Somewhere between them was a desperate hangman's humour that could not be articulated – a mutual reproach that had no substance because they were still, after all, strangers. *Better that way*, both were thinking.

'I'll wait in the car,' the real-estate agent said.

Angel walked to the gate and punched in the code; the gates swung open and he strolled inside. It was a low, Spanish-style villa with tiled roofs. There were faded pale-brown lawns, arid with neglect, and a few pieces of garden gnomery, a small toy windmill and a pool that had dried out. He picked his way along the shell path, eyeing the untrimmed edges of the lawns and the windows of the villa, where lilac curtains were drawn, and when he was at the door he paused and listened and heard the sound of an aircraft passing, but far out of sight. He pressed his ear to the door.

The key worked smoothly. Inside, the hallway was surfaced with monochrome stone and there was a chandelier with smoked-glass shades. He turned it on. All the windows and curtains were drawn shut and the living room was stifling, plunged in darkness. The sofas and armchairs were covered with sheets, the coffee table wrapped in plastic. On the mantelpiece stood a plaster Jesus of the flowing Aryan variety, its eyes turned towards the very place where Angel was standing. The coffee table was piled with magazines neatly stacked. He went into the middle of the room and clutched the increasingly meaningless axe. It occurred to him that Mendes had spooked him for fun, and that this was just a routine matter with a very slight risk of an unpleasant surprise — a risk, however, that the cautious agent had not wanted to take himself. The axe, therefore, was only symbolic. He laid it down on the nearest armchair and considered his curious situation.

It was hot inside the house and it was clear that no one had been there in some time. He ventured into the kitchen, which still smelled of long-gone gingerbread, and into a dining room where mass-produced acrylic paintings of waterfalls hung on the barren walls. The table was glossy and no dust had accumulated upon its surface. From there a narrow corridor led to a series of bedrooms. The doors were all closed, but not locked, and he opened them one by one, peering inside the rooms. The curtains were all closed here as well and the windows fastened. Cushions lay on the little beds. At the end of the corridor there was a kind of nursery with large windows through which the sun blazed. He walked down towards it and, as he did so, he heard a muffled sound, like that of something rubbing against a soft wall. The door of the nursery was half-open and from it came a sweet smell that set it apart from the musty deadness of the rest of the house. He came to the threshold and pushed the door open further, then looked down instinctively at a large bag about five feet long, lying in the middle of the floor between two baby pens.

It was made of a dark-green material like a military duffel bag, and it had drawstrings that were tied tight. Below this opening there lay a saucer of water. He had already sensed that there was something living inside the bag, because he had heard it move when he was in the corridor. As he opened the door, moreover, it stirred more frantically, sensing his presence. A subdued moaning made him want to speak to it, reassuringly, and he stooped at once and held out a hand, silent and afraid. The bag shuffled and it was clear in some way that there was a small human inside it. Maybe a child of about twelve. He was about to talk to this person, but something held him back. Angel straightened himself and glanced with a sudden panic through the large windows whose blinds had been raised. A dusty back yard could be seen, filled with large ornamental *saguaros*. The metal barrier around it had rusted slightly and a child's climbing frame stood forlornly on a floor of dark sand.

On the side of the green bag there was a single patch of blood, circular and moist, and around it lay a few grainy pellets of what looked like dried dog food. Angel retreated to the door and thought, with a slow anguish, about the axe lying on the chair in the living room. Quietly he closed the door and retraced his steps, his mind trying to reach forward into the space of an impossible future.

In the living room he stepped to the window, parted the curtain and peered down the drive towards the gate, through which the road could be seen and the front fenders of the car.

He went back to the chair and picked up the axe, but it dithered in his grip. *Get your five hundred bucks*, he thought to himself. *You won't even see their face. It's just an animal in a sack.* He turned and went back to the corridor, his eyes beginning to dim, and the handle of the axe slipped in the sweat that came off his hand.

Halfway down the same corridor, he stopped again and tried to think more clearly. He had been tricked, but surely the trick could be turned the other way? Rotating the axe slowly in his hands, he reconsidered, and gradually he realised that he was not going to cross the Rubicon. It was a vast chasm to cross, but its vastness was not even perceptible; it was more like the desert itself, formless and immersing, uncrossable alone.

'That bastard,' he said aloud. 'Five hundred for that?'

Turning on his heel, he went back to the living room and threw the axe into the same chair. There were a multitude of risks, but they could be calculated in seconds. He walked out into the declining sun, slammed the door shut behind him and strode boldly back down to the gate.

The car was still parked in the same place, and Mendes sat on the bonnet calmly smoking a cigarillo.

'Well,' he said, looking up.

'You bastard, you knew there was a dog in there.'

Angel got into the car as if furious, and Mendes lethargically did the same, grinning from ear to ear.

'You took the challenge,' he said as he put the key into the ignition. 'All I asked you to do was clean the house. Nothing wrong with that.'

'Get me as far away from here as you can.'

'Anything you say, my friend, anything you say. As long as the house is cleared, we can leave.'

'It's cleared.'

They drove south for an hour. As night swept in, they saw dark-green mountains shaped like stalagmites in the distance – the end of the desert. Lights rose up out of the dusk, towns spread along the highway like fossilised rubbish, corrals of horses lit by arc lamps, and districts of bars where those $500 would go a long way. Mendes pulled over just outside town and opened the boot. There was a suitcase with money and he pulled out 500. Angel got out as well, and it occurred to him that he might as well be on his way. He wanted to disappear into this commodious hellhole with its lollipop bar signs and ample motels.

'Shit,' Mendes said suddenly as he handed over the money. 'What about the axe? We forgot the axe.'

'What about it? I left it there on purpose.'

'You left it?'

'Yes. It's evidence – it's better left there.'

Mendes considered this and reluctantly began to nod.

'Yeah, I guess you're right. Still, I wonder if I should go back and get it.'

'I wouldn't bother, *hombre*. It'll give you bad dreams.'

Mendes looked at him with a cold eye.

'Bad dreams? I get them anyway.' He hesitated, but finally said, 'To hell with it' and sauntered back to the driver's seat. 'Where you going now?' he called over the roof of the car to Angel.

'Into this here pueblo. I figure I earned some relaxation, after what you made me do.'

'I guess you did. So we're parting ways.'

'I reckon we are.'

Mendes waved and said a curt '*Adios*'. When he was seated and the car was humming, he spoke through the opened passenger window. 'If I find you didn't clear up, Angel, the others will come and find you.'

'Let them come. Everything is in order.'

'Sure it is. Have fun with your five hundred, *cabron*. I am driving on to Mazatlan all night!'

He left Angel standing by the road, and after the boy had watched the tail lights of the Pontiac diminish, he walked over between the tamarisk trees and dipped down a track that led into the town. It was a short walk.

Magueys grew by the roads here and flame-vines spread up dark hillsides, but soon the lights from the *tiendas* and bars obscured them. He went to a hotel and got a cheap room and climbed up to the third floor. He took off his boots and shirt and washed himself down with a flannel soaked in hot water. He counted out the money again and then a second time, just to fill himself with the satisfaction of it. Then he packed it into his travel bag and went down into the street to get a shot of Sauza at a bar and a plate of radishes and *flautas* with guacamole. He ordered in a loud voice, as if defying his own unease.

Yet as he sat in that *cantina* eating his *flautas* Angel was aware of the men glancing at him sideways. Thinking back to the house, he wondered what had made him stay his hand. In the moment, it had not been fear. It was the certainty that his life would change either way, but that there was a difference in the two roads that were suddenly open to him. The calf is more free than its slaughterer, and the road of the victim is somehow clearer. A killer has nowhere to hide inside himself. Had he done as Mendes wanted he would be free now, but only as far as the outer world was concerned. His interior world would have collapsed into darkness.

His hand began to shake and he drank half the bottle of Sauza as he ate, and then finished it at his leisure. The children threading their way between tables with bunches of radishes also seemed to know what was in his eye, and beyond it. A drifting fatalism only half-aware of itself. It was simply a question of roads – those loose ends that crossed landscapes belonging to others. At the crossroads, one waited and trembled and then acted, but there was little foresight or expectation. Nor could one go back along the same road.

Having eaten, he went in search of a poker game in one of the bars. He played until eleven, losing steadily, pulling out his twenty-dollar bills and drinking at an equivalent pace, and then he went to a fairground and walked among the machines, eating bags of *nuez fina* and shooting toy rifles at teddy bears. Before long he was at another gambling table, and losing still more. He laid down heavier bets and soon he had lost $400, so that by one in the morning he was drunk and agitated and unaware of where he was. The good old boys strung him along; they could see that poker was not his game.

When Angel was out of cash he walked back to the hotel, staggering around packs of dogs and rubbish tips, singing to himself and carrying the night's last bottle of mescal. It was good that he had paid the hotel in advance. He had enough for tomorrow's bus to nowhere. He climbed up to the roof of the hotel, where there was a hammock, and crashed into it with the bottle in his lap. It must have been only a few hours that he half-slept, observing – or so he thought – brilliantly lit pellet-shaped objects high in the night sky, tiny zeppelins lit by a second moon that no one knew about. He stretched himself out and relaxed, waiting for first light, listening to the sound of the rattling cicada-heavy trees and the frogs deep inside the fields. He was certain, or as certain as he could be, that at this time the following day he would be dead and his limbs scattered among hungry crabs.

The following morning he rose early and there was a brightness in his mind, a hardness of purpose that the refreshment of sleep had instigated. It was, he supposed, the dreams of youth revived. The grackles woke him, and the sound of children in a garden next door. He found that his body was all in one piece and moreover he still had some of his money left; he decided, then, to stay in the town and play what was left to him. He had nothing much to lose and the spirit of survival had suddenly been aroused by his nightmares.

Novilla only revived at the end of the afternoon as the insects subsided and the painful glare seeped out of the streets. The back lots of the houses were filled with *manzanilla* oaks from which tyres were hung on ropes. Little girls swung inside them, like fish on hooks. When Angel was in the street he walked under shimmering coral trees, with the hum of mariachi coming from the gardens. At times he was alone in the street. His neck crawled with anxiety at the thought that he was being watched.

The *cantinas* came alive and the men stood there in their *jipijapas*, rocking on their heels and chewing pickled carrots.

They turned to watch him go by. One of them, half-gringo by the look of him, a mix of *gabo* and Mexicano, called out into the street, as if addressing only his moving shadow: '*Que onda, gabacho? Tabacha la gabacha?*'

Their laughter followed him, a dog snapping at the heels.

He went without dinner, not even a beer, and joined a card game near a small fairground. It was much the same crowd as the night before. They teased him as he drew up his chair and accepted a free Modelo.

The game went on for hours to the sound of a jukebox. Slowly Angel began to win back what he had lost and when he had got to 700 he quit and bought the table a round of Sauza shots, then walked back into the heat of the street. He turned the first corner, not knowing where he was going, and walked and walked until he came to the first of the arroyos glittering under a half-moon. There he stopped and counted his cash, feeling a vivid satisfaction that fate could turn this way and that. It was still early, too, and he thought he knew a place where he could score a second-hand car for a couple of hundred. It was a garage he had seen by the road. He walked there now by the back streets, coming through a large lot decorated with pennants where old cars awaited buyers.

He paid the $200 and drove out of the lot in a rusted Saber. It was filled with trash and the seats ran with oil, and a mile out of town he stopped by the roadside and cleared it out. It was the same road by which he and Mendes had come, the only road that ran past that town, and he had already forgotten where it came from and where it went to. It went from north-east to south-west, he thought, but he had never seen it on a map, it was just straight and inflexible as it cut across the desert, going from one unknown town to the next. He remembered merely the Pemex stations infrequently positioned along its length, the dust storms and the whitewashed posts set into the hard shoulder, and the women selling *gorditas* in the shade of blue trees. It went on for ever and ever and at the end of it was another room in a hotel where they would find him eventually, but exactly like a card game, he would never know when and nor would they. It was, after all, the same *camino real* that had made Mendes rich and which might, one dark night, bring him to the presence of the Lord of Light as a dead soul. It was paved with silver as well as dust, and as he drove on towards La Mira he wondered if his luck might change again.

THE WAVE

THEY DROVE BETWEEN PADDIES GUARDED BY WATER buffalo, and the sea appeared again, the sun setting violently behind it. They were near the Turtle Cove government hotel, by Aerial Bay. A beach of corals was fringed with Alexandrian laurels and the road came right down to the water. The houses had little rose gardens around them, lush with *nypas*, and delicately thatched doorways. Ink-nut trees bordered the gardens, where children stood silent as little statues watching them pass. Fading posters of Christian evangelists coloured the sides of shacks and walls; in spaces in the jungle she saw sudden sprinklings of white crosses. The first British settlement in the islands, Aerial Bay used to be called Port Cornwallis. Malaria and Jarawa warriors had once killed it off, and now it was a listless fishing village surrounded by mysterious islands.

The silhouette of Saddle Peak now rose up, its upper jungles obscured by the mists that coiled round it. The road they were on ran as far as Saddle, then stopped. Behind the beach stood the hotel, posed ambitiously on top of a steep little hill that commanded a modest view. The gates were padlocked and the 'r' was missing from the word 'Turtle'. Wilson, the driver, honked several times and at length a sleepy boy in a dhoti came down the steep driveway to the gate holding a key.

The Turtle Cove driveway curved steeply up to a concrete block painted a dull custard-yellow. It looked worn and shambolic, like a doll's house whose owner had grown up and walked away. Alice had been bracing herself for some time for the worst. But all the same she was glad to see that the jungle came right up to the walls and that the air of abandonment had not been corrected by a vigorous new investor. There was a row of sandals along the bottom step, and metal buckets with mops.

The exterior was lit with two paraffin lamps and the family was seated outside, cooking chai. Four young men came out onto the steps and the weedy forecourt, rubbing their eyes as if they had been asleep all day. The manager was called Manish.

He shook her hand and at once Alice liked his eyes. He was apologetic, but clearly useless, and from his tone she gathered that there were no women here, which meant that the bathrooms would be a mess and that food would be slow in coming. Her heart sank. She looked up and saw blank dusty windows curtained from the inside, while around the building cracked ball-lamps stood in the grass, untended, as long-horned cows munched around them. There was only one light on, a two-cent chandelier above the reception desk.

They went into the lobby and there was a backgammon board dusted with talc where the boys had been sitting for hours. For days or weeks, perhaps. The other guests were away on a boat trip and were expected back imminently. The boys hauled her bags and her seven equipment boxes into the lobby and piled them carefully under the light cast by the chandelier. Another light was turned on. She saw that there was a 'Lounge' with a TV screwed to the wall and a 'Dinning Room' with mauve curtains and photomurals of local beaches. Wilson brought in her two microscopes. He laid them gingerly at her feet while Manish brought the massive quantities of paperwork necessary to complete before a long residence could commence.

'Very happy you are being here,' he murmured, leafing through the forms. 'Having dinner?'

'What can we have?'

'Having fried fish. Dal. Rice. We are making for the boat trip coming back.'

'How many people are here?' she asked anxiously.

He counted on his fingers. 'Four are one Indian family – it is the General Manager of the Indian Railways and his wife and children. They are doing time pass here.'

'Time pass?'

'Yes, they are doing time pass.'

The inner part of the hotel looked like a tropical penitentiary of some kind, with cement corridors and hallways arranged in crude concentric squares. On the two upper levels, rows of turquoise doors were padlocked, numbered from 1,000 to 1,025, and hers was named 'Barren', after an island nearby. The room hadn't been inhabited in months, perhaps not in years. But there were still posters of indigenous Jarawa matrons on the walls. Sentimental tribal stuff designed to get tourists in the mood. The women, round-bellied, in languorous earrings, smiling sheepishly straight at the bed. Hotel Rules were pinned to the back of the door, the commands listed vertically:

> *Do not bring the intoxicatings into the room*
> *Do not bring the motors and cars into the room, for*
> *there is park*
> *No unparliamentary language if you please*

The dining room had fourteen overhead fans, one for each table. When the hotel was opened, government employees must have taken their holidays there, journeying up from Port Blair on a steamer putting in at Aerial Bay. A few hardy souls and their children. There was the beach at the bottom of the hill, a few willing fishing boats to take them out to Craggy and other deserted islands. The photomurals and the electric fans — concessions to comfort — were made, one suspected, a little unwillingly. The room, moreover, was lit with small neon strips that bathed it in a brittle blue-white light. An electric insect-attractor crackled continually as bugs fried themselves against it. Manish showed Alice to her place, a towel draped around his arm which signified that he himself was the cook. But she noticed at once that there was a third table set, yet as far from hers as possible.

'I thought I'd be alone,' she said as the chapattis were brought in.

'Dr De Silva and his family, Miss.'

The table was set far more lavishly than hers, with dark-blue napkins, wine glasses and a candlestick.

Manish appeared in the hallway with a broom and began to stir up useless clouds of dust in preparation for the arrival of the day-trippers, who were paying much more than she was, and as she watched him tinker with the dirt there was the sound of feet on the driveway and the sudden projection of light from a pair of torches. The Indian family had arrived. She could sense at once the hummingbird motion of two children and the tension of gentle chiding in the air. Manish abandoned the dust and darted towards the doors of the hotel, which in any case were always open. The General Manager was already there, dusting his own legs with what looked like a small spatula.

'Na, na,' he sang in English, 'leave alone', and his plump face swung into view under the chandelier as his wife came up behind him.

'These bloody children,' she laughed.

Manish called the boys. He wanted the iced-lemonade jugs on the table at once.

Into the hall came the General Manager's wife – a lofty, strikingly beautiful woman. She was dressed in a gold-specked sari with mauve leggings and she wore a pair of glasses attached to her neck by a gold chain.

'Robert,' she said to her husband, still in English. 'Can you get that naughty boy under control? We want to give him some lemonade.'

The De Silvas from Goa swept royally into the dining room. They noticed the Englishwoman at once but showed no surprise that she was there. The two children skipped in behind, a boy of about ten and a girl of about eight or nine: glossy, quick children with insolent eyes. It was a compact, well-behaved, aristocratic family with well-defined rules and its handsome geometry was obvious to Alice at once – so

obvious that she felt an immediate envy. They claimed their
wretched table first and the man, a little plump, flattened out
the napkins one by one. The children came winging around
Alice's table, inspecting her.

'You're the insect lady,' the girl piped up without
hesitation.

Mrs De Silva was called Mervyn, and she made an apol-
ogy for her daughter's bad manners.

'Nadia, come here and say hello properly. You don't call
people "insect ladies".'

'Are you an insect lady?' the boy asked.

'This is Nadia's brother, Anthony.'

'We have Catholic names,' the girl smiled.

Manish came in now with jugs of orange juice and a bottle
of dusty-looking red wine, which must have been stored
underground for years.

'I'm an insect lady,' Alice said.

Robert put on his glasses and kicked off his sandals. He sat
back and the chair creaked dangerously.

'Manish told us all about you. You are doing research into
moths. I can't say I understand it. I hope you didn't let them
diddle you?'

The English was soft, rolling, privately educated, as comfortable in the British caste as in any other caste system —
except that they were Catholics, of course.

'Diddle?' she said.

'These fellows are always diddling. Look away and they
will diddle you. We were almost cheated ourselves. Manish?'

'Yes, sir.'

'Would you say so? Come on, spit it out.'

Manish laughed awkwardly.

The General Manager swept on, 'I am here for the sun, the sea, the clean healthiness. What my family are here for, I cannot say.' He leaned forward playfully. 'I find them rather mysterious myself.'

'I'm ten,' the boy said shyly.

Nadia was imitatively formal. 'And *I* am nine years old.'

'I am Robert and I am fifty-six.'

His wife shook the white woman's hand ironically. 'You're not allowed to ask my age.'

'Mummy,' the girl said, 'can Tony and I go out in the garden and play with the goats?'

'I suppose so, yes. If Daddy agrees.'

The father shrugged. 'I suppose so, too. Though I cannot see, for the life of me, how you can *play* with a goat. Do you turn it upside down? Does it make a noise when you turn it upside down?'

'You could try,' the beautiful Mervyn laughed.

Manish lit the candles and secured the windows as the wind rose a little. He went outside and pushed the rotting shutters into position, latching them externally. In the hall the backgammon table came to surly life, and the boys gathered around it as if these exotic guests did not exist, and even if they did exist, they would not bother to think about them. It was part of the rundown charm for the tourists.

'We came from Kolkata on the plane,' the glamorous one was saying, 'what about you?'

'The same plane.'

'It's a hell of a city, *Calcutta*,' Robert sniffed, archly avoiding what he clearly thought was a parochial attempt to fussily amend a pronunciation that had never been inauthentic to begin with. 'Compared to Goa, it's like – it's like—'

'Calcutta.'

'We stay at the Oberoi at least.'

Manish came out with their meal. There were stuffed parathas and chutneys and aloo and tandoori prawns. It was laid out on seven plates, and Manish said quietly that he would feed the children in the garden; they liked the fireflies.

Robert glanced at the stick-like Englishwoman as if he wanted to find her attractive, but couldn't. Although he didn't reveal it, he found her slightly alarming. She sat there rigidly, smiling rigidly; it was odd.

From the wine came a smell of old perfume, slightly rancid, and Robert sipped it warily. He snapped his fingers and called to Manish, 'Let's have some music, shall we? Radio?'

Manish – slavishly, Alice thought, with a white liberal's disappointment – nodded and disappeared for a moment, reappearing with a grand British radio set from the Fifties, set on a castored table that moved with a slight whinny. It had marbled knobs and a grille with black fabric. Manish treated it with exaggerated drama, twiddling the knobs until a cricket match came on air. It was live, but not from India. 'Lords!' he announced rather unnecessarily. Then he switched to some sweet mainlander music, and the De Silvas rocked their hands and snapped their fingers. They obviously didn't speak the language being sung, but they got the gist.

Mervyn reached into her beach bag and took out a silver cigarette case packed with elegant mauve *beejees*. The food had hardly been touched when she asked Manish for a milk pudding and some sweetened tea. The music was lowered a little and she blew expert smoke-rings into the air above her head, while the husband did some reaching of his own and extracted a wooden flute from the bags he had left by his chair.

'Sometimes, Alice, I like to play the flute after dinner.'

'That's all right with me.'

It was rather beautiful, Alice thought, and as unexpected as it was touching, this serenade from man to wife. And yet they made her feel subtly inferior.

During the night she heard the family settling into their rooms. It began to rain around midnight, and the radio was turned off in reception as the night-watch boy went to sleep on the steps outside. There was just the soft susurration of the rain and that of the surf at a slightly different pitch. She read by oil lamp and then, thinking she would be alone, walked out to the landing to cool off by the rain. She saw at once that the girl was already there, dressed in a cotton nightie and leaning against the concrete parapet. The girl turned when she heard the Englishwoman approach and her eyes were filled with a heavy, black emotion that might have been fear, but which was likely something else.

'Nadia, what are you doing up? Does your mummy—'

The girl put a finger in front of her lips and her eyes said, 'Shhh!'

Alice crept to her side and met her eyes.

'What is it?' she whispered.

The girl was quietly grave.

'The Sand Man,' she whispered back. 'He's down there waiting for me to fall asleep.'

Alice peered over the wall into the driveway where puddles were forming. There was no one there.

'The Sand Man, Nadia?'

The girl nodded.

'I saw him earlier. He was making a sign to me.'

'I think you ought to go to bed.'

Now Nadia slowly shook her head.

'If I go to bed, he'll come through the window.'

'Come, I'll take you downstairs.'

She took the girl's hand and pulled her gently away
towards the stairs. Alice thought that Nadia was willowy and
already elegant, in the way of girls who are mysteriously
anticipating pubescence but have not surrendered to any
adult implications of their future transformation.

Nadia's eyes were straight, frank, amber-and-tobacco
and sceptical of everything outside her beautiful and ordered
and witty family. She suddenly looked up at the stairs, as if
she had seen something that had swung into sight and then
out again. She pursed her lips. Beads of sweat stood out on
her delicate little forehead. Her eyes became nervous, then
steadied. It was as if she was used to concealing things from
adults that made her look foolish in their eyes. Alice took her
back downstairs, where her family were all asleep.

'There,' she said to her, 'here's your room. Can you go to
sleep now?'

Nadia nodded.

'All right then. There is no Sand Man, Nadia. It's only the
rain.'

The girl stared at her incredulously.

'I mean it. He's just your imagination.'

'So?' the girl said. 'That's real.'

'Yes. But go to sleep now.'

THE FOLLOWING DAY ALICE collected moths in the forest at the base of Saddle Peak and then walked slowly and wearily back to the hotel at dusk. She thought about her work, about the past of a century ago. Lieutenant-Colonel M. L. Ferrar again, Chief Commissioner of the Penal Settlement in 1923, and one of the most remarkable amateur lepidopterists of all time. He had been assisted by the Indian collector Bhagwan Din.

It was Din who had presented Ferrar with a rare blue nawab, *Polyura schreiber tisamenus*, as a welcome gift. The *tehsildar* of Nankauri had famously sent Ferrer twenty specimens of the almost extinct Malay tiger butterfly, whose exact habitat was unknown to this day. Ferrar caught the lurcher and the branded yeoman once each during his tenure as Chief Commissioner, but he never saw either of them twice. The bamboo treebrown also haunted him; he glimpsed it a single time.

In the hotel a three-quarter moon shone down upon a scene of apparent desertion. As Alice went up to have a quick shower and recompose herself, she thought, *The boys must have gone off on some jaunt, perhaps a fishing trip. I suppose they do that from time to time.*

Behind the kitchen there was a small herb garden filled with pots of cumin where someone had left a clay pipe on the wall before running off. Physically spent, she decided to read in bed. She snuggled into her sheets and listened to the soft rain. It seemed never to stop. She dozed, then reawakened. As she turned the next page of *Chemical Ecology*, however, there was a muffled boom and the room shook. There was a pause, then the walls shook again, this time more violently. In the controlled stillness her ears strained, and there was a faint popping in their depths. The lights went out. A second later, the AC unit shuddered to a standstill and from out of the silence there rose the sound of the sea. Her new sandals echoed like sandpaper on the stairs as she tumbled down to the lobby. The chandelier vibrated, tinkling with its cheap glass as the droplets rubbed against each other. An earthquake? But the foundations did not seem to be rocking. She was certainly alone. No one had come back. There were no shouts from the other guests.

From below by the road came a strange noise – a cracking and crunching of wood, as if a giant bulldozer was making its way along the little road, ripping up everything in its way. There was a third boom, much louder, and by moonlight she saw something moving at incredible speed through the tamarind grove at the bottom of the hill, snapping the trees down like toothpicks. It sped towards the gateposts of the hotel, just visible, and smashed against them in an upshoot of foam and debris. She took a step back and her mouth opened to cry out. And yet it was all quite calm, quite logical. All around the gateposts a mass of shiny sea poured through the rice fields and the coconut plantations, knocking down the thin trees one by one and crashing into the houses with a dull thud. Other trees suddenly appeared, whirling around at high speed, moving horizontally without gravity like objects in a cartoon, almost gaily.

Because the hotel was on such a steep hill the commotion moved around it, washing the hill's base with multiple oily waves that curled back upon themselves and collapsed onto the disappearing road. A cow suddenly swept by, its legs stiffly upended like a table. Alice ran up to the top floor. The wave had rushed along the road, smashing the shacks like toys. Their planks and pieces of palm thatch swirled about under the moon, and then disappeared as they were carried off. And then another boom as the water hit the mountainside and met resistance. Seawards, the scum of broken trees rose as another wave moved in. A small Hindustan Motors car tumbled through the canopy of the submerged wood of Alexandrian laurels, rolling with beautiful motions as it was driven forward. The water rose furiously, its surface becoming brighter as the moon spread over it, and soon it covered the fields behind the hotel as well as the coconut groves in front of it. The gateposts were submerged and a wave burst on the driveway with a deafening crash, splitting the posts into fragments and sucking up the little fruit trees that had been planted there. Then a cloud passed over the moon and the waters turned black, their seething suddenly less visible. She held onto the balcony as if for dear life, though nothing had disturbed the hotel itself. The ground floor was perfectly dry. It was too high for the water to reach.

The waves eventually slipped back. At dawn they receded as far as the roadside farm, of which only a rectangle of mud bricks remained. As the water withdrew, it left claw-marks in the crust, long streaks and runnels filled with rubbish. Little fish lay smashed into it, along with beer cans, *pandanus* fruit, tyres, saucepans, calendars, brooms, scythes and bricks. By the gateposts a jagged pool opened up about a foot deep. Alice sat under the beautiful sun. Then she thought, *It'll be dark again tonight – there'll be no electricity.*

The day was long, suffocating, and she lay and waited. She wondered ceaselessly about the others. Where were they? They must have escaped somehow, with the assistance of some warning that, however, had not been shared with her. They had not thought to wake her up and take her with them? It seemed incredible. But then again there was the incomplete improvisation that panic always imposed. That was it. They must have panicked, swept up the children and fled for their lives. *Sauve qui peut.* It was understandable. But what about the staff? They too had not thought to wake her up and save her. All too quick, no time to think. She had to admit that that, too, was understandable in a way.

That night, a noise rose from the dark: the cicadas re-emerging. When the moon rose, she climbed up to the roof as if drawn upwards by its magnetic influence, and lay on a bamboo mat smoking her Woodbines. Miles to the east, thunder rolled over the destroyed headlands, bringing with it hotter, more boisterous air. She calmed herself, forcing herself to accept everything.

As she made her instant coffee on the gas stove in the kitchen the next morning she thought, with regret at a wasted opportunity, about the *Synechodes coniophora* she had collected before the wave struck. She had come here to acquire fame and fortune, not a family. A moth no one had yet discovered, or an ant, or anything that offered itself. That unknown specimen was there for the taking – one knows it in one's bones – and the parabola of a career in an obscure but highly competitive discipline was as rigid as any physical law. No one cared about one's misfortunes. No one cared about a woman in a man's field. They only cared about one's meticulously exploited opportunities. Hers had arrived. And then it had been snatched away from her.

It was a cruel joke, coming at the midpoint of a life defined by such jokes – the final cruel joke, you could say, confirming and controlling and consolidating all the previous ones.

Well, Alice thought, *I'm abandoned, stranded. Alone with nothing. But perhaps new niches have opened up. I can still collect specimens. It's what I came here to do.*

As she was dressing in her collection gear, she heard something buzzing against the closed shutters. Hummingbirds. They must have come along the coast foraging for titbits. She was happy to hear them. Then, as she pushed open the shutters, she caught sight of the grey-and-amber blur of their darting strikes. *Crested swifts*, she thought quickly, *insect-quaffing Apodiformes.*

She followed them outside and they darted off into the trees where the epiphytes, perhaps, offered cups of nectar. She knew nothing about them, outside of their predation patterns on airborne insects. She knew vaguely how much they ate on the move, and what mattered about them now was the suggestion that they were after dragonflies. Down they fluttered to the water and then flew straight across the passage to the nearest island. Then they came looping back past the hotel like tiny dive-bombers, shooting towards the Saddle forests. So she put on her sunhat and wellies and set off after them with a butterfly net, struggling across the field of mud that had supplanted the rice-paddies.

At its centre lay a pair of roasted buffalo horns and a package of cornflakes whose advertising colours had not faded at all. Tyres and shoes lay further on, and she saw the birds hesitate around them, probe for a moment, then speed on. They slipped into the trees by the farm and she gave chase. A stream flowed past a ruined farmhouse, fast and swollen, and the swifts danced around a large ant-mound on its far bank. They could taste ants in the air. She went up close to the mound, snapping with the Leica. But still the mound looked ruined, abandoned, and she was disappointed again. The water must have risen so far that they had decided to flee.

Beyond, the gullies led upwards at a ferocious angle and here big stones had been displaced, pushed to left and right. The moss had been scraped off. Bored, the birds departed for more profitable areas of plunder; Alice sat on the stones and listened carefully, but only the creak of timber filtered downwards from the mountain. Toadstools had appeared all around, however, red-and-cream flesh-caps bursting out of the ferns. She lay back and let herself slide into a quick sleep. It began to rain, softly and liltingly, and it was the drops that touched her eyelids and woke her. She sat up with a panic. The forest whispered quietly and she recovered. She took her net and wandered back down to the stream, which coursed noisily between banks of mauled mud.

The undergrowth on the higher ground had been stripped away by the outer edges of the waves as they lashed around the farmhouse, perhaps covering it entirely for a while. A sari was wrapped around a tree, high up, and tin spoons and forks projected up from the silt like metallic saplings. She walked down to the water, took off her clothes and bathed in the stream, which reached to her hips. She submerged herself into it and cleared the grime from her oily skin. The water was cold, violent and mixed with twigs and leaves, coloured like brewed coffee. She dried off in the sputtering rain. The skies darkened and she looked up, curious about the odd-looking stripped-down trees. As she did so, her eye caught a bulge in one of them. It was something caught in the crux of two branches. The body of a small animal of some kind.

She walked over to the tree, a massive banyan that had withstood the wave's shock. It was the body of a young girl trapped high up, and she had been dead since the moment the wave whisked her there. A clouded dread overcame the deepest parts of Alice's mind as the truth sank in and she made out the little fingers, spread as if catching raindrops. She stood directly underneath this small, sad corpse and tried to emotionally contain the enormity of it. She could not climb and dislodge the body, or she was afraid to. The tree was wet and slippery. The girl's face was turned upwards and could not be seen. Soon, however, she spotted the pink plastic sandal attached to the dangling right foot and remembered it as Nadia's.

Up the surface of the bark two columns of ants made their way. One seemed to be moving upwards and the other downwards. They were slightly golden in colour, and bloated, and they moved with a sinuosity that suggested a single centipede-like organism. She stepped back and followed with her eye the entire length of the columns. They snaked their way up into the top of the tree and she knew instinctively that they were feeding on the child.

She reached up and plucked a few of the ants from the descending column and put them into a ziplock bag. Her heart beat savagely.

As she walked back, she refused to let her emotions overwhelm her. She thought instead with anxiety that the still-intact vegetable garden behind the hotel was going to cause her trouble. When the insects had eaten the child they would be ravenous, and there was the tricky question of how to protect the tender young leaves. Cover them with plastic? But there was no plastic. Build a scarecrow? But insects could not be deterred by human-like images. They didn't see the world like that. They responded to fast-moving shadows that threatened to crush them. It was going to perplex her. She hurried.

That night Alice examined the ants with the microscope and an oil lamp. She picked one up with the tweezers. Superficially it looked like a typical *Myrmoteras* species common to South-East Asia, with a large head and spectacular 'trap jaws' armed with ferocious teeth. Trap jaws like these could bite certain soft-bodied prey insects in two. They could give humans a painful bite. Trap-jaw species hunted small, fast-moving creatures like springtails. It was an armamentarium quite common in tropical regions – some species were called 'dacetines', and many researchers had studied their methods of stalking symphylans, diplurans and, of course, springtails. As every entomologist knew, perhaps the fastest things in the animal kingdom were the explosive leaps of little springtails – their bodies were propelled by a forked appendage under their bodies – and the lightning snap of the trap jaws of the *Odontomachus* ant. From the point of view of evolution, of course, one had given rise to the other. Only this 'big-toothed' ant was fast enough to catch the elusive springtail.

Alice wondered, meanwhile, if this was a dacetine species at all. One would have said it was too big, since dacetines were usually small, though some larger species that hunted grasshoppers were also known. She put down the animal, then lowered the tips of the tweezers towards it again. The ant saw them at once – so its eyesight was excellent – and instantly performed a remarkable acrobatic operation. Lowering its long mandibles like a pole-vaulter flexing his pole, it suddenly flipped itself into the air and against the tweezers in a precision attack. Having struck the steel intruder, it bounced off the plastic wall and turned about to face it again. The magnifying glass showed the jaws opened 100 degrees, a nightmarish sight for any animal its own size. The creature was almost one-third jaw. Again, it assaulted the tweezer, as if its genes had given it this function and it could not desist from it. Falling again, it reared itself up and prepared to strike a third time. She re-closed the box and made a few notes.

Her dreams were of the wave, always the wave. Who had sent it, and where had it gone? Halfway through the night the rain stopped. She couldn't sleep deeply and the sudden silence woke her. She was sweating with desire for a man with no shape, no face. It was like an imagined husband, with his face destroyed by an axe-blow.

The Apodiformes woke her the next morning. Sunlight shot downwards through the metal shutters onto the foot of the bed. The jungle was submerged in steams, wildly noisy, as if the solar brightness had resurrected its gaiety. She rummaged around in the kitchen, found the glass jar of Nescafé and boiled herself some water on the gas stove. While she waited for it to boil, she turned on the old British radio set standing by the stove. It was all in Hindi and Bengali.

When the coffee was ready, Alice turned the heat off and went to drink outside. It was now about six. The sun had risen sufficiently to bathe the entire front porch and she could bask again in her light-yellow dress, sunning legs and arms and face while listening to the murmuring of the surf.

It was true that the sound was much fainter than it usually was. It seemed to have receded some way, though if she concentrated she could still make out the individual sizzle of each wave as it struck the coral. On the way through the second floor, she happened to pause on the open landing where, she had noticed, there was usually a choice collection of interesting crickets and cicadas. Perhaps they liked the sun.

On the road past the shrine, a hot wind blew suddenly through the destroyed pineapple trees. As she climbed higher, she noticed that the Lepidoptera were unusually dormant and that they clung to the trees motionless, while their wings quivered.

This left the spaces between the trees clear of insects, and as if to match this dormancy the ground-hugging beasts had vacated their territories as well, leaving behind a path of leaves and undisturbed twigs. She at once registered the change in the mound itself. Lower down, the surface was granulated. It was heavily ridged and lathed, like a crude piece of pottery that has only been turned a few times. Its colour had also altered. The light-toffee tone of before had changed to a rank mahogany. Approaching it warily, she measured it at fifty-eight inches, then walked around it a few times. Her thoughts would not come together properly.

Then she forced herself to turn to the rapidly decaying body of the girl, still fixed in the tree. The ants still swarmed across the bole of the tree, as if aware that they were running out of time. Their columns were even more swollen, more insistent, and they gave off a faint blue tint. She went up to them and watched them for the better part of thirty minutes. There was a smell emanating from the corpse. Alice had to steel herself against it, and make herself pay attention. She had become sure that this was a new species of ant that no one had noticed before.

She picked off more of them and bagged them. She was sure, just by looking at them with the naked eye, that they were fatter than the ones she had bagged the previous day. It was of course impossible, but she was sure all the same. The corpse had turned black and its odour was now becoming – minute by minute, it seemed – more pronounced. She had wondered all night if she should find a ladder and bring it down, for compassion's sake, and because the girl haunted her. If she could, she would bury her decently by the hotel and create a gravestone of some kind. If the parents had also been carried off, as seemed likely, the rescuing authorities could eventually re-bury her wherever the grandparents wanted in India. Yet as she contemplated this civilised procedure she found herself unable to execute it. She found herself calculating the arguments for and against. If the girl was buried, the extraordinary animals feeding on her would vanish from sight.

Every night she went out into the close heat of early

evening, pacing among the vegetables. Her fists tightened, and she was always close to tears. The water sprang into her eyes, welling behind the lids, and did not run, clogging her vision instead and making her momentarily crazed. Years alone in a small room with a microscope; alone on London streets with a suitcase, in a terraced house in Blackwell, with no sound coming through the walls; on buses, walking over bridges in expectation; tending a quadrangular garden to no purpose; eating alone in the local Thai pub. Eyes wide open like a pair of antennae, waiting for the revelation, the shock of a fulfilment that never came. Years of pacing and waiting and sitting on hard stools. Eventually the body gives up in some way, as if it no longer believes in the happiness that is entirely natural to it. It sours and darkens in confusion. One learns to be alone. There is failure. There are small successes. One learns not to expect an opening, a change, and the romantic belief in imminent revolution fades. One might publish a significant paper one day, but otherwise one simply *is*. The life of a scientist is often a stern sacrifice given as a gift to the future. The future entomologists not yet born. She sobbed, then caught herself. She couldn't go back as a failure, not again.

All week the weather was wet. The container on the roof filled to the brim and there she took her baths, reading with glasses and a long candle, with an umbrella opened over her. There was a lot to read in the hotel. Tagore collections left by holidaymakers, back numbers of Kolkata papers, the usual Tolstoy-length Anglo-American bestsellers, which warp in damp heat like blocks of wood. The last pages of *Chemical Ecology*, a couple of Booker Prize winners and some copies of Chinese *Vogue*, which were at least good for the photographs. The newspapers were the best-written, with their occasional outbursts of Dickensian diction and hyperbole. The worst-written were the Bookers. Alice read, but all the time she thought of the ants.

It seemed that the world was rapidly changing, becoming subtly unrecognisable. It was adapting to a shift that was too deep to perceive. The ants poured into a vacant niche where there was nothing alive but herself. Day by day they gnawed through the corpse in the trees until its small bones began to appear. She photographed them tirelessly, classified them as best she could, in the white heat of her excitement. She became convinced, in the end, that they were a new species entirely – a species that might one day bear her name. Immortality of a kind, or would she name it after the girl, without telling anyone why? The idea made her laugh, and the more she laughed, the less she missed the outside world.

VOLCANO

S IX MONTHS AFTER SHE DIVORCED HER HUSBAND, Martha Fink packed her bags and flew to Honolulu to attend the lucid-dreaming seminar at the Kalani resort on the Big Island of Hawaii. She had discovered the faithless Donald in the same position that the wife of Samuel Pepys had discovered the London diarist in 300 years previously, copulating with the family maid. 'I was deep inside her cunny,' Pepys admitted that night in his diary, 'and indeed I was at a wondrous loss to explain it.'

Martha filed for divorce. She collected the apartment on Central Park West and a considerable sum of money and then went to counselling. Lovers did not appear to replace the discarded husband. She became yet more enraged, went onto Zoloft and finally decided that her eighteen years of therapy and dietary rigour had not, in the end, helped her very much to face the endgame of biology itself. Growing old had proved a formidable calamity.

Nothing could save her from it. Not irony, certainly, or dieting or gyms or drugs or the possession of children and priceless friends. Nothing saves the declining human from the facts of her decline, except the promise of work excellently executed. And that had not saved her either, because, unluckily, she hated her work. She detested it more and more. A lawyer, she now realised, should always maintain extracurricular passions, and she had not. Her lifelong practicality and good humour had not sustained her, either, and her fine skin and aristocratic profile felt to her increasingly insufficient, if not wasted. There was now just Hawaii and dreams. The resort, run by two gay dancers, was next to an active volcano.

She spent a night in Waikiki in a high-rise hotel called the Aston. The city seemed compressed, airless and suffocating. A nightmare of dullness and saturation, of Burberry and Shiseido, of families braying on the far side of thin walls. Her room was filled with red neon.

She wept all night, strung out on sleeping pills. In the morning she went to the old Sheraton for coffee in a courtyard of banyans and squabbling pintails. It was now called the Moana Surfrider, with Soviet architecture all around. She sat there for several hours. She felt herself coming apart. The sun did not cheer her up, there was no charm whatsoever in the colonial effect – a style that could be called New Jersey Tropical.

She went to Pearl Harbor in the afternoon. Sappy music, the crowd hustled along like cattle. 'Each visitor can contemplate his innermost responses and feelings.' In the bus back to Waikiki she saw a poster for Dr Christian Harfouche, a preacher selling 'Signs, Wonders and Miracles'. The streets were full of federal detention centres and ukulele stores. Not a single attractive human. Suddenly she felt years older than forty-six.

She waited tensely for her flight to Hilo.

From the air, the islands regained their beauty. They seemed far-flung again, imposing, like sacred statues lying on their sides. The sea immense, like a visual drug that could calm the most turbulent heart. Not America, then, but Polynesia, though it was difficult to remember. She slept and her tears subsided.

A driver from Kalani was there to meet her. They drove down to Pahoa through a landscape of lava rock and papaya groves. In town they had a milkshake in a 'French café' and sat outside for a while, looking up at silver clouds shaped like anvils, static above the volcano. The driver told her, as if it were a detail she might relish, that he had transported fourteen people so far from the airport to Kalani for the Dream Express seminar. Most of them, he said cattily, were middle-aged women who looked like they were having a bad time.

'A bad time?' she said tartly. 'Do I look like I'm having a bad time?'

'No, ma'am. You look real eager.'

Eager, was she that? In a way Martha was. A wide freeway swept down to the southern coast and the lava flats, and the cliffs above which Kalani stood in its papaya woods. As the sea appeared, she felt a keen relief. The road dipped up and down past affluent hippie resorts, yoga retreats and fasting centres. A few flabby joggers shot by, all ponytails and tattoos. At the gates of Kalani, lanterns had been lit for the evening.

The resort was a considerable estate made up of groups of traditional spherical Hawaiian houses raised off the ground. In the thatched communal meeting place everyone ate a macrobiotic vegetarian buffet dinner courtesy of the resort. The owners and the dancers were dressed in Hawaiian skirts and were performing a votive dance to the volcano goddess, Pu'ah. They danced and clapped to welcome the new residents, jiggling their hips, rolling their fingers and hailing the volcano itself, which lay only a few miles away and had become active just two weeks before. At sundown a dull red glow stretched across the horizon.

Kalani hosted four different seminars at any one time. The Dream Express group was indeed, Martha saw at once, made up of middle-aged women wearing tense and confused expressions. Her heart might have sunk right then had she not determined not to let it. She braced herself for these sad, bewildered specimens, who were likely capable of comradeship and kindness. Her eye sorted through them, unable to keep from disapproving. The seminar leader, Dr Stephen DuBois, was a Stanford psychiatrist who supplemented his academic income with dream seminars in alternative-health centres. It was he who had devised a daily routine of herbs, combined with nightly use of a special pair of goggles that shot regulated beams of light into the eyes during the deepest periods of REM sleep in order to 'wake' the dreamer inside their dreams and make them conscious of them. He argued that by doing so one could enter a state of 'lucid dreaming' and consciously direct the flow of the dream itself. It was a common technique of dream therapy, but was rarely used in such a controlled environment as Kalani — a context from which normal reality had been almost entirely subtracted. DuBois claimed to be able to alter each participant's relationship to her own dreams by the use of the herb galantamine.

Aside from being a popular treatment for Alzheimer's, polio and memory disorders, galantamine in powdered form (it was derived from Caucasian snowdrop flowers) was said to induce exceptionally intense and memorable dreams by deepening REM. It looked like a white powder, like very pure cocaine.

DuBois introduced them all to one another. A psychiatrist from Rome at the end of a long nervous breakdown; a married couple from Oregon working through their difficulties; a female stockbroker from London who already possessed a 'friend' inside her dreams, who flew with her across vast oneiric landscapes. There were a few Burning Man types from the Bay area who came every year, young and wide-eyed; and two New York basket cases fleeing their catastrophic jobs and marriages. All in all, they were what Martha had expected. Bores, beaten-down shrews in decline and kooks. She didn't mind, particularly. People are what they are, and they were no more broken down by life's disappointments than she herself was. She was sure that half the women had faithless husbands who had run off with younger women. They had the trauma of that archetypal event inscribed upon their faces.

'It's very simple,' DuBois explained from the head of their trestle table. The Volcano Dance had wound down and a group of New Age square-dancers arrived at the adjoining table. 'Every night we'll take a capsule of galantamine and go to bed at a reasonable hour. We'll put on our goggles before we go to sleep. If the infrared beam wakes us up, we'll leave the goggles on and go back to sleep. Hopefully, though, we won't wake up at all. We'll simply become conscious inside our dreams.'

'Really?' said the Italian psychiatrist.

'Certainly. When that happens, you all have to remember a few basic things. To change your dream, simply reach out and rub a rough surface. A wall is perfect. The dream will change immediately and you can enjoy the next one. If you want to fly, simply start turning on the spot. You'll start flying.'

They all began to smile, to nod. It would be like hours of entertainment every night. Like cinema inside their heads. And because of the powdered snowdrop, they would remember it all.

'Every night you'll tell each other what you dreamed. It'll help you remember everything, and it'll help you write your dream journals. The dream journal will be a book you can take back with you when you have finished here. Something permanent and life-changing.'

Now they would get acquainted and then return to their thatched cabanas and prepare for the first night of lucid dreaming. It seemed to Martha a simple enough plan, and she was still tired from the long flight. The resort owners stopped by the table in their skirts, handsome, tanned, muscular gay men whom you could imagine vigorously fucking in hot tubs and saunas. The handshake gave her a twinge of arousal.

'Look over there,' the owner said. He pointed to the glow visible above the treeline. 'Looks like lava on the move.'

Across the smooth, rolling lawns Martha could see naked men strolling down towards the hot tubs surrounding the swimming pool. The resort was nudist after 9 p.m. After a chamomile tea and a few desultory chats, she said goodnight to the group and walked back to her cabana. A high moon illuminated the edge of the jungle.

She took the galantamine capsule, lay under the mosquito nets hanging above her bed and attuned herself to the rhythmic chirping of the tree frogs. She put on the cumbersome goggles and adjusted the strap so that it did not squeeze her face too tightly. Then her exhaustion took over. She was too tired to care that the goggles were uncomfortable or that the frogs were loud because the windows had no glass. She slept without thinking about sleeping, and soon the REM cycle had swept her up.

She began to dream at once, but later she could not remember it as clearly as she had hoped. She did recall that in this dream she was standing in a hotel bar, drinking a glass of port. Rain was falling outside and behind her there seemed to be a roaring fire. When she turned to look at it, she felt the fire's heat touch her face and she saw the piercing red beam of the machine inside the goggles flood her consciousness with its colour. Unused to this intrusion, she awoke immediately and tore off the goggles.

The first thing she heard was the frogs. The moon had moved position and shone directly into the room, touching the foot of the bed. She was drenched in sweat. She got up and went to the screened window. Nightjars sang in the papayas. She felt intensely awake and therefore restless. She put on her flip-flops and a sarong and climbed down the steps of her cabana into the long, wet grass. At the end of the lawn shone the pool, wreathed with steam from the all-night jacuzzi. She made her way to the hot tub, tiny frogs popping out of the grass around her feet, and when she reached the pool she disrobed again and sank into the water, naked. Tall palms stood around the pool. The moon shone between them.

As she floated on her back she could feel that something in this idyllic scene was not quite right. It was too serene. Then, from far off, she heard a wild whoop of male voices. She sat up. A group of naked men was running down the lawn towards her. They ran in a line, their erections flapping about, and they headed straight towards the pool. Startled, she leaped out of the water, grabbed her clothes and darted into the dripping papaya trees on the far side of the footpath. The men, impervious to her presence, jumped en masse into the pool and filled it with phalli and noise. She reached out and touched the rough bark of one of the trees, and as she did so, she found herself back in her bed, the goggles still fixed to her head. Rain was pouring outside the window.

She tore off the goggles, gasping, her body drenched with sweat. The downpour was so heavy that the frogs had fallen silent, and all she could hear was the mechanical dripping from the edge of the window frame and the rustle beyond, in the forest. Martha got up a second time and her bewilderment made her reach out and touch the insect screen to see if it was real. She wrote down her dream straight away.

In the morning the sun returned, but there was a taste of burnt wood on the air, borne from afar, and a reddish dust that seemed to linger over the treeline. In the cafeteria the group was eagerly discussing the eruption of the volcano during the night – one of a series of eruptions, it seemed.

'It kept me up all night,' the London broker said, eyeing Martha up and down. 'Didn't you hear it?'

'Nothing,' Martha said. 'Did it rain all night?'

'It rained, but there was one hour when it was pure

moonlight, peaceful as can be. I went down to the pool.' The broker lowered her voice. 'Unfortunately, it was occupied. Men are strange, don't you think?' The woman had bossy, aggressive green eyes that possessed a knack for mentally undressing other women and lingered now on Martha's cracked lips.

'I slept badly,' Martha admitted, rubbing her eyes. 'The rain woke me up.'

'Personally, the galantamine does nothing for me. You?'

Martha shrugged. 'I have nothing to compare it to.'

During the day they listened to DuBois lecture in one of the rotunda meeting halls, and Martha dozed in a corner, feeling that she had not enjoyed enough sleep. It was a hot day, and after lunch she went for a walk by herself along the coastal road where the woods were thicker. She walked for miles until she came to a grey beach under the cliffs, where sundry hippies and half-stoned locals sat drinking kava and smoking reefers. Beyond the beach lay flats of black lava that reached out into the sea. She went down onto the beach and lay in the roasting sun for a while. Her grief welled up inside her until the tears flowed down her face. No one could see her there. She emptied herself out and breathed heavily until her body was reoxygenated.

Later that evening she walked down to the lava again with some of the other dream women. One of them was a mosaic artist from Missoula, Montana, and another sold hot tubs for a living. Makeshift kava cafés made of driftwood had been set up on the rock shelves, and wild travellers on motorbikes appeared out of nowhere, racing across the lava with their lights blazing. The women drank kava accompanied by

seaweed honey out of small paper cups and watched the
red glow of the volcano in the distance; three divorced
women, two of them long into middle age, waiting for an
improbable turn of events. Ageing European hippies in feather earrings, with names like Firewind and Crystal Eye,
tried to pick them up.

Martha felt supremely detached from everyone. She
didn't want to talk about the love lives of the other women.
Everyone's love life, she thought, was more or less the same
and, to be disgusted, one only had to remember that seventy
million women were saying exactly the same things to their
friends at that very same moment.

'I only left him six months ago,' one of the women was
saying, as if they had all known each other for years. 'He
never went down on me, either. I know he was sleeping
around—'

'They're *all* sleeping around.'

'Does a fling every two years count as sleeping around?'

'Maybe we could fuck one of those filthy hippies. Firewind is quite sexy.'

They drank the kava and became more stoned.

'Mine never went down on me, either. They get lazy after
a while. No one stays with anyone ever, unless they're
Christians.'

'I wouldn't sleep with Firewind. He has blue fingernails.'

'You wouldn't notice in the dark.'

'Yes, but feather earrings?'

To Martha, the red glow in the night sky was more com-
pelling than the conversation. It seemed incomprehensible
that a volcano was active so close to them and yet no one

seemed concerned. The molten lava in the distance must be moving down to the sea. The scene must be one of terror and grandeur, yet no one saw it. She thought about it as they licked salty seaweed honey off their fingers.

She dreamed of her husband that night. She was cutting his toenails in a sea of poppies and his toes were bleeding onto her scissors. He laughed and writhed as she ripped his toes with the blades. The galantamine made her remember it vividly. In the morning she skipped the dream seminar, in which she had no longer had much interest, and rented a motorbike from the front desk. She took a night bag and some money and decided to play the day by ear. She drove to Pahoa and on through Kurtistown until she reached Route 11, which turned west towards Volcanoes National Park. Soon she was rising through the Ola'a Forest.

At the top of the rising road stood the strange little town of Volcano. It was a cluster of houses on the edge of one of the craters, lush with rainforest. She parked by a large hotel and walked into a wonderful old lobby with a fireplace and oil paintings of volcanic eruptions on the walls. There was no one there. She wandered around the room for a while, admiring the Hawaiian native artefacts, then noticed a spacious bar on the far side of the reception desk. She went in.

Enormous windows wrapped around the room. Through them the entire crater could be seen. It was a pale-charcoal colour, a vast field of uneven rock scored with ridges from which a glittering steam rose hundreds of feet into the air. A pair of antlers hung above the bar itself, next to a 'volcano warning meter', a mocking toy with a red arrow that pointed to various states of imminent catastrophe.

At the bar sat an elderly gentleman in a flat cloth cap, dipping his pinky into a dry Martini. He looked up at her with watery, slightly bloody eyes in which there was a faint trace of lechery. He wore a hopsack jacket of surpassing ugliness and a dark-brown tie with a gold pin in it. The barman was the same age, a sprightly sixty or so, and his eyes contained the same sardonic and predatory glint of interest in the forty-six-year-old woman who was entering their domain.

'*Aloha*,' the barman said, and the solitary drinker repeated it.

Martha echoed the word and, not knowing what to do, sat down at the bar as well.

'Going down to the crater?' the capped man asked.

'Yes. I just wanted a stiff drink first.'

'A good idea. I recommend the house cocktail. "The Crater".'

'What is it?'

'White rum, pineapple juice, cane sugar, Angostura bitters, a grapefruit segment, a dash of Cointreau, a cherry, dark rum, a sprig of mint, an egg white and a hint of kava,' said the barman.

'I'll have a glass of white wine.'

'The Crater'll set you up better.'

She looked around the volcano paintings, at the flickering fire, the inferno landscape smouldering beyond the windows, and finally she noticed that the man in the cap was halfway through a Crater. *Oh, why the fuck not?*

'Okay,' she said, 'I'll have one.'

They all laughed.

'Try walking across that crater after one of those,' the

drinker said. 'The name's Alan Pitchfork. No, it's not my real name, but, hey, we're at the Volcano Hotel in Volcano, so who the hell cares?'

She took off her scarf and sunglasses.

'I'm Martha Prickhater. That is my real name.'

'Oh, is it now?'

Alan leaned over to touch her glass with his. Her eyes strayed up to the ancient clock underneath the antlers and she was surprised to see that it was already 2 p.m.

'Are you a local?' she asked politely.

'Moved here from Nebraska in 1989. Never looked back. Retired geologist.'

'How nice. Did you come here with your wife?'

'Died in Nebraska, 1989.'

'Ah, I see. I'm sorry.'

'Long time ago, not to worry.'

'Well, cheers.'

She sipped the amazing concoction. It tasted like the effluent from a chewing-gum factory.

'Cheers,' the man said, without taking a sip of his own. 'Staying at the hotel?' he went on, eyeing her. 'Nice rooms here. Traditional style. African antiques in some of them. Views over the volcanoes.'

'I hadn't thought about it.'

'Well, you should think about it. You get a good night's sleep up here in Volcano, if a good night's sleep is what you want.'

'I'll bear it in mind,' she said testily.

'You should. Bear it in mind, I mean. There's no better spot for watching the sunset.'

She finished her drink, said her farewells and went back into the sunlight of the parking lot where her bike stood, the only vehicle there. She drove down the lonely road to the trails that led to the crater. She chained up the bike and wandered down, through the rainforest dripping with water from a shower she had apparently not noticed. The trail led to the edge of the lava crater, rich with the odour of sulphur. She walked out into the middle of the stone plain.

In the sun the wreaths of rising steam looked paler, more ethereal. She lay down and basked, taking off her shoes and pushing her soles into the slightly warm rock. Looking up, she could not see the hotel at all. To the south the sky was hazed by the continuing eruption of the neighbouring crater and soon, she could tell, that haze would reach the sun and eclipse it. She was tipsy and slow and her body ached for something. A man's touch, maybe. The touch of a rogue.

It was early evening when she got back to the hotel. The fire was roaring high and yet there was still no sign of other guests. She hesitated, because she was not quite sure why she had come back at all. The barman was on a ladder, dusting one of the oil paintings. He stepped down to welcome her back.

'Want a room?' he said hopefully.

'Not exactly.'

'I can give you thirty per cent off.'

It was clear the place was empty.

'Dinner?' he tried, stepping gingerly around her. 'A drink at the bar? Two-for-one?'

She peered into the bar and saw that the same drinker was

still there, a little the worse for wear, but still upright on his seat, another Crater in front of him. He caught her eye and winked. Behind him, the windows had dimmed and only the outline of the crater could still be made out, illumined by the red glow that never seemed to diminish. The men told her the hotel's clientele had vanished after volcano warnings had been issued two nights earlier.

'Volcano warnings?' she said, sitting down again at the bar.

'Red alert.' Alan smiled, raising his glass.

The barman began to prepare another Crater without waiting for her to order.

'Yeah,' he drawled. 'They run like ants as soon as there's a red alert. But Alan here and I know better. We've seen a hundred red alerts, haven't we, Alan?'

'A thousand.'

'See?' The barman served her drink with a yellow paper parasol. 'It's perfectly safe to stay the night, if you so wish.'

'I wasn't thinking of it.'

'It's a long ride back to Kalani,' the geologist remarked. 'In the dark, I mean.'

She let it go.

They turned and watched the firework display outside for a while. The eruption had intensified, and it was easy to imagine the flows of lava dripping into the sea only a few miles away. The glow cast itself against the walls of the bar, turning the room a dark red. Martha gripped her drink and tilted it into her mouth, watching the geologist drum his fingers on the bar. Who was he and where did he live? He never seemed to leave the hotel bar. He asked her how she had found the crater, and he added that he had watched her cross it from this same window.

Soon, she was tipsy again. Something inside her told her that a motorbike ride back to Kalani at this hour would be suicidal. That 'something' was simultaneously a desire to cave in, to book a room upstairs with African antiques and a view of the eruption. But it seemed, at the same time, inexpressibly vulgar to do so. To be alone in a hotel like this with two decrepit old men. She tossed back the dregs of her disgusting drink and ordered another.

'That's the spirit,' the barman said. 'It's on me.'

Alan disputed the right to buy the drink and soon she was obliged to thank him.

'Shall we go sit by the fire?' he said.

In the main room where the fire crackled and hissed, the Hawaiian masks had taken on a lurid menace. They stared down at the odd couple sinking into the horsehair armchairs. The geologist put his drink down on a leather-surfaced side-table and told her a long story about the last major eruption, when he had spent a week alone in Volcano, smoking cigars at the bar and enjoying the view. People were cowards.

'Personally, I'm not afraid of lava. It's a quick death, as good as any other, if not better.'

'That's philosophical of you.'

'I'm a geologist. You have beautiful legs, by the way. If I may say.'

She started with surprise and displeasure and instinctively pulled her skirt down an inch or so.

'No, don't cross them,' he went on. 'Don't feel awkward.'

Instead of feeling awkward, she felt warm and insulted.

Her face began to flush hot and she wanted to throw her drink in his face. She controlled herself, however, and tried to smile it off.

'Thank you, if that's a compliment.'

He said it was, and he wasn't going to apologise for it. His scaly, wrinkled skin seemed to shine under the equally anti-quated lamps. After a while she heard a quiet but insistent pitter-patter against the windows that was not rain. The man smiled. It was ash falling.

'Sometimes,' Alan said, 'I swear it's like the last days of Pompeii.'

As the evening wore on, it became obvious that she would have to stay overnight. The barman told her that she could have the Serengeti Suite half-price. She agreed. He served them sandwiches with Hawaiian relishes, and more Craters. Martha began to see double. Eventually, she decided to go up to her room and lock the door. It was safer that way. She got up and staggered to the stairwell, while the geologist sat back and watched her leave. They said goodnight, or at least she thought he did, and she pulled herself up the squeaky stairs with a pounding head.

The suite was cold, and she left the main light off while she lit the glassed-in gas fire. Then she opened the curtains and let the red glow invade the rooms. On the horizon, beyond the crater's rim, globs of white light seemed to shine behind a frazzled line of trees. She lay on the damp bed and kicked off her shoes. There were Zulu shields on the walls and pictures of Masai spearing black-maned lions under the suns of long ago. The chairs looked like something from a luxury safari lodge. She lay there and grew subtly bored, discontented with her solitude. She wondered what they would be doing at Kalani right then. Dancing in skirts to the volcano goddess around a fire, drinking their kava with marshmallow or doing 'personhood square-dancing' in the woods with paper hats. She lay there for an hour, fidgeting and feeling her emptiness and loneliness well up within her, then got up again and went to the bathroom to re-brush her hair. The antagonising red light filled her with restless anxiety, but also an itching desire not to be alone. She looked at herself in the mirror and saw, for once, what was actually there. A lean, pale, frightened-looking little girl of forty-six. She put some salve on her lips and dusted her face with powder.

The hotel creaked like an old ship. Wind sang through empty rooms. She went out into the corridor with its thick red carpet and felt her way along the hallway, listening carefully. She could hear a man singing to himself in one of the rooms, no doubt the repulsive geologist. She thought of his slack grey skin and his leery eyes and she felt a moment's quickening lust-disgust. What was arousing to her was that she was alone and no one could ever discover what she was doing. She ran her finger along each door as she passed. As if responding to her telepathic signal, one of them finally opened and the familiar face, with its leprechaun eyes, popped out.

'So there you are,' Alan said. He put a silencing finger between them so that she wouldn't reply.

His room was exactly the same as hers, but it was plunged in complete darkness, as if he had been prepared to go to bed. She sat down on the bed. Soon his hands were all over her, the scaliness visible only by the light of the volcano. His dry, slightly perfumed skin was against hers, though she refused to look at his face. Instead she kept her eye on the red glow and on the Zulu shields on the walls. He told her they were alone, as he put it, 'on a live volcano', and the thought seemed to make him smile. All these years sitting in that damn bar, he said, hoping that a beautiful woman like her would walk in. Up to then, she never had. No, sir, not until then. She had walked into the bar and he knew, he said, as soon as he laid eyes on her, that she would sleep with him.

'You did?' she whispered.

'I saw it in your face. You would sleep with an ugly old man like me.'

He gripped her shoulders and kissed them slowly, as if there were kiss-spots arranged in a predetermined line along them. His mouth was dry and papery, but not untitillating, precisely because it was a human mouth. She could accept it in the dark. From behind, he slipped a hand between her legs and she let herself roll to one side, sinking into sheets scented by contact with an inferior cologne. He pulled her arms behind her and, perhaps for the first time in a year, she forgot that her treacherous ex-husband existed. The geologist closed hungrily around her, and before long he was inside her, desperate and greedy and relaxed at the same time, and although she knew it was a dream she was not sure how to terminate it or change it.

She reached out and stroked the wooden surface of the bedstead, then the cold surface of the wall, but still the old man held her pinned down and pumped away at her. *The goggles*, she thought. When was the beam of red light going to wake her? And soon she heard rain, or was it ash, pitter-pattering on the windows and tinkling like falling sand on the sills. The man gnawed her neck, at her shoulder blades, and told her he was going to penetrate her all night long. His perspiration dropped onto her face. She flinched, but still she didn't wake up.

THE WHITE GODS

TAYLOR MILDRED WOKE BEFORE HIS WIFE THAT morning, a hundred miles from Dalanzadgad near the Gurvan range, and found a fire burning in the open-air pit that they had built the night before. The guides were awake, too, and drinking tea around their DVD player, watching *Mr Right* in Chinese with Mongolian subtitles. Their fingers glistened with butter. A Thermos of hot coffee had appeared on the tarpaulin next to his bed and, after putting on his desert boots, he took it outside to the pit and sipped from it, with the heat of the fire at his back. No dreams, no symbols in the night. He felt washed clean in some way, having benefited from those hours far from the world and its vaudevilles. The snow from the night before had melted away. A faint light bore down upon the plain. His wife and daughter were still asleep and the wind had calmed a little, though countless blades of grass trembled in unison, forming the illusion of a herbaceous sea.

He took the Thermos with him and walked, stretching shoulder blades cramped by a rough sleep, and when he had woken up a little he wondered at the scores of pieces of flat rock scattered around their camp and extending as far as a small tumulus a hundred yards to the east. They were inscribed with images clearly made by humans. Men with spears, or stars and moons broken into fragments. Here and there, an oblong stele of the same stone, as high as his waist. 'A graveyard,' Ider the guide had told him the night before around the fire, gesturing at the mounds of dark-violet and slate-coloured stones, three millennia silent, that lay around them, undisturbed by centuries of high winds.

The American had not quite believed him until that very moment. Now he saw that their horses had moved quietly away from the graves. He made a mental note to tell Hannah later; his daughter Rosalind would find it amusing as well. Who knew that horses sensed such things? He strolled over to the animals and stroked them as the sun appeared on the flat horizon. They were slightly spooked, he could tell, and their nostrils flared. It was probably just their horror at being petted by a television producer.

He went to Rosalind's tent and gently woke her from the enchanted sleep of twelve-year-olds. He placed her pair of cream Guidi hiking boots by her head and whispered into her ear, 'It's sunny outside – get up!'

They had breakfast as a family around the fire pit with the tents flapping around them. 'Warm days in the Gobi,' he reminded Hannah, 'cold nights.' But the mornings were somehow even colder than the nights. It was exactly what he had promised them for their Gobi adventure. The three men accompanying them from the Gobi Sands Company made them buckwheat pancakes with sour milk and American coffee, as Taylor had prescribed. Millionaires on private trips can determine all the smallest details; they can afford months of preparatory riding tuition on their own ranch in Rancho

Santa Fe. *We're all three of us cowboys now*, he thought with satisfaction as he watched the small horses being saddled in the sunlight.

Rosalind was now in her pretty boots, in the fox-fur hat the staff had given her as a welcoming present at the lodge a week earlier. Her long hair had been brushed out to form auburn streams that ran down her shoulders on either side. Her mother, in a lavish Shetland roll-neck and suede boots of her own – stylish even a hundred miles from the nearest town – brushed a strand away from her daughter's ear. In the heat of the fire their faces had become pink. The pancakes gave them an additional inner heat. Rosalind said that she had slept with many a dream. She had got up in the middle of the night and wandered out through the graveyard.

'You did?' her mother said.

'I picked up a stone and brought it back with me.'

Taylor glanced over at the Mongolians, hoping they hadn't overheard.

'You know,' he said to his daughter, 'you are not supposed to do that. Shall we go and put it back?'

'Why?'

'Because, honey . . . it just isn't done.'

'It's only a stone.'

'Then why did you pick it up in the first place?'

'It has a picture of a sun on it. It's *so* pretty. I'm going to take it home and show my friends.'

'I understand. It's not a bad idea. But we can't.'

The girl sulked, rolling her eyes. 'Why don't you ask Ider if I can?'

'I'm not saying anything to him. He'll be angry. We are

going to go out, you and me, and put it back where you got it from.'

The stone that she had taken was about the size of her palm. It was worn smooth by the elements and yet the image of the sun was still gracefully clear, but bent and peculiarly irregular. She passed it to her father reluctantly and he took it, without saying anything to the guides. They had been instructed not to disturb anything inside the graveyard, however insignificant it might seem. Graveyards were the property of the state.

The mounds of graves where Rosalind had found the stone lay upon the small tumulus, reached by a path worn into the hill's surface. From there, at a modest elevation, father and daughter wandered among the steles and mounds as the sun's rays crossed the plain and turned it a pale icy gold. But Rosalind could not remember exactly where she had found the stone. There were hundreds of pieces lying about on the flat top of the hillock. Taylor tossed it randomly onto one and told her not to mention it to anyone. They walked back to the camp.

'Does it matter,' she said, 'that you threw it onto the wrong grave?'

'How do we know it wasn't the right one?'

They laughed together and for a moment he took her hand and swung it playfully. At the camp, Ider was waiting for them.

'I saw you went up there last night,' he said to Rosalind. 'Did you sleep better afterwards?'

'I did.'

The guide was a palaeontology graduate, unlike the two others, who were local nomads who hired themselves out to the lodge during the tourist season. His English was perfect, honed at school in Oregon.

'Shall we go see some dinosaurs then?' Ider suggested.

They rode on five horses due north-east for three hours, passing through arroyos thick with sagebrush and nitre bushes. Over the steppes of feathergrass, herds of black horses twitched and ran with the nervousness of swarming birds. By midday it was almost warm, the wintry air transformed by sun.

In the foothills of the Gurvan they came into the shadows of desert cliffs. They stopped for their daily picnic and the freezing shots of Chinggis vodka that the Americans were slowly getting used to, knocked back with cucumber sandwiches and *buuz* dumplings. Here in the foothills, Ider explained to them, he and his professor had found a rare fragment of a Tarbosaurus. His professor had made his name with it.

They climbed up one of the hills, dry as solidified ash. Taylor and Hannah hung behind the others and the tensions between them that had paralysed their marriage over the preceding months began to loosen. The many problems with Rosalind at school and in therapy had begun to seem more distant. Was California, Hannah was now thinking to herself, really the right place for them at this stage in their lives?

'She seems happier here,' she said aloud, gazing after Rosalind as she scampered ahead with Ider. 'I wonder why? Maybe it's being away from school. Away from social media.'

'She's at a difficult age. A tender age.'

Bullshit, she thought. Instead she said, 'We must have involved her in all our arguments. It's been bad for her. We really shouldn't.'

'Well, we agreed on that before, didn't we?'

'You just need to spend more time with her. Give your career a break for a change. Try it.'

He nodded, to avoid a spat. 'You're probably right. I've been selfish, a little absent.' *But then*, he thought simultaneously, *I brought her here for her birthday, didn't I? It could be worse.*

That night a Soviet-era UAZ van arrived at camp from the distant lodge, with three young girls and a sound system manned by three boys of the same age. They were dancers from a local school. With light projected against the tumulus, they danced to traditional music in white deerskin boots and headdresses. A trestle table had been set up and a meal of mutton *korkhoz* made with hot stones from the lodge kitchen was served with vodka and lemonade. The boys played *morin khuur* fiddles in a gritty wind that drowned them out. Soon they were all drunk. The girls and boys danced together. 'Terrific,' Taylor shouted at no one in particular, 'simply terrific!' He too was drunk, Hannah noticed with disgust.

He began dancing with Ider, throwing up his arms like a ballerina. Hannah began to tire of the whole charade. A full moon, an out-of-control husband. Surely there were better things in life. She suggested to Rosalind that they retire.

Once they were in their sleeping bags next to each other they read a few pages of *The Hobbit* together, and then turned off the lamp and listened to the fading party.

'Mummy, did you hear wolves last night?'

'Wolves?'

'Ider said there were wolves. I heard them. I think they woke me up.'

'They don't come near humans, darling.'

As she said this, Hannah was not entirely sure if it was true. She lay awake for a long time, turning it over in her mind. Her daughter was highly sensitive, attuned to things that many people did not notice. Maybe even wolves. She had a slightly autistic predisposition. It was entirely possible that she had, in fact, heard wolves in the far distance. Hannah strained to hear them now. The music outside had been cut, and all she could hear were the eternally soughing desert gales that picked up at night as the skies cleared with a hard starlight. Neither she nor Rosalind heard Taylor crash into his own berth much later. He was too drunk to stay awake for longer than a few seconds.

When Rosalind started back into consciousness a few hours later she realised at once, without needing to verify it, that she was the only one in the camp awake. She sat up quickly and found her back drenched with sweat. Her face was damp and feverish.

Outside their tent the land was lit up by moonlight as if by stationary flares. In that white glare the rocks threw shadows as brilliant as the light itself. The staff lay asleep in their tent, snoring audibly through the fabric walls. Closer to their tent, she saw a longer shadow over the gravel. It was cast by a girl standing a few feet from the tent ropes. A girl who had appeared out of nowhere, it seemed, but perhaps she had come with the Soviets and been left behind in the course of the drunken revelry.

She wore a leather dress, which might have been traditional, with string sandals. Her hair was tied up in a coil on top of her head and held in place with coloured ribbons. In the bright light she looked pale, but her arms and hands were tattooed.

'Did you come with the dancers?' Rosalind asked.

The girl signalled that Rosalind should stay quiet. Then, as if stating something tremendously obvious, she pointed up towards the moon. Her face seemed for a moment to slip out of focus. Rosalind turned at a slight sound behind her and saw the horses shying away from them.

STUNG BY THE COLD air on her face a few hours later, Hannah rolled over and threw a hand towards her slumbering daughter, but found the sleeping bag empty. She sat up and called out Rosalind's name. Outside, through the zippered fabric door, she could sense the onset of colder weather. It was snowing. Lightly, but with effect.

Pulling on her boots, she thrust herself outside into a world whitened with swirling flakes. The horizon was no longer clear, and even the nearby tumulus was shrouded by the slow-motion downpour.

She called to Rosalind again, her voice falling flat in the snowscape. She already felt her daughter's calamitous absence. Hannah walked as far as the tumulus and called repeatedly, but the girl was not there. She walked back to the staff tent and saw that they were all still asleep, so Rosalind could not have departed somewhere with one of them. There were still five horses shivering in the snow. She went to her husband and woke him.

'Get up, you drunkard. Your daughter has gone missing.'

When he didn't rouse himself she emptied a small bottle of mineral water into his face.

Abruptly, commotion and panic began.

'Was that really necessary?' he snarled.

Taylor ran to the staff tent and shouted at them as well. They quickly ascertained that the Guidi suede boots were missing. So Rosalind must have taken off in them. But there were no tracks in the snow. Ider, severely hungover, staggered outside and surveyed the tents. Not a single footprint.

He called to the lodge on the satellite phone and then to a nomad camp ten miles to the south. They were the only people to have a phone that he knew of. Tending their herds over vast distances, they would be the most likely to find Rosalind if she was lost.

But already, seeing the thickening snow, a terrifying idea had occurred to Ider. How long would she last in these conditions?

He rode out with the parents in a frantic circumnavigation of the camp. An hour passed and at the end of it the snow finally cleared. A blue sky bathed the horizons. Then they understood the obvious: Rosalind had simply disappeared. Exasperated and stunned, they came to a standstill while Hannah began screaming at the steppe. They dismounted for a while and Ider talked on the phone. Rosalind had not walked back to the lodge, which would in any case have been a remarkable feat. The nomads were looking for her further away from the camp, out on the plains.

Hannah took Taylor aside and whispered to him. 'What if . . . it's the nomads who are the problem?'

'What?'

'They could have done anything. Hasn't that occurred to Ider?'

But Taylor could not see how they could suggest such a vile thing to the young Mongolian, without insulting his people. Yet still – instantaneously, through no volition of his own – the idea turned poisonously inside his mind. A young girl, alone and powerless out on the steppes. Who was he to say that they wouldn't have touched her?

On the ride back he slowly filled with rage. He talked with the lodge manager on the phone and gave his suspicions free rein.

'Who are these *nomads*?' he kept shouting.

At length a Land Cruiser arrived from the lodge with the manager himself, David Batbayar. He was a Mongol-American entrepreneur whose clientele included film stars and Silicon Valley barons. Large, but rarely seen at the lodge that he ran, he blustered and soothed like a pro. He knew Americans and how to handle them. Suave, yet also terrified at the prospect of a scandal, Batbayar tried to calm the Mildreds down. Management had decided, he explained, to wait before calling the police in Dalanzadgad.

But as they were talking, the satellite phone rang. The manager's face shone with relief. The nomads out by an old Soviet military base an hour's drive from the camp said they had found Rosalind asleep in one of its abandoned radio sheds. She was alive and entirely unharmed.

'There. Didn't I tell you? Thank Tengri!' the manager beamed.

At the abandoned communications base, a nomad on an ancient motorbike appeared. An old man in second-hand military fatigues, he had waited for them patiently. The girl, he said, was still asleep and he could not wake her. Hannah rushed in to find her. Rosalind was asleep without her boots on and lay in a pile of yellowing Russian newspapers, wrapped in a leather gown of some kind and, beneath it, completely naked. When her mother kissed her face, Rosalind opened her eyes and smiled. She had no memory of how she came to be there, or where her clothes had gone.

Back in the security of permanent *ger* tents with stone foundations and hot water, Hannah and Taylor had dinner that night with their daughter, alone in the lodge restaurant. The snow beyond the windows was now an onslaught and the steppe had apparently entered its Siberian winter.

'And you really can't remember how you got there?' Hannah asked Rosalind, who was eating shovel-loads of dumplings.

'Nothing.'

'But you got up in the middle of the night? And went for a walk?'

'She might have been sleepwalking,' Taylor said peremptorily.

'My God!' The tears rolling down Hannah's face seemed to go unnoticed.

'It's all right, Mummy, nothing happened.'

'But where are your Guidi boots, for heaven's sake?'

'I must have lost them.'

'How could you have lost them?'

The girl burst into a dry laugh. 'I'm so glad I lost them!'

Taylor noticed that something in his daughter had changed. There was something subtly glossy about her face. Her eyelashes seemed to have grown a little longer, though that was impossible. Surely he was imagining it. She had never before eaten with such an appetite. In some indefinable way her sweetness had altered. *Trauma*, he thought bitterly. *It must have been the trauma she has suffered*. But what had been the trauma?

Later he lay in the *ger* with Hannah while Rosalind slept in the unit next door. There was something wrong with her, he insisted to his wife.

'Thank God she's alive,' Hannah hissed. 'If you hadn't been so drunk, maybe this wouldn't have happened.'

'Me?'

'You were too drunk to wake up when she did.'

And you? he thought. *Did you wake up – tediously sober as you were?*

In his own *ger*, meanwhile, Ider lit incense sticks that night and prayed to the bodhisattva Migjid Janraisig.

He too had noticed the new-found strangeness in the American girl. Like Taylor, his mind had turned inexorably to dark theories. Yet he put them aside. In his dreams he met a shaman and followed her out into the desert, where they talked about the matter. The shaman told him not to trust Rosalind, or any of the others, or to speak to them as frankly as he usually did. The girl was not who he thought she was, the shaman opined. She was an imposter, a facsimile of a girl. The shaman crouched in the sand and plunged a hand into the soil and lifted it up, letting the grains fall through her fingers. She said, 'You should never have let that fool come here – that man from afar. It was a mistake. You should have her exorcised. In the Lord Buddha is our salvation.'

In the morning Ider suggested to the Mongolian staff and to the manager that they should indeed call in a shaman and have Rosalind properly exorcised. He would explain it to the Americans and ask them if they approved.

'A shaman?' Taylor burst out when Ider told him his plan.

'You are sceptical, Mr Mildred. But it will work. It will bring back her memory.'

'Rubbish. It's vile.'

'But,' Hannah said quietly to Taylor, 'with this snow, we can't go anywhere. We could try it, unless you have a better option? You were the one who suggested there was something wrong with her.'

'*Try it?*'

'We're not going to find a doctor out here. Are we?'

For a fleeting moment he wondered if Hannah was losing her bearings in a way that was not entirely dissimilar to the disorientation of their daughter.

As if on cue, and to Ider's surprise, Hannah then told her husband that he shouldn't be so contemptuous of local beliefs.

'Me,' he hissed, 'contemptuous of local beliefs?'

'It might work in some way,' she stammered. 'Let's be open-minded, shall we?'

'Are you serious?'

'It won't hurt her, Taylor. It might even heal her a little . . .'

'No.'

But the *boo* did come at seven in the evening, obstinately summoned by Ider. He was a man who lived alone in the desert forty miles away. More than eighty years old and covered with moles, but he still possessed the sparkling, mysterious health of the steppes. He arrived on a motorbike with bags stuffed full of herbs, dressed in a long, dark-scarlet tunic decorated with

severed eagle heads, and fox furs draped over his back. He was
a 'black shaman' who was antagonistic to Buddhism, not a
'yellow' or Buddhist-friendly one. His was the old religion of
the hunting tribes of the north. But Taylor refused to see him
and refused to let him anywhere near his daughter. He packed
fifty dollars into the man's hand and told him to leave.

'That intruding spirit is not a member of the fifty-five white
gods,' the *boo* said in Mongolian, 'nor one of the forty-four
black gods. Nor is she of the seventy-seven earth mothers.'

Yes, Ider thought, *the gods*. He had forgotten about this
lore during his years as a Westernised graduate student. But
if the spirit was not one of these innumerable gods, what and
who was it?

Taylor turned to Ider with a jovial sneer. 'What's he
saying?'

'He's saying he cannot help you.'

'Thank God for that, then. We don't need his help. Tell
him to bugger off.'

Ider said to the *boo*, 'The foreigner thanks you humbly
and asks you to bear him in mind.'

The Mildreds had another family dinner that night and
Hannah remarked that no other guests had so far arrived at
the lodge.

'We scared them off,' Taylor joked, now in a much better
mood.

Rosalind gazed out at the plain and her eyes seemed to
have changed colour slightly. They had a pinch of greyness
in them now.

'It's better that way,' she said slowly. 'I'm glad we scared
them off.'

'I asked the manager,' Taylor said, 'if we can drive back to the capital tomorrow. I think it'd be best, no?'

'What's the capital?'

'Why, the capital city, darling. Don't you remember it?'

Rosalind shook her head.

'Does it have people?'

Hannah and Taylor exchanged an anxious glance.

'Don't you remember us taking the aeroplane at the airport last week?

'Airport?'

'Where planes land and fly out of.'

She's like a three-year-old again, Taylor thought, gritting his teeth. *She's lost her mind.* 'Your grandma will be happy to see you again,' he tried gently.

'Grandma?'

Hannah's eye filled with tears and she began to choke quietly. 'Let's forget today and go to sleep,' she said. 'Let's forget all about it.'

At a loss, Taylor put down his fork and reached for the Chinese wine set on the table. His daughter was eclipsed to him – to them – and yet she seemed delighted with everything.

On his way out of the grounds an hour earlier, the irritated *boo* had been accosted once again by Ider, who wanted to know what he really thought.

'I told you, she's possessed,' the old man said bluntly, as though it was a stupid question. 'But there's nothing I can do about it. White or black gods have nothing to do with it.'

Ider thought over the previous two days. He had said nothing about seeing Rosalind walk to the tumulus that night, because he wanted to preserve the trust and discretion that existed between him and the wealthy foreign clients. It was a delicate balance. He had kept it to himself, in fact, for a number of reasons. He had seen her steal a funerary rock from the graveyard and bring it back with her to the camp. She was so innocent that he had had no choice but to be gentle with her. And indeed when he went out to greet her a little way from the camp, he had been very gentle with her. He had merely asked to see the stone and she had handed it over for inspection willingly. It had a prehistoric sun drawn upon it, but a curious one. Its edge was uneven, suggesting the depiction of an eclipse. 'You know,' he said to her, 'you'll have to put it back tomorrow.'

The following morning he had watched Taylor toss the rock randomly among the others. Therein, Ider knew, lay the problem. The grave had been disturbed and not restored to its original condition. All along it had filled him with dread, though he had said nothing. He could have replaced the stone himself, he supposed, but something had held him back. A subtle fear, an uncertainty. Now the Americans were anxious to be gone, understandably enough. They wanted to get their daughter to a psychiatrist as soon as possible – it was the Californian way. The family had wanted to abandon that tactic for a while at least, but as soon as a problem arose they reverted back to it in a heartbeat.

It was with uncustomary alacrity therefore that Ider organised the two cars that would drive the family back to Ulaanbaatar. He too wanted them gone as soon as possible. He had begun to feel that their presence violated a sacred space. They had blundered into a world whose supernatural rules they didn't understand and they had disturbed its elegant balance. Perhaps the girl would regain her memory when she was back among civilisation's comforts, but now he neither knew nor understood the full consequences.

There was a solemn departure ceremony, as was standard for guests. Taylor simmered with some undeclared anger to which he had not given full expression. Was he feeling a guilt that his conscious mind could not understand? This was the most generous assessment Ider could come up with.

'We're sorry for the unfortunate episode,' Ider said to him as they shook hands a little coldly.

Taylor said nothing, but directed a look of contempt at his spouse.

'I'm sure Rosalind will feel better soon,' Ider said reassuringly. But neither man believed it.

Ider watched their Land Cruiser recede to the horizon among the wild camels, then resolved to put them out of his mind as best he could. Instead, he brooded alone inside his *ger*. He drank heavily in order to clear his mind rather than to numb it. It was his duty, he began to realise, to restore the grave to its original state. The state that its creators had long ago intended. That was the least he could do in the circumstances, and he had found the courage to do it.

Accordingly, he rose early the morning after the Americans had left and drove out to the dismantled camp, armed with a shovel and a few tools. The snow had finally cleared and the ground was hard, compacted with ice. They had packed the tents at the camp, but they had not yet transported them back to the lodge. He climbed up to the tumulus and began sifting through the rocks, brushing off the snow, until he found the

rock that Rosalind had so thoughtlessly purloined. It was so
unusual that it could hardly be missed, even among so many
others. He had mapped out the grave site himself as part of his
conservation mandate from the lodge, and so he knew which
grave it had come from. He replaced it gingerly and then sat
down beside it to pray for the angered soul of the occupant.

Yet a wild and sacrilegious idea had taken hold of him
during the previous restless night. As he prayed he found
himself asking the occupant forgiveness for what he was
about to do. It was the white gods, he explained, who had
asked him to do it. He waited until it was high noon, the sky
cold and petrol-blue, as Tengri the sky god had designed it,
and then dug into the grave with his shovel until he had
reached the level where the ancient skeleton lay. Soon he had
found it. It was almost intact, as if it had been buried only a
few months earlier, the bones obviously those of a young
girl. The earth around it seemed fresh, as if someone else had
clawed away at it recently.

He stood there breathless, staring down at this proof that
his hunch had been correct, before renewing his efforts and
reversing his excavation with great lunges of the shovel.
The grave was restored exactly as it had been before. He
then laid the stone with the sun image upon it, prayed again
and sat by the grave through the afternoon, waiting for the
sun to dip to the horizon and the wind to turn savage. He let
it hit him. He lit a carbide lamp and sat vigil by the disturbed
grave, no longer sure who it was who lay buried there, or
who the girl was who had left with the Americans the day
before.

BURNING ANGEL

WHILE STILL AN INTERN WITH THE ARCHITECTURAL firm of Long & Budd, Edward Munroe had already created a vision of the duplex he would one day inhabit, in a location far from what his parents would have considered desirable. He had formed a precise idea that merely required two decades of gradual implementation. The corridors of the place he would remake in his own image would be pathways suggestive of those inside a Japanese temple. His inspiration, in fact, had been the Fushimi Inari temple of the fox god in Kyoto, hemmed in by great walls of bamboo. It was a place that he liked to say had lain at the bottom of his unconscious for half his life, since the day he had first visited it with his mentor, Aaron Kisalek, in 1987. While Edward was building his university library in Osaka ten years later he had gone there many times to renew his acquaintance with its uncanny atmosphere. Could one build a city apartment that captured its ethos?

The corridors of his duplex, twenty-seven floors up at the top of The Bridge, which took its name from the nearby Manhattan Bridge, were made of maple from a particular forest in Ontario. In summer they gave off a subtle scent. The walls were inlaid with huge New England quarry stones. Some were fragments of granite from Owl's Head, a hundred years old, which he had repurposed to fit such a minimalist conception. In the open dining and living rooms, windows occupied entire walls. He wanted the light from the nearby waters, as he often said to his guests, to be projected up into his aerial temple, filling it with the radiance of oceans. In his solarium library he gathered together a little forest of tropical plants nurtured by sprinklers and humidifiers. It was a system that produced round-the-clock fragrant steam. His future children, when and if they arrived, would have a place to play unlike any other in the city. He was sure of this because he knew all the original architect-created homes in the city as well as he knew his own hands. His creation was always going to be in defiance of what had already been achieved in the medium of space.

When other architects came for dinner, he felt them sizing up the scale of his ambition and the exactitude with which he had fulfilled it. The details were so finely placed that even the most envious had to concede a silent victory to Edward.

A man of taste is a cheap thing; they are two a dozen. But a man able to make his taste both visionary and material — there you had Edward Munroe, *Praemiun Imperiale*. His wife Alicia was a journalist who wrote about art and design. They often appeared together at their dinner parties dressed in identical black Japanese *haora* jackets, like a pair of elegant fishermen who had wandered into Manhattan from a remote island in the Osumi archipelago. They had their own sashimi master-knifeman on call five evenings a week, an *itamae* who rented one of Ed's empty studios.

It was in the year of their fortieth birthdays, after many failed attempts, that Alicia conceived. It was then that Edward hatched the idea of hiring not just a daily visiting maid, but a live-in one who could organise a household that would surely fall into chaos in a few months' time when the two of them became three. He visited an agency and was shown the books. He admitted that he was not exactly experienced in this matter and was therefore not sure what he was looking for. Old or young, American or foreign, experienced or new to the trade? Or should one go by the face, following one's gut? A face, even in an agent's book, radiated its own truth. He decided to trust his instincts. He believed that a younger woman would be better when it came to energy and enthusiasm and, conscious of his social politics, he thought that someone American might be unusual, enabling him to evade the embarrassing look of a rich white man hiring a Guatemalan girl.

The difficulty was that the book he was leafing through contained only Central American women. Only two or three were white, and two of those were on the senior side. There was one twenty-three-year-old white girl and her name was Hope. It was a fairly ordinary face with open, even vacant eyes, her blonde hair cropped short. It was not a face he could attach anything to. It was neutral, colourless. She was from Maryland originally. The rate was too low to refuse.

'She has references?' he asked the agent.

'Everyone on our books is fully documented. Her former employer was a family in California. Their name is Krasner. I can show you their letter, if you like.'

'Could I call them?'

'I'm sure it would be fine with them. They seem to have been very pleased with her.'

'Was there any reason—'

'Hope said she wanted to move to New York. She's also hearing-impaired. I believe she wanted to take some classes here.'

'Impaired?'

'She wears an aid in one ear. She can hear a little, with it turned on. The Krasners even seem to have thought it was an advantage.'

They shared a quiet laugh and Edward nodded. 'Yes, I suppose it could be, come to think of it.'

'Not that you would be hiring her out of pity. I was very impressed with her myself.'

'In what way?'

The agent turned a little sentimental, Edward thought, and she glanced sideways, as if collecting insignificant thoughts for the benefit of a lucrative client who might well pay more than she was asking.

'She is very punctual, very serious. You just *know* that she's a hard worker. Do you know what I mean?'

'Since I haven't met her . . .'

'Well, I see a lot of these girls. Believe me. I screen them out very carefully. It's a gut thing, an instinct. There was something I had to admire about Hope. Being somewhat handicapped and moving to New York by herself – I thought it took some courage.'

He considered this rapidly and found that he agreed with the sentiment: it must indeed have taken a dogged courage for a handicapped young woman to make such a leap into the unknown. Her courage, then, could be matched with his moral temerity and generosity in hiring her. This, at least, was how he might frame it for his wife and, for that matter, for himself.

'When is your wife expecting, if I may ask?'

'Six months. She will take time off. But we'd like to get back to normal working routines sooner rather than later, if it's possible. If you see what I mean.'

'It's the main reason people come to us.'

Edward wasn't sure if Hope was really his choice, and so he asked the agent if the girl could come to their home for an interview – was it done like that?

'It's done any way you like. When would be a good time? But first I should ask you how much time you would expect her to spend with your baby. I mean, I understand she'll be hired as a nursemaid as well as a maid, but we want to be sure that she can handle the stress. Normally older women who have children of their own seem to handle these things a bit better.'

'They probably do.'

'Maybe you and your wife should talk it over first.'

'She was busy at work today. But, as you say, we'll talk it over.'

Before leaving he wanted to know where the girl was living now.

'She's in Borough Park, I believe. I think she has a room on Fifty-Fifth Street. Do you want me to verify that?'

'No, it's quite all right.'

He had never been to Borough Park and had only a vague idea where it was. Maybe he and Alicia had gone to a Chinese restaurant there once. It was rather Chinese, wasn't it? Brooklyn, but darkest Brooklyn.

It made his rescue of Hope even more satisfying. Nevertheless, it was a stiff sell to Alicia. The girl was obviously young – maybe too young. She had no experience with a baby. Had she worked with children at her previous employment? Edward said he believed that she had. How old had they been? He admitted that he wasn't sure. He hadn't thought it through much at all.

His inclination to hire Hope was based purely on his liking for a dimly photographed face. But then, so what if it had been? Was he supposed to have selected a face he didn't like?

'I HAVE A FEELING,' he said defensively to Alicia later that night as they dined together at home, 'that we are going to like her. Really we are. She has a hearing impediment. But do you remember George Vasilis telling us that he once had a half-deaf maid and that her impediment made her rather *douce*. That was exactly his word. I know it sounds a bit far-fetched. But I think I know what he meant.'

'*Douce*?'

'Well, *sweet* doesn't quite capture it. It's not the same as *douce*.'

'How about *deaf*?'

'Oh, come now. Aren't we being a little harsh?'

'*Douce* and *deaf* then.'

He threw up a single exasperated hand, then let it fall. He muttered, 'All right, all right.'

'You mean I will have to shout at her all the time?'

'Not at all. She has a hearing aid. They're sophisticated these days. I looked it up online. Apparently even totally deaf people can now hear aeroplanes passing overhead.'

'Can they hear screamed orders?'

'No, don't be unfair – you won't be screaming. Nobody's going to be screaming at anybody.'

'Really?'

'Hope can hear things. We can also text her on her phone. So there's that.'

'Text the maid?'

Privately, Alicia had already decided not to make too much of a fuss about hiring a maid who would probably only last six months. It might be better simply to let her husband arrange it and then make her own decision later. But there was a technical point she wanted to clarify. Did deaf or partially deaf people have problems not merely hearing, but also speaking? She felt compelled to ask. The girl would have to run errands, converse with people, tell her about how the baby had behaved during the day. It was not a simple thing. She wanted to know if the agency could guarantee that their investment in this unknown girl would be worth their time. Could Ed himself say that?

'Why don't we just meet her?' he said. 'Nothing is more important than meeting another human being in the flesh. We'll know in a minute if she's the right one. Maybe in less than a minute.'

When the girl came to the lobby of The Bridge at six in the evening three days later, he went down alone to meet her. In that towering space filled with ferns and a small waterfall, lit by cathedral windows that looked out upon a crescent of clipped lawn, she cut a tiny figure that was dispiriting to his eye. He had to admit that he was a little surprised. He had secretly hoped for a taller and more stately apparition.

The real Hope was timid and pale, dressed in a plaid shirt and leggings, her skin sickly-looking and slightly given to rashes – malnourished, he would almost have said. She was going to leave a bad impression on Alicia. The owners of fifteen-million-dollar apartments swept past her as if she was not even there.

Edward stepped towards her and extended his hand to Hope to show that he was the one she was seeking. The movement caused her to freeze. It was, he thought, the building that had awed her, and which had robbed her of her wits. He shook her hand and introduced himself and then thanked her for coming all the way there at such short notice.

He whisked her to one of the eight high-speed elevators. Under her shabby clothes, she seemed to be trembling slightly. *Well, the building is over-the-top*, he thought, *but it's not that bad*. Inside the elevator she managed a first weak smile. He had twenty-seven floors to explain their situation: wife, baby, work schedules.

'I didn't ask about cooking,' he said nonchalantly, while looking at the back of her head in the elevator mirror. *Rather fine*. 'But if you can't cook, we can send you to Cordon Bleu.'

And then, thunderstruck, he realised he had forgotten the most essential thing about her. That she couldn't hear. His eye moved to the earpiece discreetly tucked in place in her right ear, and he watched her eyes tracking him, noticing that he had noticed. 'I'm sorry,' he was about to say, but he was now unsure exactly how much she had been able to hear. She looked at him directly and a quick humour suddenly flashed in her eyes. She had understood. But the ambiguity was unresolved as the doors opened and they stepped into the Munroes' icy home. The girl was less fazed now. They went into the living room, where Alicia waited for them with three glasses of Prosecco. Between the two women there was an immediate frisson. Alicia rose and shook Hope's hand and told her, with obvious exaggeration, to make herself at home.

'I hear,' she said very slowly, as if talking to a child, 'that you have a hearing aid. I see that you are wearing it. Can you hear us?'

Hope nodded, and the Munroes understood instantly that speaking was not going to be habitual with Hope.

'Maybe,' Alicia went on, 'you have trouble speaking. But please don't worry about it. For now if you understand, you can nod or shake your head and use hand signs. I know it's not easy for you.'

The girl raised a hand and made a strange sign. The Munroes glanced at each other, and it occurred to Edward that it was a sign equivalent to 'okay'.

'In any case,' Edward resumed, 'my wife is about to have a baby in a few months and . . . I'm sure the agency explained it to you. You can live with us. In fact you have to live with us. Would you like to see the room?'

Hope gave an affirmative nod and Edward said to Alicia that he might as well take her there now. But Alicia had turned an eye upon Hope's untouched glass of Prosecco.

'Do you want a sip at least?'

Hope held up two crossed fingers and Edward offered his spontaneous translation: 'She doesn't drink!'

'Well, that's a plus,' Alicia said.

Edward took Hope to the room he had prepared at the back of the apartment. The girl's shyness, her impairment, had begun to make him feel sorry for her. She would have to be protected a little.

He wished he could ask her about her previous employment and whether – to put it tactfully – there had been any difficulties that had caused her to leave. But he wasn't sure it was the appropriate moment.

He showed her the elegant and tidy room, which had its own sofas and armchairs, an en-suite bathroom with views of the Brooklyn shore. There was a small bookshelf and an Apple TV set up. It must have represented a vast upgrade from what she was used to. He watched Hope's expression as she took it in. There was a quiver of delight in her eyes, an equally slight tension in the closed fists. It had exceeded her expectations, and this meant that he had her in his pocket.

However, he had no intention of driving a hard bargain with her. What he wanted from her was compliance. And then agreeability, gratitude and, above all, submission to his wife. The idea of learning a little deaf language was also gratifying to his moral compass. He'd be sharing his wealth, spreading the happiness a bit.

He made an inquisitive 'Okay?' and, quickly, she corrected it to the right one in sign language. They shared a moment of merriment. He approached the aid-piece in her ear and said, 'Can you hear a little?'

She nodded and they shook hands.

'Room and board,' he said slowly, 'all included. Laundry is okay to do?'

She assented and, after a slightly awkward mutual pause, they went back to the front room.

Here Alicia was brooding, upright by the windows, looking out over the now-blue waters of the East River. A subtle hostility seemed to have hardened in her towards the entire arrangement, but it went unspoken. After Edward had gone down with the girl to find the Uber he had called for her, he asked Alicia if her impression of Hope was favourable and whether the following week was a good time for her to move in. Alicia had clearly been mulling the matter during his brief absence.

'I suppose so,' she said vaguely. 'What about you?'

'I like her a lot. Do you not?'

'I do like her. She's quite fragile-looking. Is she all there?'

'All there?'

'Is she sound? You know what I mean.'

He felt for a moment that his judgement was being called into question and bristled.

'I'd say she was sound,' he retorted. But it was with as little drama as he could muster. 'She seems sweet and even a little terrified to me. Isn't that the perfect combination in a live-in maid?'

'Don't be sarcastic.'

'Well, I'm half-serious. It *is*.'

'As you say, *douce*.'

'I say we give her a try.'

ON THE DAY HOPE moved in, he went down to greet her once again, curious about who might accompany her in her

momentous move. In the event there was no one but herself
and the taxi, along with a forlorn suitcase and an umbrella
with damaged spokes. He asked the doormen to get rid of the
umbrella and, as they walked to the elevators, promised to
get her a real one.

In the elevator there was a slight awkwardness between
them, provoked by this sententious offer. When they were in her
room he decided to leave her there for a while to acclimatise.

During the afternoon he showed Hope around the kitchen using improvised signs and, when verbal indications
were unavoidable, speaking close to the small machine inside
her right ear. He had prepared a page from Bittman's *How to
Cook Everything* for a simple poached-salmon dish, and he
made Hope understand that she was to make a recipe every
evening according to a different page in that book, at 7.30
p.m. punctually every day unless they were eating out. It was
an easy place to start with her training. This done, he checked
the contents of the fridge to make sure all the necessary
ingredients were there. Salmon, capers, dill and cream. Then
he went to work at his firm's quarters in Soho, leaving a short
note for his wife before leaving.

The day passed without commotion, alone at his station on
the third floor of the neoclassical palace on Greene Street
where XTN had its offices. Below his window, people loped
about in the heat without alacrity, sheltered by the shadows of
the canyon-like street. Edward felt quietly disembodied and
distracted. He thought about the slope of the maid's shoulder
above the ragged hem of her old shirt. There was an elegance
to it, an awareness of itself. For a moment his focus slipped
and the screen in front of him lost its meaning. Hope was not

all that she appeared. (This was an optimistic intuition on his part.) She had some brightness to her. To use an old-fashioned word, she was canny rather than inert. A pleasant surprise.

In the late afternoon he decided to walk home to get in some exercise. By sundown the streets were already emptying. The city had not recovered its zest from successive crises and his walk home along Spring Street had none of the claustrophobic energy of years past. Now it was easier to pass along the sidewalks. But by the time he got to Cleveland Place the crowds had thinned out entirely and only a few fellow ghosts drenched in sweat passed alongside the Corinthian columns of the Sixty Spring Street building and the railings of the little park. He ploughed on down Centre Street, with a storm thickening the air, and stopped for a few minutes at Rowing Blazers to look through their collection. He had been fancying a cream terrycloth blazer with navy trim for the rest of the summer. But in the end he didn't buy it.

On the terrace of Nickel & Diner he saw a few familiar faces to whom he nodded, but a little further down he was alone as he walked. Soon he was on Henry Street, coming under the bridge. He stopped at a grocer's to buy a pineapple. The home stretch of Pike Street was in shade, already cooler, and he found himself looking forward to seeing what Hope had done with the salmon. Under the soaring tower of The Bridge he stopped in the gardens, sprayed by machines and automatic timers, and cooled himself down after his walk. He was looking forward to unwinding with a gin and tonic; indeed, he would have to teach Hope how to make it for his late-afternoon homecomings.

*

RECOMPOSED, EDWARD WENT UP in the elevator. When he opened the door there was a powerful and summery scent of pesto emanating from the kitchen. The table was set for two in the glass-walled dining room, and Alicia was already there with Hope, the two of them caught in a lovely dusk light.

There was an opened bottle of white wine on the table and Alicia was two glasses in. He was slightly taken aback. She was drinking again, and Hope was not making what he had suggested. But he decided to be relaxed about it. Hope was at work making pesto and there was no sign of any salmon. Across from his wife stood what looked like a perfectly made gin and tonic. Hope worked with her back turned to them as he sat, and he noticed at once that she was dressed in sharp new clothes, obviously courtesy of Alicia. She was seemingly now quite at home in her new kitchen. She didn't appear to have noticed him at all. *Well, well.* He tasted his gin and tonic: it was, indeed, perfect.

'I suppose you taught her,' he said quietly to Alicia.

'You don't need to whisper. She can't hear us. And no, I didn't do anything. It's all her.'

'She made a gin and tonic?'

'All by herself. I didn't say a thing to her. How could I? But I'm happy you asked her to make pesto tonight. It's exactly what I wanted. I was dreading you asking her to make some dull salmon dish or something equally school-foody.'

'Ah.'

'It was thoughtful of you.'

'No, you're welcome.'

It was gnocchi with pesto, sophisticated and light. Hope had clearly made it before, perhaps many times.

She served them silently. She barely met his eyes. A surprising coolness. He wondered if the two of them had been communicating prior to his arrival. Might Alicia have said something to Hope about personal interactions and the necessity of coolness in employer–maid relations? It was annoying if she had, because from now on Hope would be stand-offish and dull, and that diminished the amicable mood. They ate more slowly than they usually did and he felt irritable.

'I'm growing used to her already,' Alicia said without lowering her voice. 'One thing I like is that we can talk freely without worrying about what she thinks. It's quite liberating.'

'You think?'

'I don't feel guilty about it, if that's what you mean. What Hope doesn't hear doesn't hurt her.'

'I have no desire whatsoever to hurt her.'

'You know what I mean. We can *comment* without worrying if she'll take offence. So I can say the pesto is perfect and the gnocchi is underdone. It is, isn't it?'

'A little.'

'So now we can say it.' She smiled and winked at him. 'What do you think of the clothes I gave her?'

'They're not yours, are they?'

'I measured her up this afternoon and then got Felicity to go out shopping for me. I think I did rather well. Hope's never going to be eye-candy, but it's an improvement on what she looked like at midday. She looked like a member of Antifa. Perhaps not as chic as that. It was alarming.'

'You're exaggerating.'

'No. She looked like she'd come from a shelter. Are you sure she didn't?'

'I don't think the agency would be taking people from shelters.'

Alicia looked severely at the maid hunched over the preparation of coffee and biscotti, and her lips tightened.

'She might have gone through a hard period. Drugs, abusive boyfriend. She looked like that.'

He shook his head. 'No. It wasn't that. It was just a rough life. We should go easy on her. A rough life is a rough life. How would we know?'

Hope went back to her room after the coffee had been served, and husband and wife enjoyed a half-hour by the artificial gas fire watching raindrops spatter against the floor-to-ceiling windows. Later, as they lay in bed together, still not talkative, they read books, each isolated in their own world. Alicia fell asleep first.

Day by day the pregnancy was changing her internal rhythms. She fell asleep more readily, stayed unconscious more profoundly and for longer. If Edward was honest with himself, it took a little pressure off him. He continued reading and soon he felt more awake than ever. He put down his book and wrote messages on his phone. The rain grew louder and he turned off the light at last. Soon, however, he began to hear a rustling noise from the corridor outside their room. It was an immense passageway that led to a common area with antique consoles, and from there into the kitchen and dining room. At first he was amused by the idea that it might be a mouse. A mouse, in the upper reaches of The Bridge: he would personally feed it himself, if that turned out to be the case. But soon he knew that it was not an intruding animal.

Getting up and putting on his silk kimono, he crept to the door and opened it. Only the night lights were on, exactly as they had left them, and he could see the darkened kitchen lit by the nocturnal glow of the real bridge a few hundred yards from it. He padded his way back down to the kitchen and turned on the lights. Burglary was impossible in The Bridge, so that left very little room for conjecture. He thought at once of Hope and it occurred to him that perhaps she was hungry and had quietly crept back to the kitchen to avail herself of the fridge. He had not given her explicit permission to do that, but it was her first day and he decided to be lenient. On the countertop he spotted a few stray crumbs and his theory was confirmed. He went on into the front room, echoing quietly with the rain beating against its windows, and sensed that the magazines neatly stacked on the Roger Capron coffee table were oddly displaced, but only very slightly. Since he supervised them himself with an exacting eye, it was something that he was well equipped to notice.

He straightened them back into their original order and felt, for a moment, vulnerably exposed in the middle of his own room. It was as if a ghost had swept through it, disturbing it simply by virtue of her motion. He looked behind him at the long silk curtains, moving slightly in the circulating breeze created by the air conditioners. Then, moved by an irrational idea, he stepped up to them and pulled them apart.

He was almost surprised that no one was there. Even a little disappointed. He went back to the bedroom and on the way passed by Hope's door. Her light was off. Yet he was curious, not quite satisfied at being so empty-handed. Pressing his ear a little closer to the door, he thought he could make out a very faint sound, like music. She must have left the TV on while she fell asleep.

Returning to bed, he lay awake for a while longer, trying to imagine if she had really raided the fridge in her pyjamas. If that continued, as he hoped it would, he would sooner or later run into her and there would be a rather delicious awkwardness. He would let her off, but there would have to be a private understanding between them. Just the two of them. All maids, he had heard, took a cut on the side without their employers knowing. And he had even been advised by a friend to turn a blind eye to it. It was like an invisible moral tax that one had to pay, in return for a quiet life.

DAYS AND THEN EVENTLESS weeks passed, with only small yet pleasant surprises. Hope ignored all his meal orders and requests and made up her own menus as she went. She divined their moods brilliantly – and far better than he could do himself – so that soon he stopped giving her suggestions and left everything to her intuition. This made everything easier for him. Moreover, he accumulated all the credit for it from his wife, to whom he never admitted that he had relinquished control. In Alicia's mind, he had merely become more sensitive and more responsible.

It was exactly what he wanted her to think, and so he let her think it. Gradually, and yet still slightly, her stomach began to swell. On the weekends they took to driving out to his family's house on the Old Montauk Highway, Hope in tow. They set up the barbecue on the deserted stretch of beach, thick with brushwood and salt-spray roses. The

modestly imposing clapboard house rose behind them, lit by
a mass of candles.

Edward was certain that Hope had never seen or experienced anything like it before and he therefore exerted himself
to make her feel at ease. He took her through the house and
explained all the implements in the basement and kitchen that
made it tick. He gave her a room in the attic, facing the sea,
and since he and Alicia occupied the room below hers, he
could monitor at night the motion of her naked steps.

He instructed her to get up early, at six, and prepare breakfast on the deck. When they rose three hours later it would
be there, the Maine honey and the yoghurts and strawberries
from the Montauk market. The egg brioche-toast and the
Beurre d'Isigny, the coffee made five minutes before they
arrived, perfectly timed. The milk warmed and whisked, as
they liked it.

It was astonishing how infrequently Hope needed to be
corrected. Even the eggs, a tricky matter, were always done
exactly as they needed to be. Afterwards, he let her spend
some time by herself, allowing her to roam the beach for an
hour or two while he worked in his study and Alicia did her
yoga and read on the deck. At lunch they came together
again, with the deck half in sunlight, and the employers starting their wine run for the day.

Hope served them carefully, watching them from the kitchen window as they ate alone. During the afternoons they
all drove together up to the Montauk lighthouse and walked
around it. Or else they went into the village to buy champ-
pagne and order provisions for the evening meal.

The girl seemed wide-eyed in the Montauk gourmet

stores. Yet she executed every dish perfectly on her own. It must, he reflected, be down to her prior training at other households, into which he had not delved in much detail. They would usually drive back to the house by five, and by six he would be making a bonfire on the beach, with Gershwin booming across the sands, unheard by distant neighbours and ignored by the local police.

It was on one such night, during the second week of August, that he made his fire after a swim beyond the rollers and noticed that Alicia had fallen asleep in the hammock on the deck. Dinner was set, and Hope was standing at the edge of the deck, watching him.

He motioned for her to come down to the beach. When she was there, he gave her a branch of driftwood and invited her to toss it into the fire. He made a sleeping gesture with two hands under his cheek and pointed to his wife in the hammock. They smiled about it. He pointed to her espadrilles and made a kicking motion with his own feet to suggest that she could take them off. Then he walked barefoot himself away from the fire and towards the surf, letting her follow him. By the huge waves the noise was deafening to him, but of course not to her. The moon on the sea, moreover, appeared to make her calm. The moonlight made the lights of the house recede, creating its own world separate from the bourgeois illumination of his father's mansion. It was under its effect, he thought, that they were drawn magnetically closer to each other. The music was now so faint that he could hardly hear it. Only the impetuous bonfire was there to remind him of his daily habits, formed since boyhood. Here, in this place, he could do what he wanted because it belonged to him. Even that stretch of sea belonged to him.

His eye remained trained on the deck and the girl appeared dazed, as if sleepwalking. There was a wonderful liberation about not being able to speak to her. A casting-off of habitual restraints and inhibitions. He didn't have to think too much. Losing control of his mind a little, he acted in slow motion, as if moving through water, reaching down and kissing her cheek.

To his surprise she didn't flinch away. There was not even any astonishment in her eyes. She merely waited for him to do something else, to speak or repeat the timid kiss or else something more bold.

They walked back to the fire and sat there throwing pine-cones into it. *Well, what about that!* he thought. *She has accepted me.*

At dinner, Edward was in a superlative mood.

'I could stay here until Labor Day,' he said, taking Alicia's hand and suggesting that she might want to do the same. What was the rush to get back to the malodorous city? 'Have you noticed that all the rentals around here have tripled in price this year? Everyone wants to get out of New York. It's a dying city.'

'Then why don't we leave after the baby is born?'

'It's a genius idea. Why don't we? We like the house, don't we? I can work from here and commute in, when need be. Even in winter I'd prefer it.'

They ate the linguine with clams that Hope had cooked and from time to time the girl darted out quietly to tip the bottle of Chablis into their glasses. Alicia flashed her a questioning look, simultaneously placing a hand over her glass to diminish the size of the serving, and when Hope had retired again to the kitchen she said to him, 'She looks rather rosy and healthy, don't you think?'

'It's the sea.' He felt a childish moment of triumph.

'Is it?' she said. 'It must be. I suppose we all look a little better.'

In fact, he thought, it was indeed Hope who had blossomed in the new environment. He had barely noticed it until that night. But now that he did perceive it, her brighter complexion was obvious. Not only that, but the stilted manner of communication – a voice constantly pressed to a digitally controlled hearing aid – had come to feel quite normal.

'*You* certainly do,' he lied.

The sea began to calm, the swells grew less temperamental. His bonfire started to die and he watched its drifting sparks with satisfaction. Soon his wife had reached out for her nightly pills to help her sleep, which she now took in increasingly heavy doses. It was as if her doctor had permitted it. He had wondered before about her intake. But in the end he decided to let her do as she wished without interference; he was pleased that she had responsibly reduced her wine intake accordingly. Therefore he said nothing each time she reached for the pills and knocked them back with a glass of water, as she did now. She leaned back with a contented smile and they were at peace together.

'I'm going to bed earlier and earlier. I wonder why I didn't start this regime earlier in life. It feels so rejuvenating.'

'It's definitely better for us.'

He drank the last of the wine and felt Hope watching them from the kitchen, as she always did.

'I'll help Hope clear up,' he said. 'You should hit the sack and wake up at dawn. We're at the beach after all.'

WHEN ALICIA HAD GONE, he waited for Hope to reappear while eating from a saucer of chocolates that she had laid there earlier. As they melted in the hot air they stuck to his fingers and he used a napkin to clean his hands. It was then that Hope reappeared with a small dish filled with water. She offered to do it for him. He let her, not saying a word. When she had finished she looked up at him and smiled. They cleared the table together and then he went down to the beach to seal the fire and scatter the embers in the sand. Hope, he could tell, had mounted the stairs to her attic room because her light there briefly came on. He paced back to the surf and wondered what to do. The light was itself, he felt, a tacit invitation.

As soon as he re-entered the house he heard Alicia's snores from the master bedroom. He dutifully went to their room to undress and then lay down next to her. In that spacious room built in 1948 one could hear the sea at all times, but without being disturbed by it. He listened to it now. Then, as his ears became attuned to every sound, he heard the girl above him walk across her room in bare feet. It seemed to him that she was talking to him through her feet, tapping out a Morse-code message of some kind. Finally it faded away. He lay unable to sleep, trying to summon the courage to reply to the message. At length he rose, put on a dressing gown and sat by the window, staring out at the moonlit beach. He guessed then that Hope had left the house by herself. Of course. Perhaps she had returned to the beach. He suddenly knew what to do.

Slipping out of the house silently, he made his way down the wooden steps that led from the deck to the beach. The sand was now brilliantly illuminated. Wandering up the beach, he looked for her, knowing that she was waiting for him somewhere. The house next to theirs, several hundred yards distant, had been empty all summer and the dunes covered with dry grass and Japanese honeysuckle were plunged in darkness. Yet the moon lit up the house itself. He was passing it when a small flicker of light caught his eye from the bushes.

Hope had taken a lighter from the kitchen and had flicked it open to attract his attention. As he stumbled towards the honeysuckle, it was not until he was in the shadows that he saw her lying on the sand on her side, as calm as if she had been watching him all along, dressed only in a pair of denim shorts and topless. The wind whipped sand over them and he had no reason to waste any time with words, which she could mostly not decipher anyway. He took off his clothes and threw them in a heap in the undergrowth. Later, he almost forgot them when he walked back alone to the house, dishevelled and filled with wonder. It was Hope who had indicated that he should go back alone and that she would wait for some time on the beach. He was reluctant, but finally agreed, and at the last minute he ran down to the surf like a schoolboy and jumped into the waves. It would be the alibi for his absence, if one were needed.

*

HE REGAINED THE MARITAL bed at 3 a.m. and lay awake still longer, waiting for something tremendous that would not come. He never heard the girl climb the steps to her own room, or her footsteps crossing the ceiling. But before falling asleep he went over in his mind the violent kissing, the sand encrusted in her mouth, and the earpiece that fell into the pine needles and was temporarily forgotten.

When he woke he was caked with salt and he heard at once Hope and Alicia laughing together on the deck. He came down to the usual breakfast and a sunlight alive with bees. The two women looked up at him as if surprised in some *flagrante delicto* and Alicia showed him that she had already buttered a piece of toast for him.

'I had the most wonderful dream,' she said as he sat down at the table, completely befuddled and drowsy.

'Coffee, first.'

On that front, Hope sprang into quiet action, and the pot was fresh.

Alicia went on, 'I dreamed I went out on the beach while you were sleeping and went for a long swim beyond the rollers. Where the great whites are. When I came back, the house was on fire. I didn't know how.'

'On fire?'

'Yes, I know it sounds awful, but somehow it wasn't. How can I put it? It was a joyful sort of fire. You were outside, dancing and singing. Then I realised that it was you who had set the fire. I thought to myself, *He's burning the house so that we can be free and go travelling around the world like we used to.*'

'Isn't that a rather naïve interpretation?'

'It depends how you look at it. Not necessarily. But the

dream did change. Soon I realised there *was* someone in the house.'

'Ah, for Christ's sake.'

But she laughed.

'No, it wasn't someone human. It was like an angel of some kind. She just stood there, burning, but she was not in any pain.'

He drank the whole cup of coffee and then another. His mind was elsewhere, back in the previous night. Or else with the girl, who was now in the kitchen, watching them from the shade.

'So much for dreams,' he muttered. 'They're never as entertaining for other people.'

'I just thought it was curious.'

'They're always curious. That's what's so tedious about them.'

'Oh, but I didn't think it was tedious. I thought you'd find it curious, too. That's all.'

Later in the day Edward played tennis with a friend in Amagansett and drove back slowly, stopping at Salivar's Dock to knock back a rum-and-Coke at the bar, under the taxidermied remains of the great white shark that had once stimulated the imagination of Peter Benchley.

He took his tumbler and strolled along the jetties as the dusk came down and the lights became reflections in the small harbour. When he was small, he had watched boats returning with huge sharks tied to their winches, but now the seas were less fertile. He and Alicia often came to Gosman's Dock for a fish dinner but they had not been for a while. He wandered past Gosman's now, still holding his incongruous tumbler of rum, until he was at the open sea and the long but narrow beach, fronted by tumbledown wooden shacks. Their decay had surprisingly not been reversed by the wealthy residents who otherwise dominated the scene. The road was covered with sand. It had not changed since he had walked there in the Seventies with his father. The same grasshopper sparrows, the same dry crabgrass, or so he thought he remembered. Yet it had altered subtly for the worse, though he could not say how. A quiet deterioration at the invisible centre of things. All he wanted to do for the next few hours was sit at Salivar's and recall the old types who used to haunt it thirty years ago. It was said that Edward Albee used to be seen there, and even Lauren Bacall, though he had never seen either. But Alicia was calling him and he had to drive back in time for their evening meal.

Once home, he ate in his tennis whites, the rackets laid at his feet. Hope lit the glass oil lamps around their table of salads and Greek-style fish covered with olives. They were all in a strangely festive mood by the time the home-made pina coladas were being poured. But his inner festivity, Edward was sure, was different from theirs, since it was fuelled by the fresh memory of the previous night's escapade. Unremarkably, he wondered if it would be repeated that night. Or perhaps every night that the three of them remained at the beach, isolated from the mundane world. He even imagined, as he and Alicia got tipsier, that she sensed what was going on and didn't mind. They hadn't made love in months and, to his surprise, he was quite happy with the arrangement. If she did sense it, he thought, she would not be threatened by a deaf maid from nowhere, who could be dismissed with a sudden snap of the fingers. In a sick way, it made sense for all of them. Or perhaps it wasn't sick at all. The dinner that night was the best of their sojourn at Montauk. Afterwards the couple went for a walk in the moonlight, past the same Japanese honeysuckle, and Alicia asked him who lived in the gloomy empty house next to theirs.

'Some people called the Farlows. They live in California now. I used to collect their driftwood when I was a kid.'

'And they just leave the place empty?'

'I should trim their honeysuckle for them and send them an email about it. But I won't.'

Behind them Hope cleared the table, silently and efficiently. Alicia said that she liked her more and more. She was 'a find'.

'Isn't she?' he said.

'You couldn't have found better.'

Later, Alicia took her pills again and went up alone to bed. He waited on the deck, drinking little shots of Schnapps. An hour went by. Then he heard snores from on high and was satisfied, to a reasonable degree, that the delights of the previous night would repeat themselves. Agitated by lust, he got up and went down to the sand with his glass full and strolled down to the surf, downed the shot and threw the glass into the waves.

He already knew that Hope would be waiting for him under the Japanese honeysuckle, and would be every night that they remained in Montauk. So she was. This time she was more practised, and he noticed that she had not brought her earpiece with her.

It went on for longer, and he lost himself in the moment

more completely. It was four by the time he staggered back to the house, hoping that Alicia had not woken up. But there seemed to be an enchantment at work. For the remaining four nights it was much the same.

Alicia never woke from her deep sleep while he slipped in beside her, covered in sand and sweat, fearing to wake her if he took a shower. But if she did wake, he could always say that he had been for a restless midnight swim. In the morning, their routines continued as before. Nothing was said. The secret between Hope and him grew nightly until it was too large to worry about. In any case, four days after Labor Day they returned to New York and, once they were there, the nature of the problem altered.

HIS ROUTINES WERE ANAESTHETISING, he thanked God. A daily walk to the office, an everyday lunch at a subdued city winery, long afternoons alone at his station designing architectural models, occasional Chelsea lunches with clients at Del Posto and the corresponding walk home through the subsiding heat of September afternoons. The mood in the household was now quietly expectant as the pregnancy began to evolve.

Hope made them their fruity gin and tonics every night before dinner. She then retired in order to leave them alone, as she had been trained to do. This too was a routine that was pleasant precisely because it did not require exceptions in order to be practicable. It made itself.

By nine Edward was invariably alone with a glass of Scotch. He sometimes went to The Bridge's public glass-enclosed swimming pool on the rooftop and swam a few laps in the aquatic semi-gloom, soothed by Art Deco lamps and the last flare of sunsets seen through the mighty windows. He was usually alone there by ten in the evening. He lingered among the potted palms to read a novel or send messages to clients in different time zones.

One night he fell asleep in one of the loungers and woke up a little after midnight with stars shining through the glass enclosure. With a start he realised he had been there since nine. An old millionaire he knew vaguely was doing quiet laps, a man who seemed to be slowly and quietly evolving through daily immersions into a kind of humanoid seal. The two of them exchanged a nod before Edward went back down to the apartment, feeling groggy and out of sorts, letting himself in and going back to the living room for a nightcap. With one swig of Balvenie he felt, as before, the presence of a ghost behind the high curtains in the main room. Before he could move to them, however, he threw a glance over the coffee table and spotted a pair of earphones lying there next to an iPhone. How strange. He went over to pick them up – of course, Hope must have left them there for some reason. So she *had* emerged from her room after she had ostensibly turned in for the night.

He then detected a very faint hissing coming from the earphones and raised them to one ear. It was rock music being played from the iPhone, but not at a particularly high volume. Perplexed, he placed them back on the table and considered what it could mean. Then, very lightly, a soft gust of air touched the back of his leg and made him turn towards the glass doors leading out to the deck. They were open. He was sure he had closed them earlier, so he knew at once that Hope was out on the deck by herself.

He crept to the doors and peered out. As he had anticipated, she was standing by the corrugated glass wall, looking down at the river in her pyjamas. He came up to her and touched her shoulder, but it didn't make her flinch. She already knew that he was there. She gripped the wall with both hands, and tears poured down her face. It was some drama from her past life, he was sure, one that was too complicated for her to explain to him. It did not immediately occur to Edward that it might be connected to him. But then he was forced to consider it. Had he hurt her in some way? Of course he had. He had led her into an impossible situation. All his virtue-signalling and self-satisfaction had been a pathetic sham, a ruse to permit himself to do something immoral. Paralysed, however, he held back. He was in the home that he and Alicia had built so patiently, and there were rules – areas of indiscretion that could not be entered. She turned to face him, and his eye was drawn down to something in one of her hands, held precariously. It was an envelope. On its surface was the name of a clinic in Queens. It was for him. Hope collected herself and handed it to him.

He was going to open it in front of her, but she stopped him, kissed him on the cheek and walked away from the deck, back into the front room. By the time he had followed her, the earphones and their owner had gone. He returned morosely to his Scotch and opened the envelope. It was a pregnancy test: positive. She had done it the day before, without telling him.

*

HE DEFLATED ON THE sofa and felt his temples pounding. The drumming increased in intensity and then gradually subsided. Stunned by the unexpected circumstances, he let the Scotch calm him down so that he could begin to think his way out of this newly arrived labyrinth.

He needed to talk to Hope first. Turning off the lights, he ventured to her room and quietly knocked on the door. When there was no reply he tried again. He whispered her name, then realised how ridiculous he was being. He knocked again and waited. He tried the handle, but she had locked the door. So a game had begun. There was no way he could enter, and there was no way he could talk to her except through Messenger on his phone, if she was still awake. He returned to the front room and sat in the darkness, texting her.

Over and over, he told her that he was sorry. There was nothing else he could say. Soon, however, he understood that she was either ignoring him or she had gone to sleep. In the morning there was no occasion to approach her and so he texted her throughout the day from his office.

He insisted that they had to talk later that night after Alicia was asleep. They had to stay calm and talk it through. Calm, he insisted again and again – calmness was what they needed. After dinner he waited for the right opportunity to arise when they could be alone, but Alicia was restless and talkative that night and she didn't take her sedatives until nearly midnight. He waited alone on the balcony for an hour, but the maid did not appear. It was an obvious snub, a manipulation, and his rage rose – a rage made impotent by the sudden inversion of power. In his own house, for which he paid, he was being blackmailed in some obscure way. Emotionally blackmailed, but blackmailed all the same.

He crept back to her door, knocking as softly but insistently as he could. As before, there was no response and he returned, filled with panic, to the living room. So it was going to be a discussion via text. But it made sense, since it was easier for them both. Hope could not express herself fully through mouth and ear. A text came soon afterwards, asking Edward if he had thought it over. But he wanted to know why an abortion needed to be thought over. It was obvious there was no other possible solution for both of them. Did she need to have that explained to her?

'Calm down,' she replied. 'It's my decision, not yours.'

He had to control his fury, and reply submissively. Yes, it was her decision, of course. But there were consequences.

'For me?' she wrote.

He might have asked if that was a threat, but that would have been a dangerous road to wander down so late in the day. Controlling himself, he adopted a cool and comforting tone instead. He asked her, instead, what she wanted to do.

'Leave,' she replied, 'and keep the baby.'

It was one option, he had to admit. He ran through the scenario in his head. She would leave under a pretext, to deceive Alicia, and he would pay Hope a fair sum to keep quiet. It was difficult to put this into words in a text message without abandoning all pretence of gentlemanly integrity, a quality that was central to his vanity. But it had to be tried. He typed out four messages laying out this scenario and waited for a reply. Half an hour passed. While he waited, he realised belatedly that he had committed an obviously foolish error.

Text messages were evidence, which Hope would obviously retain for her own use. *Moron*, he cursed himself and squeezed both fists until his knuckles went white. He needed to think it out all over again. She had evidence against him now and it was too late to retrieve it. Therefore he had to be gentle and persuasively cunning. He coaxed her now, sending emollient messages asking her to come to the balcony and meet him. She didn't want to? No matter. They could do it tomorrow. He meant what he said when he offered her an easy and discreet way out. But there were, he said, other options, too. Hope could stay and they could all be happy together – she could stay and she could have the money as well, but only if she followed his advice as regards the abortion. As a gentleman, he added, he would abide by her decision, either way. He was sorry for what had happened, and all he wanted was to find a way out of the predicament for her, not just for himself. It was the truth – he really did.

But there was no quick response to his overtures. Every night from then on he texted her from his living room and she replied to him from the bedroom only a hundred yards away – though by the calculations of New York real estate, a hundred yards was an unimaginable distance.

Though he tried persistently to enforce a showdown, Hope avoided being alone with him. Yet this avoidance was never melodramatic. On the contrary, it was quiet and understated. The passions on the beach seemed as if they had taken place in another lifetime. He assumed, in fact, that she must be suffering torments and doubts, unimaginable fears, that it was merely confusion and shame afflicting her. Softly, softly, he kept telling himself, let Hope resume her sanity. She would come round and the *Titanic* would be saved.

But weeks went by and the iceberg ahead of them was not removed. Edward began to plead and then to threaten. He could not demand that the agency intervene, because of the scandal it would arouse; but on the other hand, he could certainly make sure that Hope was unemployable from then on. It was an idle threat, however. She told him that she was undecided, unsure what to do. How much would he pay if she agreed to disappear now, before the pregnancy was visible? She suggested a preposterous sum that he could pay into an account whose details she gave him; he scoffed. He wrote back that he now had text-message evidence against her as well. 'So what?' she replied. She tried again with the same demand and, deflated by her confidence, he relented a little in his tone. But time was ticking away and its forward motion was not to his advantage.

One night at dinner Alicia cast a look at Hope as she made them dessert in the vast kitchen and said, with an unmistakable satisfaction, 'She's putting on a little weight, don't you think?'

He was taken aback and quickly tried to extinguish the idea. 'Hope? Not at all. If anything, she looks a little slimmer.'

'Don't be ridiculous. She's definitely fatter.'

He looked as well and saw that his wife was correct. Moreover, the difference was not particularly subtle.

'Maybe a little,' he conceded. 'But what do we expect? She's doing all the cooking.'

'I just find it funny that we're both getting fatter at the same time.'

'But for different reasons.'

'Well, obviously. Why did you need to say that?'

He struck a nonchalant pose and looked back at Alicia's eyes to reassure her. 'No reason. But I think it's all in your imagination.'

She smiled. 'Not really. She *is* fatter.'

So the emergency had come upon them quicker than he had anticipated. That night, after Alicia had fallen asleep, he went into their apartment-sized bathroom and rifled through the medical cabinets, which they had built up over the years. Alicia had always kept a couple of abortion pills from the earlier phase of their life, and he found that she had not thrown them out, even after years of neglect. The boxes had not even been opened. He was sure she would not notice them being opened now, but to be safe he would simply remove them and affect ignorance if the matter ever came up – which he was sure it would not.

He took both boxes, one of mifepristone and one of misoprostol, and went to his study on the floor above, where he was alone without any adjoining rooms. He put them in a locked desk drawer and texted Hope one more time. 'I have a solution,' he wrote. 'I think it's best for everyone.' And he named the price for his continued peace of mind – a sum more than he had expected to offer, but which had come to him on the spur of the moment as he imagined solving the problem with one deft gesture.

'Add a zero,' she wrote back.

It was now a sum so large that it would be difficult to cover up if Alicia or his tax accountant spotted it, and they might do so years hence, as the family finances were being inspected.

'Be reasonable,' he shot back. 'I'm already being generous. Very generous.'

Eventually, however, he relented and agreed to the extra zero, but he had already resolved not to honour it.

Calmly, Hope stipulated that he had to pay it first.

'All right,' he repeated. 'But it'll take a few days.'

'I have time. You don't.'

It was true, he thought ruefully.

'I'll do it,' he wrote. 'As long as you promise.'

Later that night he went back down to the bathroom and looked through the medical cabinet again, knowing that Alicia's sedatives were stored there. It was a formidable stock of pills and he calculated again that one box gone missing would not be noticed.

Yet he had not a concrete plan about how to use them. His unconscious was moving ahead of him, mapping out a path. He was so desperate to get the problem resolved that he had decided to follow his instincts blindly.

Taking the sedatives, then, he once more returned to the study and texted the maid. But this time she did not respond and he guessed that, as was usual, she had gone to sleep – or was waiting for *him* to fall asleep. On this occasion he decided to stay up as late as possible and then monitor the downstairs rooms as best he could and, so doing, he waited until the early hours. Finally giving up, he returned to the lower floor and found nothing untoward except in the kitchen.

On the counter lay the same crumbs that had annoyed him before, and unmistakable signs that the fridge had been raided yet again. Looking inside it, he saw that there was a carton of lemonade, which only Hope would drink, because neither he nor Alicia liked it. Raiding the fridge was not strictly according to the rules but he didn't mind, and the lemonade was after all for her. What irritated him was that Hope thought she could take food from under his nose while blackmailing him. She was playing cat-and-mouse, and the mouse was getting the upper hand. Was that it?

Now she was waiting for Edward to transfer a vast amount of money into a Bank of America account that might not even be hers. He entertained the idea that it was possible she had an accomplice and that he had been set up artfully. It was a clever con, perhaps, and it pivoted on an unborn life that could be erased later anyway. Once he had paid her the sum she was demanding, there would be very little he could do to prevent Hope from disappearing and blackmailing him later with a paternity suit. He would be comprehensively ruined. That was the outcome he had to avoid at all costs. He had to evaluate her plan and seal off all the exits of which she might avail herself.

The lemonade, he thought to himself.

THE EVENING PASSED UNEVENTFULLY. Alicia seemed list-less and disengaged and they ate in silence, lightning flickering in the distance. At around nine he thought he could hear the merry sound of disturbances wafting up from the streets near The Bridge. It was an almost weekly occurrence now, but it had been going on for so long that it had become a background noise whose future ramifications were no longer discussed.

After Alicia had turned in and Hope had retired as well, Edward went to the kitchen and examined the lemonade carton in the fridge. It was only a quarter full. Taking it with him, he went up to his study, poured out the remaining lemonade into a cup and then crushed the sedatives with the back of a spoon. He then dissolved them into the contents of the cup. Pouring the lemonade back into the carton, he then returned the tampered item to the kitchen fridge. This done, he went back up to his study and worked quietly until midnight.

To his mind, it was like setting a mouse-trap. Eventually there would be a 'click' and the animal would be snared. At one o'clock he went barefoot down the steps to the living room and saw the girl lying unconscious on the sofa, with a half-eaten bagel on the coffee table before her. How smoothly it had worked.

He stood over her for a moment and planned the next fifteen minutes. Returning to his study, he retrieved the abortifacients and then sat down next to Hope and relished a moment of triumph of which he knew he was unworthy. He had outwitted the outwitter.

He carried Hope back to her room, careful not to make any sound, and locked the door from the inside. When he had done this, he laid her on her bed and made sure that her breathing was normal. He then slipped a mifepristone pill into her mouth with a sip of water and tilted her head so that it went down. He had read that there were few side-effects from the first pill, that most of the bleeding and cramping came from the second pill, the misoprostol normally taken forty-eight hours later. The mifepristone merely stopped the pregnancy in its tracks. But one could also take the second pill right away. He wondered if he should take the risk and do this. It was clear that he had little choice. He couldn't very well drug her a second time. He waited ten minutes and then administered the second pill.

She slept on peacefully for another hour as he watched over her. Edward took the opportunity to look over her room, hopeful that he might be able to discover something about her. A single drawer of her old clothes neatly folded, a few books and a pair of reading glasses: the books, volumes of poetry. This was a surprise. Then, in a lower drawer, he found a small stash of baby clothes, also neatly folded. Stunned, he turned them over once with his hands – clothes fresh and springy, waiting for new life.

An unfamiliar feeling of guilt swept through him. But just as quickly as it arose he suppressed it, sweeping it away back into the shadows. So what if he had not understood everything about Hope's intentions – how could he have? And why would understanding her have made it easier for him, given his circumstances? It would have changed nothing.

He crept back to his study after retrieving the carton of lemonade and washed it out at his sink, then threw it into the trash. He would dispose of it safely at a later date. This completed, he returned to Hope's room and sat by her for another hour while her face glistened with sweat. She murmured in her sleep. Eventually he had to withdraw, quietly leaving her door slightly ajar, and made his way back to the master bedroom.

Once in his pyjamas, he lay awake waiting for something dramatic – a cry in the dark, a scream even. But none came. Tortured by anxiety, he nevertheless fell asleep quickly. He woke before Alicia, driven by his panic and fear, and made his way to the kitchen without stopping at Hope's room. But the girl was already there, calmly making the morning meal and the coffee.

She was turned away from him and since she could not hear him, he could observe her for a few moments without disturbing her. He had no idea what her calmness meant. Perhaps the pills had had no effect on her. His heart sank. And then, as he looked down at her bare feet and the backs of her calves, he saw that they were drenched in blood.

A small puddle of it had pooled between her ankles. Yet Hope patiently made the toast and the eggs, as if it was nothing. Edward came around the counter until she looked up, and there was no expression on her face. He pointed down at her feet with a look of horror, and she smiled as if there was nothing to be concerned about. Then he noticed that she was wearing her earphones, the faint clamour of heavy metal seeping out from them. He made a sign to her and stepped closer, taking her hand for a moment. He did so gently, aware that it was the first time they had been alone in weeks, if one excepted the previous night. He made her put down the toast and led her away from the kitchen and back towards her room. All the while she was docile, as if entranced.

At the room he laid Hope back down in her bed and dimmed the blinds. The bed was also covered in blood, but he would have to deal with that later. More urgently, he had to make her rest and let her sleep for a while. He said, after taking off the earphones and making Hope hand over the iPhone, that she should forget the day's chores and stay in bed. He would look after her. She seemed to understand. And yet he could tell that she was out if it, that she was in shock. She reached up and placed one hand tenderly on his cheek.

OUTSIDE IN THE CORRIDOR there was now a line of bloody footprints on the floor. Alicia was still asleep, as far as he knew, and so Edward had a few minutes to rectify the scene as best he could. A doctor making awkward enquiries was out of the question. Finding a mop and bucket in the kitchen, he swept the corridor clean of blood and rinsed the mop hurriedly. As he was doing this, as bad luck would have it, Alicia called out for him from the bedroom and he was forced to make his way there as quickly as he could, leaving the mop standing against a wall.

She was awake and sitting upright, waiting quizzically for him.

'I heard a noise. What are you doing?'

'Making you toast and coffee.'

'Where is Hope?'

'She has a headache, so I'm letting her off for the morning.'

Alicia began to swing her legs out of bed and he rushed to her side to deter her. 'Lie down,' he urged, 'I'll bring you coffee.'

A little reluctantly she gave in. As he left, she called after Edward, 'You cut your face shaving. Didn't you see?'

He felt the blood on his cheek and winced. If the room had not been dark, she would have seen Hope's bloody palm-print.

He had to wash down the kitchen entirely and then take the mop to the guest bathroom and run it under the water until the blood cleared. At last he was able to return to the coffee and toast, and he made both in a panic. He fumbled until he had assembled a tray of botched toast and over-strong coffee. Then he carried it to the bedroom and took a shower while Alicia ate. When he exited from the bathroom, she was brushing her hair and putting on her housecoat. She said she should go and see how Hope was doing.

'No,' he said, 'I'll go. You just relax. It's nothing serious, I think. I get the feeling she wanted to be alone.'

It was half an hour later when he finally returned to the maid's room. Hope had fallen unconscious again in the bloody bed, and he wondered if he should move her and clean everything up or whether he should let her sleep. In the end he decided to pull the stained sheet from under her, roll it up and take it to the laundry room himself, where he could wash it separately in the machine. He then found some of Alice's sanitary pads from the bathroom and left them by the bed for Hope. The mattress was also stained, but he calculated that the blood would dry eventually and could be covered with a cleaned sheet. It was imperfect, but he would have to make the best of it.

THE KITCHEN WAS NOW cleaned. Hope was still uncon-scious in her room and Edward had restored his home to its original settings. He made himself a coffee and waited for Alicia to emerge. It was not yet nine o'clock and he was exhausted. When she appeared, Alicia remarked matter-of-factly on the strange smell in the kitchen area. 'Boiled kidneys,' she said, wrinkling her nose and looking around the countertop. 'Can you smell it?'

'Maybe it's the bacon.'

'No, it's like animal blood. Did you kill something in here?'

'Me?'

She smiled. 'It's a joke. I can't imagine you killing anything. But can you ask Hope to give it a spray with air freshener later on?'

'I can't smell kidneys myself. But all right.'

He worked from home that day and served Alicia in bed, as she was feeling tired. This way he could keep an eye on Hope as well. She slept for the whole day, but at eight Edward came down for a glass of wine and found her back in her casual uniform, stationed at the stove making escalopes.

Alicia was already there as well and the three of them sat around the counter while Edward and Alice ate salted Italian crackers with cheese. The atmosphere was not in the slightest bit abnormal. *It is impossible*, he thought, and watched Hope vigilantly.

Her hand did not tremble. Her mouth did not waver. Her gaze, when directed at him, was empty and calm, black and lifeless at its core. He thought to himself that she did not fully know what had happened, not consciously. She must have assumed it had been a miscarriage and that she had suddenly lost the ace in her hand. He might have felt sorry for her, before. But now his resolve against Hope had hardened. She had tried it on and he had stepped around her artfully. *Well played, you bastard*, he thought and resolved to let not a single flicker of revealing emotion ever cross his face from then on.

FROM THE OBSERVATION DECK on the twenty-fourth floor, where the Night Owls bar catered to the residents who preferred not to venture out into an increasingly volatile city, Edward sat alone every night after work with a Manhattan Iced Tea and relaxed in the privacy that the bar's dizzying elevation afforded him. He knew hardly anyone at The Bridge – a nod here and there was all that was ever exchanged – and there was certainly no one to whom he could confide a secret. Most of his friends had moved out of the city long ago, and the ones who had remained rarely made sorties to Lower Manhattan.

He could see police roadblocks on the bridge, their lights flashing against the girders, and sometimes sirens wailed in the dark streets below – dramas one never bothered to ask about later, small conflagrations at intersections that came and went in fifteen minutes leaving a few broken bodies and pieces of broken glass over which he would step the following day on his way to work. These were nothing compared to his own narrowly avoided disaster. Over time, however, matters appeared to have calmed themselves, and he became convinced that Hope herself entertained no memory of the events of that vile day. That she had forgotten everything except that she had miscarried. She could no longer demand money from him and this, he reasoned, was why she had become meek again and so quietly returned to their mutual prior agreement.

And for his part he had done the same. A rupture with her, and a disagreeable episode with the agency, was not in his best interests. For who knew what sordid details would suddenly emerge if questions were asked and answered? Better that they return to normal and wait for the baby, which was due just after the New Year. Edward's nightly drinks therefore became more optimistic. What did it matter if rioters were being arrested on the bridge in plain sight or if confrontations under it occasionally turned lethal? It had nothing to do with him.

Relations with Hope became, if anything, more congenial. He bought her little presents, which he left for her in the kitchen; he went out of his way to be pleasant with her, to encourage her. As Alicia became more immobile, Hope became more indispensable, her cooperation even more essential.

Over Christmas he and Alicia kept their respective parents at bay and spent the holiday at home. Doctors came every day, and Edward undertook to work at home until the end of January. He prepared the baby's new room, set up the cot and the toys, and the alarms and cameras. The last days of the pregnancy coincided with a New Year that they celebrated alone, inviting only Hope to join them for a glass of champagne in the solarium, from where they watched that year's fireworks over the East River. The girl, he thought, had matured in the last six months and now she was comfortable with them, relaxed in her duties, as he had intended all along, the dramas of the summer far behind them — and he blamed himself too, he thought, as he watched her from behind. Not that he wasn't relieved to have avoided having to fork out the dreadful sum Hope had demanded. Still, he had tricked her and he felt he owed her a kind of debt. He would one day give her a generous reference for her next employer. It was the least he could do, and he would do it.

WHEN SPRING CAME, THE baby's eyes focused and recognised their faces. But it was Hope whom the baby seemed to recognise first and to whom she responded most eagerly. Looked at from a certain perspective, it was not surprising. The maid was with the baby constantly. Yet the attachment between them felt jarring to Alicia and eventually to Edward as well, though they didn't speak about it openly.

When the baby woke in the early hours, it was Hope who was there first. They were grateful for it. It was why they had hired her in the first place. Alicia slept through the nocturnal cries, and it was Edward who lay awake listening to the deaf girl rocking the cot and speaking to the baby with barely audible guttural sounds that might almost have been a form of singing, for all he knew. A form of singing or a form of talking. Some nights he would get up and go to the door of the room to listen to it. Hope cradled the baby in her arms and talked to her in sounds that were not words, as if between themselves they had found a language all their own.

At last Edward asked Alicia if she had noticed the same thing.

'I researched it,' she said, concealing the unease that she

really did feel. 'It's common for a baby and a nurse to have that bond. I think it's beautiful. Imagine if they *didn't* have it.'

'It would make everything more difficult, I suppose.'

'It means I can return to work. We can get back to normal. If anything, I think you should increase Hope's pay.'

'Her pay?' he protested: she was certainly being paid enough. It was almost double what the agency had originally asked for.

'Increase it anyway,' she insisted. 'I think she's heroic.'

'By the way,' he replied, nudging that irritating subject to one side, 'shouldn't you and I go out for dinner finally? It's been months. Literally months. I can't believe you haven't brought it up.'

'I never even thought about it.'

'I think we should go somewhere insanely fancy. Because, fuck it. You deserve it.'

'You pick.'

He felt like being excessive, yet a little stuffy. 'Daniel?'

'You'll have to insist.'

'I do insist.'

He asked his secretary to find a table for the following evening, and it was done. Before they left The Bridge they gave Hope a list detailing the things she should not forget during their absence, though they knew it was hardly needed. It was the first time they had left the baby alone with the maid and, for that matter, the first time they had dined in the city in several months.

They were at the restaurant by eight. The stucco-rich room was half-occupied, but filled with camellias and branches of flowering cherry. They were known there and Alicia's pregnancy was remarked upon. The staff showered her with congratulations. They ate outside on the terrace on Sixty-Fifth Street and felt the relief of not eating at home for once. Gazpacho with Peekytoe crab, Muscovy duck with sumac and a bottle of Commanderie de Peyrassol rosé. They had grown closer, as people always said about couples after the arrival of a child. They talked about Alicia getting back to work. She suggested that they keep Hope on for at least another two or three years. She was sure Edward would agree.

'Two years?' he said quietly. 'That seems an awful long time. But I see the point. She seems to get on so well with Claire.'

'We can fire her with a month's notice, if we have to. We're allowed to. So I say we try it and see.'

'All right,' he said unenthusiastically.

'Feels odd to be in a restaurant again, doesn't it? It feels like a beautiful tomb.'

He looked around at the terrace and silently agreed. 'Even if it's a beautiful tomb, I missed it.'

He thought back over the summer, to the brutal lust on the beach under the Japanese honeysuckle bushes. The terror scenes at the apartment, the drugging and the blood. It no longer seemed as if it could have been real. A little fantasia to mark the end of spoiled youthfulness, which of course was not the same as youth. He took Alicia's hand during dessert as if to reassure himself. Finally it had come round. Normalcy had returned, if at a price. He rather thought he had fought for it with a certain amount of commendable tenacity.

What if he had not? All would have been lost, all ruined for nothing.

IT WAS JUST AFTER ten when they reached The Bridge and they stopped in at the Night Owl for a nightcap before retiring.

'I'll text Hope,' Alicia said as they settled in by the vast windows.

'Claire is asleep,' the girl texted back. 'Enjoy yourselves.'

'I'd say,' Edward put in, 'that gives us licence for two rounds of bad sherry.'

They were there for an hour, enjoying themselves for the first time in a long while. At the apartment doors they kissed, half-drunk, and fell into the apartment, having left their shoes at the door. Alicia went directly to the baby's room, but found it empty. She called down the corridor. 'Are they in the front room?'

'Not here,' he called back.

She shot out from the baby's room and went to the solarium and then the dining room.

'What about Hope's room?' she called.

But he was already there. He pushed open the door and saw at once that it was unoccupied. Not only that, but Hope's small collection of belongings had been evacuated entirely. He went straight to the drawer of baby clothes that he had opened previously and found it equally bare. There was something unmistakably methodical about it, something final. It was immediately recognisable for what it was. *She's gone*, he thought, but without the incredulity that he would otherwise have expected to feel. His reflexes kicked in and he stormed back to the front room, where Alicia had collapsed on the sofa and was frantically texting Hope. But the maid was not replying now. She had not left the baby there – she had taken her with her.

'Perhaps,' he said, 'Hope got bored and went for a walk. She took Claire for a walk.'

'What? At night?'

'She must have done.'

'What about in The Bridge? She probably went for a walk inside the building. Call the staff.'

Within a few moments he had called downstairs and asked them to search all the public spaces.

'I'll go myself,' he then announced and slipped out to find the elevator to the Hanging Gardens on the floors below. He had told Alicia not to worry. Hope was bound to be there somewhere. The silly girl had taken it upon herself to disobey one of their cardinal rules.

Alone, he wandered through the Hanging Gardens, the fountains bubbling uselessly through the night with their coloured lights, the palms reaching to the glass roof stewing in the artificial humidity. But there was no Hope and no baby. Intuitively Edward sensed they had never been there. He went to the swimming pool as a last resort and was not surprised to be disappointed. So Hope must have exited the building altogether. When he returned to the apartment he found Alicia breaking down and ready to call the police.

Her suspicion was that Hope had gone for a walk outside. She had either been attacked or had lost her way in an unfamiliar neighbourhood. He didn't believe it, but he acted for a while as if he did. He called the police accordingly and, when they arrived, that was what he told them. The maid was deaf, handicapped and she had wandered outside and become disorientated. The sceptical expressions on their faces reflected his own disbelief, but that was not the moment to say what he really thought. The maid had waited patiently to exact her revenge.

WHEN HE CONSIDERED IT later, the months of investigation and counselling that followed drearily, day after day, seemed preordained in some way. They were tragically inevitable in the light of the secret that only he held within himself. But to whom could he confess it? To his surprise, no one ever asked him about his relationship with the maid. It simply could not, and did not, occur to them. It was then that he was grateful to himself for not caving in to her demands for money.

If he had done, it very likely would have been detected at that point. He would have had some gruesome explaining to do. Instead, he weathered the predictable questions until the investigators themselves became quietly exhausted and a fatalistic quality came into their voices.

Midsummer and no result. They questioned the agency and discovered that the maid's prior addresses had all been invented. The agency had not performed due diligence after all. Hope had forged all her references. None of the families cited had ever heard of her. She had never been a maid at any family house in California. The number she had given the agency was not that of the family, and it had gone dead. At the building in Borough Park no one had ever seen Hope, and the apartment mentioned by her was occupied by a family who had never met her. The police had followed all the leads and had arrived nowhere. After three months, the days of devastation and silence between Edward and Alicia began to grow concretely hopeless. A nationwide search had similarly gone nowhere. Hope had vanished in a way that a normal careless person could not vanish.

There was only, as his secret weapon, the bank-account number that she had given him. But he could not use it without alerting the police to the secret transaction between himself and his maid.

Armed with her account number, they had a better chance of finding their child; but at the same time his marriage would be destroyed, and probably his reputation as well. The one piece of information Edward had could not be used. Slowly he began to realise that this was exactly what Hope had intended to do to him. Still, he had the account number. He could take it to one of those agencies known as 'skip tracers', of which New York was full. It took him an hour to find a reputable one that came recommended by a friend. It was known as Empire and was located not far from his office on Canal Street. It was a one-man operation.

Skip tracer Gary Hollis was licensed and had spent half of his fifty years tracking down disappeared people fleeing from debts. Edward asked him out to lunch and they met at Tribeca Grill, where there was enough of a crowd to make them unnoticeable. Hollis was fat, sweaty, in a bright viscose shirt with a pattern of halved lemons, and armed with a notebook. A man who seemed to dislike his wealthy clients, precisely because they were wealthy and nevertheless had their contemptible secrets.

For Edward, it was the sort of thing one sometimes had to endure. He divulged to the fat man all the details of his own secrets. As he did so, he realised that he was telling another person his story for the first time. The relief was so great that the whole thing came tumbling out in long, chaotic sentences.

'And this account number is all you have?'

'Yes,' Edward admitted, appalled at how pathetic it was.

'Normally we track people down who owe money. A kidnapping is a little more unusual. You won't object if we give our discovery to the police?'

'It's what I am hoping for. I can hardly arrest her myself, can I? But you could give me a grace period, too.'

'How long?'

'Just a few days. I thought . . . I thought I would go see Hope myself and see if I can settle this between us peacefully.'

'It's an extraordinarily bad idea, Mr Munroe. Generally we find that people are at their most dangerous when they are being tracked.'

'She's a deaf girl. Maybe she is confused, she wants to get back at me. She doesn't know what she is doing.'

The fat man gave his prospective client a lugubrious glance.

'I would say she knows exactly what she is doing.'

'Emotionally, no.'

'Emotionally?'

Hollis promised Edward a grace period during which the

client could do as he liked, as long as this was in the contract and he paid a little more for the privilege.

Money, Edward said coolly, was not the problem. How long would it take to perform a skip-trace search on a bank account?

'It depends. Maybe a week, to be sure. You can pay to send me out wherever she is, if you like. To trace her.'

'I think I can handle her. Just find me her location.'

'Can I ask you: was there something about her that you noticed that didn't add up?'

'What do you mean?'

'Anything.'

The music, Edward thought. *The headphones.*

'Nothing really,' he murmured. 'But then I am not familiar with people with handicaps.'

'I see. Well, I'll call you in a few days when I have something.'

It took Hollis a week to discover that the owner of the account was a Rose McLaughlin of Barstow, California. They had tracked her down to a trailer park a few miles into the desert, near a place called Bagdad. The next town along Route 66 was called Siberia. There was nothing in Bagdad these days. The forlorn Bagdad Way ploughed through open desert until it got lost in the Cleghorn Lakes Wilderness. But Twentynine Palms and its fashionable hidden resorts lay on the other side of those mountains, and there were small settlements here and there where she might have gone.

There was no trail from credit cards or leases. Perhaps, Hollis suggested, she or her family owned a trailer and drove it around, far off the radar. There was little way of knowing.

Did Edward want to inform the police of this discovery or keep it to himself? With greater resources at their disposal, the government agencies might be able to find her quicker.

But Edward hesitated. 'Just a week or two more,' he suggested.

But after two weeks she had not made an appearance.

Day and night he struggled with his dilemma, unable to find the courage to turn to the police without secrets. He felt sure that eventually, and even soon, Hollis would locate her. He could make up an excuse to fly out to California and resolve the matter. Naturally he knew that it was a demented course of action for him to follow. But he felt a personal grievance against the maid and wanted to resolve it face-to-face.

This he could not tell anyone, and especially not the grieving mother. He constantly reassured Alicia as best he could. He did so night after night, as their solitude and desperation deepened. Then the weeks turned into months and the madness enveloped them completely.

He blamed himself for hiring the maid, for using the agency and for not noticing things about Hope that surely she had displayed.

'But we treated her like family,' Alicia would say, 'and yet she acted as if she had something against us. It's out of nowhere.'

'Nowhere,' he would echo.

'I wish I could kill her. I wish I could hire someone to kill her.'

'It's a fine idea. I've thought the same thing myself.'

He called Hollis every night. Hollis was waiting for a sign

to surface. It would be, he explained, like the bubbles released by a mammal hiding underwater. Sooner or later an animal had to surface in order to breathe.

IT WAS A YEAR before the inevitable sign appeared. When it came it was a handwritten cheque issued in a grocery store – the little slip-up that disappeared people always make eventually. It was in a tiny hamlet called Shoshone, near Death Valley.

Shoshone. Edward looked it up and pored over its two dozen structures on Google Maps. A person might flee to a tiny place thinking it would make them more invisible. But a tiny place was the worst location to hide if your pursuer happened to know that you were there. How long could it be after he landed there before he spotted her? A matter of hours. He felt triumphant after so many months of anguish and hopelessness. Once again, however, Hollis counselled him against flying to California and driving out to Shoshone. It would be a mistake – a dangerous one. Better to notify the police and let them handle it.

Edward, however, was not going to back down and accept defeat and scandal when he was so close to gaining the victory that he had worked so hard to obtain. There was no chance of it. Without discussing it further with Hollis, he booked his outbound ticket to Las Vegas and told his wife that he was flying out to meet a client, as he often did. There was no need for much of a ruse. Deep down, he felt that she was relieved to be rid of him for a few days. In this he was probably correct. He packed a light summer suit and some sports casual wear, along with a bucket hat and desert boots, as if he was embarking on a voyage into the interior of an unknown country.

HE ARRIVED AT 6 p.m. in Las Vegas and hired a car at the airport, driving directly out onto State Road 160 towards the California border. It was a land of stone hills, mesquites and old telegraph piles, whose characteristics he knew well from his many visits to Nevada and California for clients. The road was now empty as it rolled through Mountain Springs.

Soon he was on 372 going west, shadowed by a line of telephone poles. He passed a sign for Death Valley, twenty-seven miles, and for Shoshone Junction, nineteen miles. From there the road was open under a glacial moon, straight and unlit by lamps. He passed through clusters of burnt-iron outcrops with *ocotillos* glistening in the blue light.

Then the road levelled out and he came into Shoshone, heralded to the left by a tiny airstrip with a lone propeller plane parked upon it. It was a hamlet of imperial palms and dark-brown hillsides which seemed to have been created by a long-lost industrial furnace. A post office, a market, a gas station. By the roadside there was a saloon called the Crow Bar. Across from it stood the Shoshone Inn, a motel under mesquite trees with dark wooden doors and barbecue pits outside them.

He took a room, went to the pool under the mountains and swam for an hour to get the grit out of his skin. Then he re-dressed and walked across the road to the Crow Bar. The village was a tourist staging point for explorers of Death

Valley, and a few ageing couples sat around the bar. As quietly as he could, he let drop to the barman that he had a friend living in the neighbourhood, and offered up the name of Rose McLaughlin.

'She's a deaf girl of about twenty with a small child. You wouldn't fail to notice her.'

'There's no deaf girls anywhere around here.'

Edward shrugged as if he wasn't bothered either way, then persisted with the question. 'What about a girl with a baby?'

'None as I've seen.'

But the question was overheard by his wife. The woman stepped out from a back room, interested in the matter.

'There's a girl with a baby on the road to the left of the fork by the inn. It's the Old State Highway. It goes up to the trailer park.'

'Oh?' Edward asked her if she had seen the girl.

'She comes into the store down here. Ask in the store. They sell to her, so they'll know.'

He crossed back to the general store, but found it closed. He was tempted to drive up the Old State Highway and find the trailer park and, in the end, with some misgivings, he did so. It lay among luxurious palms, but there was only one trailer there and its handsome equipment didn't seem as if it would belong to the deaf girl. He drove back to the inn and slept for ten hours.

At first light he went back to the general store and found it welcomingly open. The woman at the store said she knew the girl with the baby – she drove down from the desert, where she was living. But it wasn't in the town trailer park. It

was some place further up the road, a rental right at the edge
of the badlands, where her boy sometimes made deliveries.
The house was called Mesquite Shades. It belonged to an
old-timer who knew her husband.

'And what colour is her pickup?'

'Dark green. I see it around. If you sit here all day, you'll
probably see it go by.'

'It's strange that she lives out here alone, being deaf
and all.'

'She ain't deaf.'

'You talk to her then?'

'Of course I talk to her. You talk to your customers.'

At midday Edward drove back up the same stretch of
road that he had explored the night before, until he reached
the trailer park and its lone occupant. An old man was hosing
it down, with a radio set down next to him. Further on, he
passed a few shacks and cabins. Half of them were empty or
abandoned. At the very edge of the settlement lay great gra-
dients of black boulders and fields of salt-like earth. Here he
found Mesquite Shades.

It was a low, dark-pink shack with a metal chimney and a
large dirt yard with metal fencing that had fallen down. The
green pickup was there. From the tumbledown road there
was a long drive of desert grit that rose slightly to the shack,
which looked uninhabited.

Edward parked at the road and decided to walk it. As he
trudged in the silent heat sweat began to fall between his eyes
and he felt slightly confused. Then he saw a glint of blonde
hair like a shimmer of metal. A tiny child in diapers standing
by a water pump which had rusted away almost to

nothingness, a relic of a bygone age. He stopped, thunderstruck, and shaded his eyes.

The little girl stared back at him blankly, naked but for the
diaper, and he saw that her eyes were blue. He looked up at
the door of the house, submerged in dank shade, and then at
the windows with their grimy curtains. Yet the child could
not be alone. It was then that he heard something behind
him, a soft rustling of some kind, and he turned so that his
eyes were struck by the sun. In that same instant something
struck his temple and he staggered to one side, then dropped
to one knee and fell into the granular dirt.

Rolling into darkness as if down a long slope, he let himself tumble until he came to a stop and there, maybe hours
later, he awoke to find himself inside the house, in a bare
room decorated with ancient crockery, which looked as if it
had never been used. He was alone, but was tied to a chair in
the clichéd way of many a movie. At once he smelled the gas-
oline in which he was soaked, and which dripped from the
hems of his trousers onto his now-bare feet. Where had his
shoes gone? Through the windows he could see that it was
dusk and the desert trees were falling into soft darkness. But
from the back rooms of the house there was a different commotion. A swirling of smoke. With it came a scent of burning
paper and rubber.

He shouted so that someone outside might hear, but then
he remembered that the house was far from any neighbours
and the tiny hamlet was itself an almost empty place. No one
would hear him. Screams and supplications would not matter, either. Distantly, he heard the pickup rev into life and
idle, as if waiting and watching. Then it reversed down the

drive, slowly and without alarm, and made a loud turn in the
road outside.

Even from there, the house in flames cast a glow that lit up
its windows. Yet no one would notice the illumination until
enough minutes had passed for the vehicle to leave unnoticed,
moving up silently to the main highway, which led north to
Evelyn and then, eventually, to the Funeral Mountains.

ABOUT THE AUTHOR

Born in England, Lawrence Osborne is the author of the critically acclaimed novels *The Forgiven*, *The Ballad of a Small Player*, *Hunters in the Dark*, *Beautiful Animals*, *Only to Sleep: A Philip Marlowe novel* (commissioned by the Raymond Chandler estate), *The Glass Kingdom* and *On Java Road*. His non-fiction ranges from memoir through travelogue to essays, including *Bangkok Days*, *The Naked Tourist* and *The Wet and the Dry*. His short story 'Volcano' was selected for *The Best American Short Stories 2012* and *The Forgiven* was made into a film starring Ralph Fiennes, Matt Smith and Jessica Chastain. Osborne lives in Bangkok.